This book is dedicated to the 1992 Modesto Water Polo Junior Varsity City Champions. You were even better at goofing off than you were at playing polo. Fire in the hole!

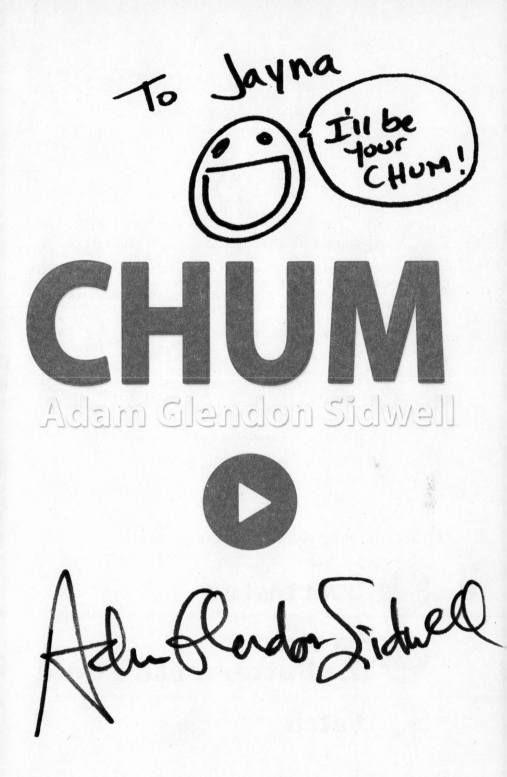

CHUM

FUTURE HOUSE PUBLISHING

COVER ART: CHRIS HARVEY

FORMATTING: JEFF DICKSON

ALL RIGHTS RESERVED.

ISBN: 0989125335

ISBN-13: 9780989125338

Other books by Adam Glendon Sidwell:

 Evertaster

**Evertaster:
The Buttersmith's Gold**

 Fetch

▶ CHAPTER 1
DESTINY

Oh, Destiny, you are a curious thing, the way you've been stalking me, the way you've been lurking under that Hollywood sign, or biding your time beneath those bigger-than-anyone skyscrapers or fancy pants museums ever since I moved to Movieland, USA.

Me. Levi Middleworth. Me, a thirteen year old kid. A guy who's never had a girlfriend. A guy who doesn't even know which jeans are the right ones. And here you come out of nowhere on a Tuesday at the end of summer and make it all happen just like everyone ever dreamed it would.

See, there I was just minding my own business down at this pool called the Plunge, soaking up the H2O, puttin' in my laps for the day, pumpin' my pecs; you know, trainin' — and boom! This Big Chief all squished up in a trim green suit makes me an offer I'd like to refuse, but banks on the fact that no one ever has.

But hold on. Let me explain. I didn't up and leave the spud farm in Idaho and come out to California because I heard you can get discovered in the grocery store checkout line; I'm much too sensible for that. I came because Dad made me. He was going to take this promotion — whether I liked it or not — so here I am, eight months later, the summer after my seventh grade year at Palms Middle School wrapping up and the eighth grade looming ahead.

I'm still not sure how things work around here. Who goes where and to whose house on what weekend or how you get invited to which pizza place. Who knows what people do for fun? So I spend an hour or so every day at this pool, training and holding my breath and working my arms until I'm strong enough. Strong enough to meet Destiny, I guess, because I want to be ready. After all, I'm no schmo — I watch TV — I know that anyone who's worth anything — magic knights, karate warriors, sometimes even stock brokers — they've all got Destinies, so I'm almost positive I've got one too. Besides, swimming makes you feel good.

So I swim, and swim, and swim. I can see the shining shimmering sun prance across the bottom, and I chase it, kicking my legs real hard together like I'm a dolphin. When I'm underwater, it's silent, like the world's on pause, all except for me, and I grow my own fins and flick my tail like I'm the one true porpoise. A porpoise with a purpose. Then boom! The guy —the one who's about to make me the offer — is standing at the end of my lane.

I think of what an idiot I've been, because he certainly saw me, and I'm a whole thirteen years old, and dudes my age shouldn't be acting like dolphins. Especially if they don't want the whole world to know.

The guy at the end of my lane looks like a lifeguard, or maybe the pool manager, or at least somebody important enough to squeeze himself into such a trim green suit, and he's looking down at me from behind a pair of dark, dark glasses, waiting for me to stop swimming when I get to end of the pool.

So I do another lap, just for fun.

"Ever try the ocean?" he says when I finally finish.

I think for a minute about how to respond, because this guy looks like a card shark, even in the sunlight, and not the kind of guy you trust your secrets to.

"Of course not," I say. Lakes and streams and rivers back home in Idaho all the time, but the ocean? The shore to shining shore of the PACIFIC? There are things in there I can't see. Things I don't want to know about. Things the surfers say won't hurt you, but they're just kidding themselves; I've watched the evening news.

"I've had my eye on you. For days now," he says. I think that's creepy. I haven't noticed him, so I bite my tongue, hoping he'll explain. "You've got form," he says; he's all cooped up behind that pair of big black sunglasses, so I can't tell if he really means it. I flex my lats.

"Maybe. But what's it to ya?" I don't want to sound rude. I just can't figure him out.

He kneels down by the poolside. His face is white — too pale for summer — a layer of powdery cosmetics covering his hippo cheeks. Everything about him seems squished, like that green suit of his is a python that's swallowed him from the bottom, and only his head and hands have squeezed out the top.

"There are all sorts of personalities out there, but there's so much more to it than that," he says. His voice is tinny, almost digitized. "You've got the intangibles. A certain charm and grace no money can buy. It's that something everyone in this town wants but half the sidewalk stars in Hollywood don't have."

I shouldn't believe a sentence of smooth talk like that, no matter how true it sounds. "And so…"

"I want to make you famous."

A dozen seconds later I've pulled on my t-shirt and I'm sitting in some office at the pool, the seat soaking up my chlorine, and he's telling me how it will all go down.

"Reality TV," he says. I shudder at the thought. Idiots running around like idiots? Lots of cheering and crying. People forced into failure. Rats in a lab. It's risky, but if anyone can be the exception, it's me.

"There's a boat headed for the island paradise of Betteravia just off the coast. I'd like you to be on board as one of a select few contestants. There will be challenges to meet, on and off the boat, hence our need for a swimmer of your caliber."

This is good. He knows talent when he sees it.

"The final, remaining contestant will receive one million in cash."

That number's so huge I can't even count that high.

"And we get national coverage."

"I'll mull it over," I say trying to put my bored eyes on, but I'm bursting at the seams. I couldn't have hoped for this. It's just what I need.

He half smiles. He still hasn't taken off his sunglasses. The blinds in the office are closed, so no one can see us.

"Another thing. It's important — for the integrity of the show — that no one knows who the contestants are while we're filming. Or that you've come."

That seems weird. I raise an eyebrow at him.

He doesn't flinch. "It's standard studio non-disclosure and intellectual property rights protection policy," he says, shrugging it off.

Lawyer talk. He removes a very long piece of paper from his pocket with tiny letters packed onto it like ten thousand black gnats smashed on a windshield. Looks like a lot of blah- blah, whatever-whatever to me.

"You're eighteen, aren't you." He's not asking. It's more of a statement.

I shrug. This year's growth spurt squeezed another half-foot out of me. Of course he thinks I'm eighteen. I'm humongous. It must be my training. I shrug again.

"Then sign here, and I'll tell you where to meet us," he says. He's got me pegged.

Those studio folks must know what they're doing, so I sign it, even though I'm just a minor. Dad would kill me if he knew. But he's a trucker, not an attorney.

The man in the trim green suit smiles. He folds up the contract and slides it in his pocket with a hand that's slimy smooth – almost plastic.

"Six a.m. Friday morning, at the Marina," he says. "Bring this." He hands me a card with his left hand. That palm is all fat, like toothpaste squeezed from his sleeve.

I take the card and get out of there. Once I'm in the parking lot I take a gander.

It's signed, "Cecil B.D. Somethington." The name doesn't even sound real. Maybe it's not. His hand wasn't. He was probably built in a lab, an alloyed ally in the Android Alliance, sent to Earth to scan for talent the likes of which his galactic masters have never seen.

A car drives by. I kick myself. Anyone could be in there. Maybe someone from school. Maybe someone who saw me.

Sometimes I worry that people might be able to see my thoughts projected up above my head like a movie. That's a problem. I'm thirteen. Robots are fine when you're in diapers, but you're not supposed to dream up stuff like that at thirteen. It's silly, and someday, it's going to have to stop. So says Dad anyway.

So I think about what I'm going to do instead, how I am going to show up on Friday at six a.m., that I am going to get on that boat. The truth is, I need this to work. This is exactly the kind of thing that's supposed to happen in Tinseltown: any ordinary person just walking down the street can turn into something bigger than life. This has to be exactly what my Destiny had in mind.

"Chum TV," reads the next line on the card. "A friendly studio based on friendship." That sounds kind of nice. I suppose I could use a friend.

▶ CHAPTER 2
VIDEO STAR

I found out about my Destiny when I was only four years old. Mom came into my room one night, woke me up, and told me all about it. "You're going to do amazing things," she said, then kissed me on the forehead. She left after that, and whether it was to Timbuktu or Kalamazoo, I can't say, but people don't lie when they're speaking the last words they'll ever say to you.

So ever since way back when, I've had my eyes open, waiting, watching, checking around every corner, lifting up every rock, peering out over the next horizon.

Sometimes I felt blundering, hopeless, like my Destiny was never coming, like I wasn't going to amount to anything — and then — bada bing! Today something big comes and taps me on the shoulder.

It's about time.

So as I pedal my bike home from the pool, I think this has to be it. It's finally my Destiny, and I'm going to win the million bucks for Dad and myself, and walk into the eighth grade next year fully famous — in the good kind of way — when I hear a voice that reminds me nothing's been settled yet.

"Levi! You need to update your status."

Marcus. I get squeamy all over, like snakes just crawled up my finger-nails. I'm stopped at the light and Marcus Earl, this guy from school, is hanging out the window of the car next to me, blond hair plastered across his forehead with a set of beefy black-rimmed glasses that are mostly for show. He's got on a too-tight V-neck lavender t-shirt. For some reason, he's wearing his shiny black and silver smartphone around his neck like it's a necklace. I hate that thing. I look at him like he's crazy.

"It's been more than three days," Marcus says holding up his fancy phone. "It still says 'BBQ Chicken Pizza'."

I can't think of a single reason why that matters. "It was good pizza," I say.

He rolls his eyes like he's been inconvenienced. "People get tired of reading the same thing. What is the point of statuses if they don't say what you're doing?"

"You could write 'I'm updating my status'," I say under my breath.

"What?"

I don't want him to know what I said, so I change the subject. "Why the medallion?" I say, pointing to his phone.

He lets out a sigh that's almost a groan. I catch my mistake right away. I shouldn't have asked him anything. It makes him feel smart and supe-rior, when he knows something I don't — it gives him something to hold over me.

"Look, I wrote a whole post about this. It describes everything." He points the flat face of the phone at me like it's a gun, and I know this much: he's vlogging, and I'm the subject once again.

"You could —"

"I'm not telling you," he cuts me off, "Just read my page like every-one else does. It's too complicated to explain without the links. You want everyone to log on for you?"

I start to burn inside. Right then I want to yank that shiny phone off his neck and shatter it like a light bulb. I want to, but I won't. It's too far away, and if I make a move now, he'll know how bad I want to kill him, and he'll suspect why. I can't let him know he has the upper hand. I can't give him that kind of power. Especially not on video.

The light turns green. "Text me!" he shouts, and the guy behind the wheel – it's his upperclassman cousin Gumbo – guns it.

I pedal home, frustrated, wondering what Marcus would say if he knew I was the only guy left on the planet with a flip phone. He's an idiot. He friends me — I still don't know why — we're not friends — as soon as I move here, then a few months later posts the video that ruins my life.

I couldn't really help doing what I did that afternoon so many weeks ago. There were only five days of school left. Why couldn't I just have stayed cool and made it to the safety of summer? But no. I was in the locker room after swimming some laps. It was really late, and no one was around. I was coming out of the toilet stall — thank goodness I wasn't naked — in just a Speedo, which is almost as bad — and I don't know why, I was being stupid I guess, and I thought I was alone — but I wrapped myself up in these super long strands of toilet paper and stuck them to my wet skin like noodles, then grabbed a broomstick and started fighting off the TP-tentacles so they wouldn't suck out my blood. I started saying stuff like "I'll sunder your cytoplasms!" and "tyrannical tentacles!" really loud. It was an epic fight to the death; I almost didn't win, when I saw Marcus in the corner with his phone, recording the whole thing. I stiffened up. I didn't think anyone was in there, since school had been out for hours. My face started burning, then my neck too, and I wished life had an erase button, or that I was dead.

I didn't know what to do. So I ran. Ran all the way home in my Speedo, with only my towel wrapped around me, doing my best to hold on to my socks and shoes and backpack as they tumbled down all over the school parking lot, and then the sidewalk and street.

Two days later he posts it.

That's why I hate him. It's also why sometimes I hate myself. I had no idea I flailed so much, or that my legs looked so skinny from the side. Barf! I look like a dork.

Marcus should've been suspended, since it was on school grounds, and in the locker room, but no one's complained, so it's not like the principal knows about it. I'm not going to say anything to anybody no matter what, especially now that summer's started. Imagine how many hits he'd get if there was a scandal. Sometimes, you've just got to lie low and hope that nobody will notice how dumb you looked all over the web when school starts next year.

The comments were the worst:

> LOL
> Is he a retard? :X
> Has to be. Look at 0:32 He's doing the windmill. LOL!!!
> !! I think he poo'ed his pants !!
> Isn't this from Pirates of Panzerfaust? He looks like this
> one episode where the captain fights off a giant jellyfish.
> That shows for noobs.
> @Gangstastylz uhhh, yeah my idiot cousin watches that
> show
> hey… that looks like Levi

The last comment was my death-sentence. Somebody out there knows that it was me. There must've been a hundred more after that. As of yesterday, this little video had 217 hits. 217 unnamed people watching, waiting like moles to rat me out when I walk through the doors of Palms Middle

School next year. I won't know who to trust. They all know my big secret, and I don't even know who they are.

The other worst part is, that one guy's comment is right. I was being the captain from Pirates of Panzerfaust. There's this show I used to watch back in Idaho — I don't anymore, it's way too fake — about these Germans during World War II that don't want to be Nazis, so they steal this submarine that's shaped like a turtle and go around saving people off the coasts of Africa. The captain — his name is Captain Bombardigo — is super awesome at sword fighting and getting everyone out of the traps set by their arch nemesis Viceicknick. But I don't watch that stuff anymore. Too bad it's too late. After that idiotic video everyone'll think that I do. Dad says that show is dumb and for wussies.

What's weird is — and it's fine since I tuned out anyway — the show got cancelled for next season. Apparently, something happened to the actors and they all quit at once, at least so says the news. All these die-hard fans with nothing better to do staged a huge protest at MIT — this college where all these C++ brained rocket-science-nuclear physicists go — demanding that the show go back on the air. People get so obsessive. Those were probably the same guys who built exact copies of the submarine's bridge in their living rooms, or got married dressed as Captain Bombardigo. There was nothing that the TV people could do anyway though, because — this is the craziest part of all — the actors totally disappeared. No one can find them. People on the blogs say they've gone into hiding. Whatever.

I lock my bike under the stairs and climb up to our tiny apartment. We've only got one bedroom, so I sleep on the sofa. There's not much space in this city.

There's a note on the fridge: "Beach Day on Tuesday?" It's from Dad. He's been obsessed with the ocean ever since we moved to Los Angeles, so he'll go whether I want to or not.

I don't care too much for the ocean. I miss the rivers in Idaho; now that was clean water. There weren't things bigger than me in there.

I get some cheese puffs and boot up my laptop on the couch. It's like looking at a picture of a dead guy's guts; I don't want to, but I can't help it. I have to check the video. Click.

861 hits.

Marcus Earl is an IDIOT! I should unfriend him. Put him out of my life forever. But, wait. No. If I do that, I can't watch him. If I can't watch him, who knows what he'll do? I'm just one of 1,213 on his friend list, and I think he thinks that I care.

My cursor wanders. I can't stop it. Click. I punch my own forehead. Somebody's posted a link to their page, where they've copied the clip and turned it into a music video. 7,644 hits! "S-s-s-sunder your cytoplasm!" croons my voice metallically, over and over. I don't know how they did it — some tuning software I guess — but I sound like a robot singing through a tin can.

Uff! I start to feel all hot again, and tense too, like I've just caught rigor mortis. If I crawl under my mattress, maybe no one will find me until after the apocalypse, or at least until eighth grade is over.

The only hope I have is that all those thousands of hits came from people who live in Malaysia or Kurdbeckistaq, or somewhere far away like Kentucky, and I'll never actually meet these people who think I'm a fool.

Good thing Dad will never see this. The internet's like another country to him — totally foreign. If he saw me acting so dumb, he'd fly off the handle. "You're not a kid anymore," he likes to say.

Well, whatever I am, Dad's going to leave early for a trucking run or meeting or something on Friday, like he always does, which gives me a chance to make a break for it that morning. Once I'm on that boat, I'll be in the clear. I don't care if that Cecil guy is really an android. I've got to do something with my life. I've got to sail to that island. I've got to be on TV — and then they'll have to think I'm awesome.

That's what TV does. It makes you invincible. It makes people know you, and after that they really want to meet you, and they say your name like it's a song. You can't make fun of a guy when he's handsome and staring back at you from the TV screen inside your house like the boss that he is.

Something bounces off the living room window. The glass shakes so hard, I'm surprised it doesn't break.

I jolt upright and dash to the glass and peer outside. The window's smeared with snot, and the sun's gone down, so it's almost dark outside. Three dudes with hoodies cinched over their heads run off down the street. I throw open the door and pound down the stairs, but by the time I get to the sidewalk, they're already gone.

Punks.

Then I see what hit the window. Up above me, hanging down from the tree, swaying from a length of twine, tied to a branch next to our living room window is a sliming stinking mess of sticky-wet tentacles dangling from a squishy sack. A dead octopus. There's a piece of cardboard pinned to it that says "Dear Captain, you're a Gumpalo."

My chest gets tight and I hope no one's looking since my eyes are burning hot. It's a message — an insult from the sea — and clearly, it's meant for me.

▶ CHAPTER 3
THE *PHILANTHROPIST*

Those jerks with the hoodies are so dumb, they don't even know the difference between octopus tentacles and toilet paper jellyfish ones. Captain Bombardigo fought off a giant jellyfish in episode 37, just like I did that day in the locker room. There has never once been a single giant octopus on the show.

They were probably from school. Must've seen the video. Not sure how they found me. Not sure what I did to them. I don't think I've been a gumpalo, whatever that may be. That must be something that other kids know about, but I bet they wouldn't say, so it's not like I can ask them. I'd look it up, but I'm not going to. That's how much I don't even care what the word gumpalo means, and that they wrote it on a hate-note just to me. What's wrong with people?

I cut the octopus down from the tree so Dad won't see it when he gets home later tonight. It's all watery and red-yellow and totally dead. I feel kind of bad for the little squisher, so I bury him in the alley out back, in the only square foot of dirt I can find. There's not much dirt here like there is in Idaho.

Sometimes I miss it — the dirt I mean. People did stuff in Idaho. My one friend and I would spend all day swimming across the river, or tying rope swings in the trees. People don't like that kind of thing in Los Angeles. I wonder what my friend's doing now.

"Hey," is about all I say to Dad for the next couple of days. I don't want him to get suspicious, and he doesn't seem to notice I'm up to something.

On Friday morning I wake up really early — my body knows what day it is. I stay on the sofa, pretending to be asleep until Dad leaves for work. As soon as he locks the front door behind him, I jump up and pack a change of clothes in a backpack, pull on my shorts, and strap on my sandals. My sandals are the sturdy kind — the ones you can run through rivers in.

I go outside. The morning is brisk, but only in a Los Angeles kind of way, which means the chill gives up before it can get under your skin. It'll be warm by 7:30.

I pull out my key to unlock my bike. The railing where it's normally parked is empty. It's gone.

I get frantic. I haven't tried to use it since Tuesday. I circle the apartment, and groan. There it is, tangled up in a bush. The guys with the hoodies must've broken the lock and chucked it back there. I can't believe I didn't see it sooner.

I snap and break away branches until I can finally yank my bike free. I'm scratched and angry, and it's almost six a.m. The front rim is bent like a potato chip. I'm so mad I could bite the metal in half. I throw the whole useless thing back into the bushes so hard, it disappears beneath the leaves.

I can't miss the boat, so I run as fast as I can to the bus stop. I'm pretty sure there's an early bus that takes people to the south end of Venice where Lincoln Ave. passes by the In-N-Out. If I can make it, I might have a chance.

My heart is pumping blood like a hammer onto my brain, and my breath is starting to get shallow, and my lungs stab when I see the bus at the stop. I jump in just as the doors are closing, and slide my dollar into the cash machine, wheezing the whole time.

Another quarter hour and we're at the Marina. I pull the chord, jump off the bus, and sprint as fast as I can to the docks.

Luckily they're not far. A minute later, and I'm sweaty and panting, when I see water. There's a forest of masts scattered along the docks in neat little rows, ropes and rigging hanging from their branches like vines.

One ship in particular is bigger than the rest — a gigantic orange and blue pirate ship over 300 feet long, its three masts half as tall as redwoods. Its paint is peeling and chipped. Its pale green sails are wound up tight. It's been modified — with metal scaffolds, lighting equipment, and what looks like microphones or cameras, all bolted, lashed or taped to the wooden deck, railing, and masts. Everything is covered in blinking orange and blue and yellow light bulbs, like a Christmas tree or Las Vegas. The whole thing looks Frankensteined, like it was pieced together by a mad man.

That's got to be our boat, which means I may have made it after all.

I sprint down the sidewalk and into the zigzag of docks. There are people milling about there: a couple of blondies in pink miniskirts and furry bear boots, a super-jock moving in on them for the touchdown, half-a-dozen nose jobs, some tattooed butterflies, and one balding fat man. Altogether there are eight pairs of Italian sunglasses, four shirt stains, seventeen attitudes, and a handful of dreams smeared like lip gloss over the crowd of two dozen would-be contestants filing up the gangplank to the ship.

I jump a waist-high chain link fence without bothering to look for a gate — no time for that now anyway — and run past two small, white, portable canopies and a couple of cameras. There's a generator sputtering somewhere, sending amps up some black chords snaking across the dock to lights and cameras near the gangplank. Just below that is the water. Above the gangplank, surrounded by light bulbs, is a big, yellow smiley face with a blinking neon sign underneath it that reads "CHUM".

I start to get excited. I'm so glad to leave it all behind that I get the same jumpy jitters I had the first time I tried to back flip off the high dive.

I hear people saying names that sound important, though I don't know who they are. "Oh, well me and Shiny Sorenson…" says one guy, or "Herb Dillinbaum's my agent's friend," says another.

Before I can figure out what I'm supposed to do next, I see an all too familiar face in a pistachio colored V-neck shirt and skinny jeans slither between the touchdown kid and the fat man. Marcus!

I groan. Of all people, why? This was my chance to get away, to make a fresh start, and now my problems are tailing me like a barnacle on my hull. I turn on my mental self-checker to make sure I won't do anything weird, but there's no guarantee it will work.

I march right up to the beefy black glasses on his face. His gigantic curly-haired cousin Gumbo is with him. "What are YOU doing here?" I demand.

Marcus pretends like he's happy to see me. "Big B!" he says. I hate it when he calls me that, like we're best buds or something. I have no idea where it came from. "I was hoping you'd show." His smartphone's still hanging around his neck. He points it straight at me. I have a wild guess why he wants me around — he wants to film me. I get him hits.

"How did you know I'd be here?" I ask.

"I'd heard you signed on," he says.

That doesn't make any sense. I hadn't told anyone about Cecil, or Chum TV, or the meeting at the pool.

"How?"

Marcus grins at me with a set of perfect teeth. I can tell he's very pleased with himself once again for knowing something I don't. "There are ways."

I scowl. I'm burning up inside. This changes everything. I was supposed to leave my past behind. Now it's followed me, and I'm not sure I'll make any good impressions with him around.

Someone at the top of a gangplank hollers, "All aboard!" and all the plastic people start crowding toward the ship and filing under the blinking neon sign. There's a little bit of shoving, some arguments, a tiny bit of mass hysteria. I almost don't want to go now, but I can't let Marcus think I'd stay behind because of him either, so I wedge myself in line, as far ahead of Marcus as possible. The touchdown kid's right in front of me.

The gangplank is angled up toward the ship like an escalator. It's a good thing it's steel, since the deck of the ship is triple my height and just as far away.

I can see the water below. It's so dark green, it's almost black. Probably ripe with sewer runoff.

"Phones in the bucket!" says a double-wide man with a scraggly gray beard in a pearl-white captain's shirt and dark navy slacks to the blondie at the top of the gangplank. He looks like Captain Ahab in a Love Boat uniform: there's a curved sword strapped to his belt, golden loops buttoned atop his shoulders, and his teeth are all crooked and jammed. I'm surprised he doesn't have wooden legs. But I can't really tell that he doesn't. The blondie drops her mobile phone in a metal pail.

"Card!" says the guy next to the Captain. He's dressed like the Captain, only he's as tall as a skyscraper, and he's got a clipboard and a set of silver teeth. Blondie hands him a card. He searches her, then lets her through.

They do the same for the next guy, and the next guy, and I climb higher up the gangplank until eventually it's my turn. I put my old flip phone in the bucket quickly, so Marcus won't see, and hand the skyscraper-tall guy the Chum TV card Cecil gave me. The skyscraper guy searches me. "Stand on one of the orange X's," he says and points me toward a wide deck between the wooden masts where everyone's lined up in rows. Sounds like boot camp, I think, and find my way to an empty X next to one of the blondies.

The boat is monstrous. It's at least a few stories high, not counting the masts, and that's the part not covered in water. The wood is warped and light blue on the deck, and there's a tangle of ropes overhead, and metal scaffolding surrounding the masts, all with blinking yellow and green and blue light bulbs screwed into rows of sockets, just like one of those Saturday morning game shows. The bow of the ship sticks out in front like a spear. There's a raised captain's deck near the rear, like a house with a flat roof, and a big wooden steering wheel on top. Altogether it's longer than a football field.

Cecil is standing aloof on the captain's deck, next to the railing, dressed in the same trim green suit he wore at the pool. I wonder if I should wave, when I see he's got his sunglasses on, and he's probably not looking my way. I put my hand down.

"You're cute," giggles the blondie next to me. I look over. She looks like she could be on a magazine, with her skinny dress and pink lips and perfect wavy golden hair. At first, I'm flattered, then I wonder if she means it in more of a cheek-pinching kind of way. After all, she looks old — old enough to have a job or go to college even.

"Uh, thanks," I say.

The blondie extends a manicured hand. I shake it. "I'm Candy — it's my screen name," she says.

"Levi," I say. She glances at my jeans, which are actually just some off-brand cargo shorts. She blinks a whole lot, like she's desperately confused. "It's my real name," I say. She giggles again.

I'm still not sure she understands. She seems nice though.

Isn't this great?" she says, then doesn't wait for me to answer. "I mean this ship! The show! I've been acting forever! Though I've never had a part."

Yeah, it's great, I think, knowing Marcus is here too. But wait — something's odd. How can she be an actor who doesn't act? "What do you do then?" I ask.

She beams, "I spend a lot of time at clubs. Sometimes the mall. Or the beach. You have to go places where people will notice you. You have to buy a lot of dresses. That's how Shiny Sorenson got discovered. I read about it in Famous."

"And that works?" I ask.

"Uh-huh," she nods, smiling, then wrinkles her forehead. "At least it has for the last six years."

I frown. Six years? Never had a part? That kind of depresses me. First, because I feel sorry for Candy. Second, because I guess I'm not the only one who thought being on TV was a brilliant master plan. She thought of it too. She might even have a Destiny, which means my comparative advantage is zero. I could be in way over my head here.

A short guy in the middle row with pockmarks on his face stares down the crowd. He growls. The fat man's in the front row, and a bald guy next to him. He's much older than me too. Most everybody is. Good thing I'm tall for my age.

Marcus is arguing with the Captain at the top of the gangplank. "I've got a Nowblitz feed!" he says clutching his phone. "I'm streaming video of everything I do, direct to my blog, 24-7. Those can't be interrupted."

I snort. I didn't realize it was live. He's got it around his neck so it can see everything he does, every minute of every day, whether you want to be broadcasted or not.

Suddenly, Cecil is alert. He leans over the railing on the captain's deck, and makes a cutting motion at his throat toward Marcus. The Captain grins. "What?" says Marcus. He's trembling. I can tell he's scared. The Captain grabs Marcus by the shoulders and jerks him in close, then draws a dagger. He cuts the cord holding the phone and tosses it way down into the green-black water. It kerplops.

Marcus looks like he's lost a limb. I'm elated. The Captain is my new best friend. In half a minute, that phone is a few dozen feet underwater with the rest of the guys who crossed the mob.

"Take an X," shouts the skyscraper-tall guy, and shoves Marcus toward the deck. Gumbo likes to play his cousin's bodyguard, so he follows close behind.

In minutes the engines are turning, some crewman dressed like the Captain cast off some ropes, and the boat idles slowly away from the dock.

Marcus looks defeated. Like I said, there is nowhere I'd rather be.

▶ CHAPTER 4
THE GAME OF CHUM

So I'm feeling pretty good as the Captain grabs hold of the wheel and steers the ship slowly out past a rocky break wall that protects the Marina from the waves.

We turn the corner and there it is: the ocean, big blue-gray water from here on out to nowhere — an endless, infinite, never-ending plane, without a landmark to its name. There are no mountains — just an ever-changing meadow so big, I can see the Earth curve away. I had no idea the world was so big.

As soon as we're clear of the Marina, the double-wide Captain barks some orders, a dozen or so crewmen set the rigging and unfurl the pale green sails, and in a few minutes more, the hull is cutting through the waves like a karate chop, the boat thumping up and down as we head out to open sea.

I'm stoked, even with the rise-drop-thump of the ship as it bumps over each new wave. The sea wind's curling around my cheeks, the sun is warming up the morning, and I'm headed out to somewhere I've never been. I'm beginning to think I might even learn to like the sea, when some girl on the X in front of me turns around and throws a damper.

"I think I saw you in a video," she says. A blaring red siren goes off in my head, and I spin around to face her.

She's wearing a pair of shin-length, blue and red plaid shorts and two perfectly round yellow smiley face earrings dangling from both ears. It looks like she made them herself. She's a red-head, she's kind of cute, and she actually looks like she's my age. She might even go to Palms.

She's exactly the kind of person I didn't want to prance around like a pirate in Speedos for, but I'm stuck on my orange X on the deck of a ship that's at least two miles from land by now, and I've only ever swum one mile at a time. This is what I was trying to avoid next year, and it's happening already. It's okay though, because it would probably never work out between us anyway.

"What video?" I ask, trying to play it cool while my innards dry up like raisins.

"The one where you're Captain Bombardigo," she says. "Why? Do you have more?" The girl's on to me.

Candy, the blondie next to her, giggles again. "You're an actor too?" she asks.

"No. No. I'm not," I say, putting up my hands as if it'll block whatever's coming next. Both girls are quiet for a moment. I feel like an idiot.

Then the redheaded girl with the smiley face earrings grins. "I built one of those blunderbusses the Torqueod crew back-wired with devolvers from the episode where they fight the clone-lions."

I do a double take. So she watches the show. Or maybe this is a trap. My head's totally reeling. I try to think of something to say. "For Halloween?" Everyone makes stuff for Halloween.

She laughs. "No. For Maker-Con."

I have no idea what she's talking about. "?" I say.

She groans. "It's a convention. You know how Comic-Con betrayed the artists?" she asks. I shake my head. I know how Comic-Con is a place

Dad won't let me go, where you dress up like superheroes so you can study awesome artwork and learn the true meaning of comics, but I hadn't heard about said betrayal.

"?" I say again.

"Comic-Con's evolved into a Hollywood hype machine!" she says. "It's forgotten its roots! Artists started Maker-Con so they could showcase their work." I don't know if I see what the big deal is. In fact, I secretly wanted to go to Comic-Con, before I found out it was for geeks, but now a girl my age who seems like she's cool is saying that it's gotten lame, which means that at one time she liked it, so I'm very, very unsure about anything anymore. One thing's for certain, though: she's got principles.

"I'm Holly," she says.

Like Holly Hotstuff? I think. That's a name I want to remember. "My name's Levi."

"Charmed," she says, turning around. So that's that. I guess we're cool then, I think to myself. And that's nice, because she actually knows about what I did in the locker room, and she didn't seem to care. In fact, she even seemed to like my video.

I feel a glimmer of hope inside me. There could be others who liked it too.

The double-wide Captain — the thug who looks like Captain Ahab in a cruise ship uniform — waddles to the front of the captain's deck so he can face everyone and turns on a TV. It sparks, then a picture of our ramshackle boat fizzles onto the screen. It's our boat.

He pulls out a set of note cards. "Welcome aboard the Philanthropist," he reads with a shout. All the contestants on the X's give a cheer. I can tell they're here to win.

"I am Captain Poursport," reads the Captain. So that's his name. Not Ahab — it's Poursport. I don't think I've ever seen someone with a beard so bristly-gray. I'd say he looks ridiculous, in that brass-buttoned shirt of his, if it weren't for his menacing sword.

"And this is my First Mate Killjoy," the skyscraper-tall guy with silver teeth snaps to attention. He must be Killjoy, the one who flashed his teeth at me.

"From the moment you set foot aboard my ship, a complex and sophisticated array of cameras has been recording your every move," says Captain Poursport.

Marcus's cousin Gumbo's face flashes up on the TV screen. Then a bald guy's, then mine. I can see my light brown hair is messed off to one side, as usual, like it exploded out of my skull. I sneak a hand up to my head and try to fix the damage.

There's a half dozen cameras with telescoping lenses duct taped to the metal scaffolding at base of the mast. One zooms in on my nose. There are two more cameras above me, two more at the bow, and several taped along the sides of the ship at irregular intervals. A little red light glows next to each lens, like the eye of a vampire bat. The whole set up seems so improvised.

"Every second of your life on board this ship, from the deck above to the cabins below, from the bow to the stern, will be taped, edited, and televised to millions of viewers across the nation," he reads. What looks like a remote controlled toy tank with a mounted camera duct taped on top zips back and forth across the deck and stops in front of Candy. It aims its lens at her. She takes one look at it and applies a fresh coat of lip gloss.

I steal a glance at Holly. This is it. This is my chance to show the world what I'm made of. Then I steal a glance at Marcus. Don't mess this up, I think.

"You will be provided with the most luxurious accommodations, a helpful staff, and fine dining." The TV shows tables covered with gourmet

pastas and sizzling sausages. Next there are pictures of the quarters —
antique wooden tables and dressers, lava lamps, fluffy, red velvet pillows
with golden tassels, oil paintings of purple elephants. It looks like a floating mansion. There's a murmur of excitement.

Then a map of the Los Angeles coastline appears on the screen. I recognize the Marina and Catalina Island. They're mere spots in all the blue.
The Captain points out another, smaller Island between the two I've never
seen before. Some music starts playing. It's epic, with crashing cymbals
and big echoing drums. Thrills rise up inside my lungs.

"This is Betteravia," says Captain Poursport over a building chorus.
"Several days from now, after sailing up and down the coast, the Philanthropist will arrive on this idyllic island paradise and one of you will be
declared victor — the winner of one million dollars cash!"

There's an audible gasp from the crowd. Betteravia. It sounds so
majestic, so perfect, like a world without sadness. Immediately, without
knowing why, I want to go there.

The Captain turns to the next note card. The music dies. "But first,
each day you are aboard this ship, you will be pitted against your fellow
passengers in a game of skill and malice — the Game of Chum," he says.

A new picture flashes up on the screen. It's a small figure — probably
made of rubber —of a dude with a big round smiling yellow head and
two enormous fists. He's got his thumbs sticking out, reminding us that
everything is a-okay. He's dressed in a white polo shirt and dark navy
slacks, kind of like the guys in the crew. It reminds me of the smiley face
earrings on Holly Hotstuff's ears.

"This is a Chum," reads the Captain. "A Chum is a curious little
creature."

"Each day, there will be enough of them hidden around the ship for
all but one of you to find. A Chum is your best friend. Without a Chum,

you cannot advance to the next round. So each day, at least one of you will fail to find your Chum, and so one of you will be eliminated."

One of the blondies in the front row raises her hand. She looks like Candy's twin, except that her dress is bright red. "Um, so you mean it's like a treasure hunt?" she asks.

"Yes, like a musical chairs treasure hunt," says Captain Poursport.

Suddenly, all the yellow and blue and red lights flash on, then blink off and on again like a computer terminal gone haywire. Merry-go-round type music starts playing, and Captain Poursport looks up at Cecil. Some guy in a red baseball cap is sitting next to Cecil on the captain's deck. He's got a megaphone in one hand. Cecil glares through his sunglasses at the Captain and Captain Poursport growls and sighs, like they're forcing him to do something he'd rather not.

Captain Poursport starts swinging his legs and arms in a slow, reluctant jig, then picks up speed as the music grows louder. He sings:

> *This, is a Chum, and… no matter who you are,*
> *You'll need a Chum to get you through the day.*
> *This, is a Chum, and when you're feeling blue,*
> *This little guy will help you on your way.*

The crew joins in the song, and I'm surrounded by live musical theater in real stereo. The Chum on the screen bounces and flips around.

> *Because no one ought to go through life alone….*
> *We've made a friend for you to own…*
> *This, is your Chum!*
> *Once you've found him, be sure to guard it with your life,*
> *Since he and she and him and her, will stab you in the back for*
> *sure . . .*

CHUM

Go! Find your Chum!!!

Captain Poursport and his crew make a big showy finish, dazzle fingers and all, and the Captain straightens himself like he's trying to regain a shred of dignity. Everyone gazes around, trying to figure out what just happened. I don't know what to think. They're probably just as weirded out by this as I am.

The guy in the red ball cap barks through his megaphone. "Cut! Cut! Come on people! Applause! You've just been given an Emmy award-winning performance and this is the kind of response I get? More pathos! Alright. We're going to have to do this over, from the top."

A murmur and a sigh pulses through the crowd. Everyone looks confused. I am too. This is a reality show. It's supposed to be real. We're not supposed to practice. "Oh, please!" shouts Holly Hotstuff.

The guy with the megaphone — he must be the director — ignores the protests. "Look, I need some good TV," he shouts. "You know how many saps are dying to be on this show? C'mon. Let's give it more feeling in all the right places this time."

There's another groan. Holly Hotstuff rolls her eyes for me and I smile.

The Captain starts his speech over from the very beginning. Everyone gasps and ooh's and aah's dramatically, but it's not enough for Mr. Director up there, and we have to do it two more times. My feet start to hurt, and I need a sandwich, and the sun is getting high in the sky.

Finally we do one more take and the director claps his hands. "That'll do," he says. I flop down on my orange X and rest.

"There's nothing real about this," says Holly. I laugh a little, but mostly on the inside. I don't want her to think I'm into her or anything. It might make her nervous.

Candy #2 in the front row raises her hand again. My eyes dart back and forth between her and Candy #1 right next to me. If it weren't for their dresses, I don't think I could tell them apart.

Next to Candy #2 is a fat guy. On her other side is the super jock who was standing in front of me in line. He's big, his head's shaved, and he's wearing a gray football jersey with the number eight on it. He looks like he might have been a high school football player. He's not the kind of guy you want to mess with, that Touchdown.

Touchdown's already massaging Candy #2's shoulders. Fatman in the front row is watching, like he wishes Candy #2 were his. "Umm, Captain?" she asks.

He turns around.

"So what happens if you lose?" says Candy #2.

"I'm so glad you asked," the Captain says. He smiles sadistically, pulls a copper baton from his belt and flips a switch. The nightstick sizzles like a bug-zapper, little bolts of lightning surging down its length. He swings it at Fatman, catching him full in the chest. Fatman collapses, slamming to the ground, a convulsing heap of electric flesh.

People scream. Touchdown and Candy #2 jump back. I go to red alert. Fatman's twitching, howling in pain. In a flash, Killjoy and three more crew men come out of nowhere, grab Fatman by the legs and arms, and heave-ho him over the side of the ship like a sack of sausage. There's a dull splash, and just like that, Fatman disappears beneath the sea.

▶ CHAPTER 5
THE PRISONER'S DILEMMA

The fire alarm in my head goes off. Everything's gone wrong. I can't believe this is happening.

"Man overboard!" cries Captain Poursport. He laughs; there's nothing funny about it.

I rush to the ship's railing, along with everyone else.

"He'll drown!" screams Candy #2 at the top of her lungs. She's crying hysterically. Touchdown is hyperventilating.

I press up against the railing. The sea's turned deep and blue, and there are waves building up in pointy mounds. Fatman's head bobs up above the surface; he's alive! He spits and sputters, trying to breathe. He's flailing, and for a second, it looks like Candy #2 might be right. I look for something to throw. There's nothing. Every rope and buoy is tacked down.

"Help!" cries Fatman. The Philanthropist ignores his plea, callously sailing on, spewing a widening wake of white foam between us and Fatman. There's nothing we can do. "Help!" he says again, with panic in his voice; this time it's fainter. Soon he's nothing but a bobbing cork far away, alone amidst the endless waves.

There's a jet ski at the rear of the ship near the captain's deck. I turn and dash toward it. Maybe I can turn it loose. Killjoy and his gang cut me off. "Get back on your X", he growls. He shoves me to the ground. He's got a copper spark club too. He pulls the trigger, and hot electricity shoots down the length. He swings it at me. For a second, I think I'm going to get electrocuted too, when he pulls his swing short and misses on purpose. He flashes his silver teeth at me. I get the hint: I move, he attacks.

I back away; there's nothing I can do for now. He's got the upper hand.

By now land is a pale and hazy strip of brown horizon, with trillions of gallons of deep, blueberry-soda sea between Fatman and home. He's an ant crossing the desert. How many miles to shore? Five? Fifteen? I've only ever swum one at a time. And that was without ocean tides. He might as well walk to the moon.

A huge bald guy with a blonde handlebar mustache that reaches down to his chin points over the side. "What was that for?" he shouts. Everything he's got is clenched — teeth, knuckles, eyebrows, forehead — they're all clenched, he's so fuming mad. He's built strong, like a tractor. In fact, he even has a tattoo of a tractor on his shoulder.

"A demonstration," says the Captain. "It's how we'll be ending each round."

"You going to throw me overboard too?" shouts Handlebar-mustache man, like he's daring them to try. There are protests on all sides. Everyone's wondering the same thing. Pockmark-face guy grins a pointy-tooth grin.

"Sure as sunshine, if you don't find yer Chum!" laughs the Captain.

So that's it. That's how it's going to be. If you lose, you're tossed overboard, without even walking the plank. It's a game of survival. The big blue ocean looks wider now.

"Eeeeh," moans Candy #1 and faints right next to me. She hits the deck kind of hard. I kneel down next to her and shake her gently. Her eyes flutter open. Everyone looks worried. Marcus is squeamishly green.

"We didn't sign up for this!" shouts a curly, dark-haired woman in a shiny silver sequin shirt that reminds of fish scales. She's tubby around the middle, and wearing high heels with her jeans. There's a clamor of agreement on all sides.

"Come now!" shouts the director through his megaphone. "We need the drama level way up· here," he stretches his arm straight up over his head. "If your poor performance earlier is any indication, there's no way around it — we have to raise the stakes."

There's more yelling. The contestants in front of me crowd toward the captain's deck, shouting their complaints up at the director. My ninja cortex tells me to get ready, in case there's another fight.

Handlebar mustache guy is pacing back and forth, fuming so hard, his bald head's wrinkled on top; he looks like he'll blow a vertebrate. If it weren't for Killjoy's spark club, he'd probably pound Killjoy or the Captain to pulp.

Mr. Director's megaphone squeals. "To be perfectly clear, you did in fact sign a contract which 'indemnifies the Studio from all negligence and harm caused to you for dramatic purposes.'" He's holding up a contract with his other hand.

That does it. Handlebar charges the captain's deck, his huge fist cocked, like he's going to do some damage. Killjoy is quicker — he swings his club and — thwack! — brings it down squarely on Handlebar's gigantic shoulders. Handlebar drops fast; he sounds like wet meat on pavement when he hits the deck. He's knocked out cold and twitchy.

Sailors pour out of the fore and aft of the ship, spark clubs in hand. They form a wall between the contestants and Mr. Director, like they're waiting for a riot. Cecil looks cool as a melon up there. It seems like he's been through this before.

Several of the crew ignites their clubs, and just the crackle and pop of electricity is enough to scare the closest contestants back a few steps.

"Have we already forgotten?" says Mr. Director. "One million dollars is at stake here. I don't think I need to say that again."

Suddenly, the crowd quiets down. I can tell they're still mad, but no one wants to say it.

I can't believe that worked. Someone gets thrown overboard and all you have to do is mention money and it all goes away? This is stupid. Holly turns around. She gives me a 'who are these people?' look.

"Look, you are all entitled to your own opinion," says Mr. Director. He presses a button next to his chair. Some chains clank, and a hatch at our feet in the deck in front of us grinds open. A set of stairs leads down below. A neon blue and gold sign on the underside of the open hatch flickers on. It's an arrow that points down below deck. "Management" it says.

"If you've got grievances, take them up with the management," says Mr. Director. The armed sailors form two lines that funnel into either side of the hatch, like the sides of a V.

Cecil descends another set of stairs on the captain's deck that I can't see. Soon, he's out of sight.

Handlebar is awake now. Shaky, he lifts himself up from the ground. His head is still twitching from the shock, like he's got a nervous tick. "I think I will," he growls. He limps down into the hatch. One of the sailors follows him, spark club ready.

Candy #2's right behind him. She was standing right next to Fatman when he got electrified, and she looks just as mad about this whole thing as I am. They practically drowned him! Who knows what will happen to him out there? I feel like we've been lured here under false pretenses, and I want to give management a piece of my mind. I decide to join them.

I go straight for the hatch, when suddenly I feel the crowd's eyes on me. They're awkwardly silent. Nobody wants to make eye contact. It's hard for me to tell what they're thinking. I can't believe they're not mad about this! I thought they wanted justice!

Glamour Sequins Girl, the curly-haired middle-aged woman wearing the shiny fish-scale sequins on her shirt, shifts back and forth on her feet, her eyes on her toes. She was one of the first to scream and protest, but now she doesn't look so sure. Maybe she changed her mind when they mentioned the money. It seems like a lot of people did.

I pause and turn back to Holly. She knows how stupid all this is. "You coming?" I ask.

She looks at me. She's very serious. "I'm not sure it will do much good at this point," she says. "The game is already afoot."

I should feel disappointed. Instead I flush a little warm. I think I'd get along pretty well with this girl. She's seems smart, and different. And she might be right; I'm not sure they'll listen to me.

Then I notice out of the corner of my eye that Marcus is staring at me. His lips are shut tight, and he's kind of looking down his nose at me, like he's waiting to see what I'll do.

"Brownnoser," mutters Touchdown. I catch him looking my way.

I stop. Why did he say that? Maybe this isn't the right thing. If it was, wouldn't everyone else go down the hatch too?

Maybe I... No. I try and shake off my self-doubt. I don't care what Touchdown says. I have to try. They threw Fatman overboard! I can't let that slide.

I turn toward the hatch again. There's a stir on my right and on my left. There's guilt on Glamour Sequin's face. Maybe she's afraid what people will think of her, if she stands by while others make complaints.

I go down the first stair, and instantly there's shuffling and some shoving behind me as others start to crowd their way toward the hatch. I guess no one wants to be the only one who doesn't care, especially if everyone else seems to be full of sympathy. Maybe they feel like they have to complain.

It's not long before there's a line of bodies behind me, all pressing ahead, waiting for their turn to have their say. It makes me feel kind of good, knowing that I'm one of the first.

I go down the narrow wooden stairs — there are only ten of them. I have to be careful not to hit my head. It's darker down below.

At the bottom are four closed, narrow doors, each one marked by a glowing yellow neon arrow pointing down at it. The third one flashes. The door opens.

I look around. A skinny beanpole guy with freckles lines up inside my personal space right behind me. I guess that's my cue, so I step through the door. It shuts behind me.

Some lights switch on. I'm in a cell that's bright and white and almost nothing else. There's a camera, with a beady little lens squinting at me hard, a silver table, and a pair of silver metal chairs — one for me, and one across the table facing me. It's the kind of room you'd expect would have a two-way mirror for interrogation, only I haven't done anything wrong.

They could beat me in here. Or torture me too. I guess I'll have to wait and see. Maybe they're already doing it to Handlebar and Candy #2 in the rooms next door. I search the cell for means of escape, just in case it comes to that. I try the door I entered by. It's already locked. There's a door on the opposite wall.

"It's just a TV show," I tell myself, trying to cling to normalcy. Tell that to Fatman, I think.

I reach over the table to see if the opposite door is unlocked.

It opens, and I pull back my hand and sit down real quick, like I've been waiting there the whole time.

It's Cecil who enters. He's still wearing his sunglasses. He's got on his trim green suit. "Hello," he says. His voice sounds as pleasant as a tinny voice can.

I take a breath. At least it's not the Captain, or Mr. Director. I know Cecil. "You didn't tell me…" I start. I'm going to yell at him.

He pulls a spark-club from behind his back. I scoot back and spring to my feet, toppling my chair. I won't go down without a fight.

"Please Mr. Middleworth," he says, pleasant as can be. He sets the club down on the table. "It's been deactivated." He holds both hands up to show they're empty. One is slimy smooth.

I relax a little. "Then what's it for?" I ask, pointing at the club. He brought it here for a reason.

He shrugs. "It's yours," he says.

That doesn't make sense. I'm not one of the sailors. You won't catch me frying my fellow contestants.

"Please, sit down," says Cecil. He takes a seat opposite me. "You had something you wanted to see me about?"

How can he pretend he doesn't know! He's playing innocent; I'm not falling for it. I take the safety off my finger and point it right between his eyes. "You drowned the fat guy!"

Cecil shakes his head and frowns. He's quiet, then he shakes it some more, slower this time. Finally, he speaks, "Just how far from shore do you think we are?" he asks.

I can't tell. The mountains were my only landmark when I was on deck, and they were covered in world famous Los Angeles haze. "Five, six miles!" I say. "Enough to kill someone!"

Cecil does more of his head shaking. "More like one," he says. "The GPS can confirm it."

ADAM GLENDON SIDWELL

I assume Cecil is telling the truth — for the moment — so I can run some calculations in my head. 5280 feet in one mile, which equals 1760 yards. 4 lengths in the pool is 100 yards, so that's about 70 lengths or so. That's a lot of laps. It can be done. By me for example. Just not by everyone. "You don't even know that guy can swim!" I say.

"Mr. Middleworth, how do you think Mr. Roberts was cast for this show?"

Mr. Roberts must be Fatman. Or was Fatman. "I don't know," I say.

"I found him surfing at Manhattan beach. Don't let his size deceive you. He is a very, very strong paddler," says Cecil. "And quite buoyant to boot."

Maybe that's why I was recruited at the pool. "What's your point?" I say.

Cecil pulls a small black tablet computer from his pocket. It's beeping. He points to a flashing red dot on the screen.

"Captain Poursport clipped a tracker to Mr. Roberts before he threw him overboard. My point is that he should make it to land sometime before nightfall," he says. "He will be exhausted, but perfectly alive."

He's lying. He's got to be. There's no way he can guarantee Fatman will live. Or any of us for that matter. The whole thing jangles my nethers way too much to be true.

"And truly, I do owe you an apology for the barbaric treatment you've received at the hand of Captain Poursport and his crew," says Cecil. He sighs. "It takes constant effort to keep that man's brutality in check."

Is that supposed to be nice? Cecil's apology is unacceptable. This whole thing reeks, and I want to keep myself away from it. I get an idea. "I won't play," I say. It feels good, to stand my ground like that. I hope I'm doing the right thing.

"Oh?" says Cecil. He's calm, unmoving. He leans forward in his chair. "But you're already playing. You have been since you set foot aboard this ship."

"You can't make me find the Chums." I say, folding my arms.

"Then we won't be able to advance you to the next round." His face is hard as stone. "And I'm afraid I cannot keep the Captain from enforcing the rules of the game."

So there's no choice in it? If only there was a way to call the mainland. That must be why Captain Poursport took our cell phones. "This has got to be against the law!" I say.

"Nope," Cecil says, "We checked the law, and it's just bad manners."

Cecil knew exactly what he was doing when he lured us onboard this ship. "We're prisoners here!" I shout, smashing my fists onto the tabletop. I'm out of my chair, ready to lunge across the table and grab Cecil by the throat.

Cecil points at the camera in the corner. Its red blinking eye is aimed at me. "You're on TV, Mr. Middleworth!"

I flatten my hands and count to ten. He's right. There's no telling what they would do with footage of my rage. They're holding all the cards. I've got to put my best foot forward. I've got to choose my words with care.

I consider my options. Cecil has me cornered. The crew outnumbers me. Plus they have a couple million volts on their side. If I don't play, I won't find a Chum. If I don't have a Chum at the end of the round, they won't hesitate to throw me overboard too. What they did to Fatman is evidence of that.

"Are you quite in control now?" asks Cecil. He waits, but I don't answer. I'm getting hot around the ears. "Then here's what happens next," he says. "If you decide to forfeit, you may make yourself comfortable until the end of the round, at which time you will be subject to the rules of the game as administered by the Captain and his crew."

"You mean you throw me overboard," I say.

Cecil nods once. "It is unfortunate, and it is extremely embarrassing, not to mention forgettable, when one is eliminated in the first episode of the television season."

I cringe. I know how it goes. The guy who leaves with his tail between his legs. They barely get an exit interview. It's humiliating.

"Or, you choose to participate — which seems to be the reason you came here in the first place — and I'll activate your club."

"My club? Why would I need that?" I say. There must be something they haven't covered.

"To defend yourself of course."

"From what?"

"From the other contestants," says Cecil.

I'm not going to believe it for a second. They wouldn't betray each other like that. They wouldn't be willing to fry each other for a million dollars. Not Handlebar. Not Candy. Not Glamour Sequin girl. Or maybe Glamour Sequin Girl. Definitely growling Pockmark Face guy.

"The game is in motion, Mr. Middleworth. The others are having the same interview as you in the adjacent rooms. They are being offered a similar choice. Some of them have already made it. Are you willing to gamble that every single one of them feels as strongly about forfeiting as you do?"

He has a point there. Let's say one of them decides to play. Then I'm left unarmed. No one wants to bring a toothpick to a knife fight, much less come empty handed. All it takes is for Pockmark guy or Marcus to plug his cattle prod into you and crank up the volts, and you're out cold and hurting. I'd lose the round for sure.

Those are just the kind of guys who would do it too. Then they grab the goods, and the rest of us get the deep six. That is, if anybody else decides to sit around and let themselves lose. I don't want to be that guy. I don't want to be left unarmed.

I was stupid to come down the hatch. I should have stayed on deck. We could have all refused to play together, to start a mutiny. Handlebar would have stood his ground. Candy #1 would too. Holly — well, I'm not sure what she would do. If only I could talk to them, we could band together. Instead I'm trapped. And they are too.

Maybe Cecil and Captain Poursport meant for us to come down here, so they could separate us. That way they could keep us from banding together.

Cecil is quiet. He's staring at me, studying me. At least it seems that way behind those big black glasses. "I'd like to speak to you off the record for a moment, if I might," he says.

I can pretend not to listen, but I'm a prisoner here. He's got a captive audience. I cross my arms.

He taps the screen on the black tablet computer in his weird shiny hand, and the red light on the camera goes out.

I'm glad he turned off the camera at least. It feels like I've just stepped off the podium after public speaking. I can relax a little.

Cecil reaches for his glasses. I've never seen him take them off before. I'm almost afraid of what he'll do, since I'm pretty sure they're welded to his face, and removing them might tear his skin off. I hold my breath. He takes them off, and there's a chubby face underneath. I sigh.

His eyes are pale blue – uncomfortably so – like somebody squeezed all the pigment out. I look away, so he doesn't think I'm staring at them.

He folds the earpieces. "I want you to have a fighting chance of making it to Betteravia," he says slowly, almost softly.

I'm confused. He's talking like my Dad did that one time he got emotional – I've rarely seen it since.

"You remember what I told you that day I met you at the pool?" Cecil asks.

There were so many things. One especially sticks out. "That you want to make me famous," I say.

A tremor runs through Cecil's chest, pushing out air in short bursts. He must be chuckling. "I suppose I did say that, didn't I?" His eyes are so pale, it's unnerving. "And I believe that will happen. I also told you that you had something – a certain quality about you that is hard to find."

Of course that's all true, but I'm not sure what he's getting at.

"I think you can win this game," he says. "That's why I chose you. It's my privilege as producer to cast for this show. I decide how to make it a good season, which means I have to pick winners, and potential losers. I'm sorry, but not everyone has the same fighting chance going into it. I've been producing for a long time Levi. We can tell fairly well beforehand just who is likely to triumph, and who is not." He folds his hands.

I'm listening. "You have the intangibles — call it courage, call it intuition, call it dynamic athleticism—," he shakes a finger gently at me. "—there's something that I saw when I plucked you out of the pool that day, something that said, 'this man is going to make it to Betteravia, and that's just the beginning.' I want to see just how far you'll go in the world, Levi."

I don't know what to say. His eyes are watery, almost sad. I didn't expect him to open up like that. I didn't expect him to understand.

He presses his thumb and forefinger on his normal hand to his eyes, and squeezes them shut. When he opens them again, he looks right at me. "I'm leaving the choice in your hands," he says. He slides the club across the table toward me.

He's right. This is my chance. The one I knew would come. It's what I was meant to do. Destiny, I think.

I pick up the club and heft it, just so I can take a look. It's solid, about the weight of half a wooden baseball bat. It's got metal prongs on the end, and more running down its length in a spiral pattern, plus a hand guard like an old cutlass. I have to admit, it's kind of cool -- like a pirate sword from space.

Cecil stands, pushes the door open and steps back to let me through. I hesitate, but I know what I have to do. I step out of the bright white room and into a gloomy passageway with wooden planks and support beams climbing up the walls and crisscrossing the ceiling. There are two wooden staircases there, each one a single flight; one leads up, the other down. A glowing red neon arrow points upward. It reads "Forfeit." A glowing green arrow points down. It's bigger, and it's flashing on and off, casting a green glow over all the wooden planks. "This Way to Chums," it says.

I clip my spark club to my belt and charge down the stairs as fast as I can.

⏵ CHAPTER 6
THE GAME IS AFOOT

There's a buzz then a tinkling sound as soon as I reach the bottom of the stair, and my spark club surges full of power, like it just plugged into an invisible socket. I make a few practice swipes in the air like my ancient samurai ancestors would do, then hit the trigger. White bolts of electricity sizzle between the prongs. It crackles, and the walls flash white, blinding me; I almost drop it. Stars float in front of my face. It startled me, I guess. I put it away on my belt.

Only in case of emergency, I think. I couldn't bring myself to use it on anybody. Except maybe Marcus.

There's a dark, narrow hallway at the bottom of the stairs. It's so narrow it'll scrape my elbows off if I don't hold them in close as I run. Everything is cramped down here, like I'm in a clubhouse built for little kids. Submarines are the same way too, from what I hear, except this place is made out of wood. The further I go, the less light there is — all I get is a few dusty sunbeams filtering through narrow gaps in the boards overhead. The whole place is musty too, like it's short on air, and moldy as bread.

I'm not sure what to do next, except look for Chums, so I keep running.

The hallway dead ends. It's lit up by the numbers 1, 2 and 3, each outlined in flashing light bulbs at the end of the hall. There's a red door under the number 1, a blue one under number 2, and a yellow door under number 3.

I stop. This decision could make all the difference. I'd heard a poem once about exactly this thing, except it was in a forest, and it was a split in a path, and there wasn't a million dollars in the poem. I try to guess which one a champion would choose. Nothing too obvious, but nothing too unlikely either. You have to outwit the masterminds behind these things.

So I choose the yellow one. "What's behind door number 3?" I mutter, and push on it. It swings away from me. Behind it is a small room the size of a closet. There's a faint blue flashing arrow pointing into a square hole. A ladder leads downward.

I get close enough to peer down over the edge. It's dark down there, and hard to tell how far down the hole goes.

I set my feet on the rungs and squeeze my shoulders down, then lower myself into darkness. It's only a few round rungs then a short drop to the ground. My sandals hit the floor.

This hallway is different. It's even narrower, and it runs directly underneath the one above, as far as I can tell. It's darker too, since the sunbeams don't make it this far down. I'd have a hard time squeezing past anyone who got in my way. There's a cluster of three cameras, all pointed in different directions, screwed into the ceiling, blinking and staring at me, watching my every move.

I flash a smile. I need to show the folks back at home who's champ.

Beneath the cameras are three round openings cut into the wall, just large enough to crawl into, one on top of another.

I choose the highest one, because it's the hardest to get to, and that's what a winner would do. I scramble up to it, using the other holes as steps, then rest my belly on the tube until I can heave myself in and get on my knees. It's metal — this must be a newer part of the ship. I crawl inside, and the tube turns right. So do I. I imagine this is what a hamster feels like.

In a few feet the tube bends straight down. There's a floor six feet down, so I twist around to my back and slide feet first down out of the tube. I hit the floor with a thud. I'm in another damp, musky passageway a few yards long. There's a single, electric light bulb screwed into the ceiling. It casts a weak yellow light in a narrow pool around it. Everything else is dark.

The hallway branches off to the right and left in a T. A dark figure rushes across the end of the hall and disappears.

I can't tell who it is, but it's just like I guessed — I'm not the only one who's decided to play. The game is on.

I stumble to the end of the hall. Whoever ran by is gone now. There's another light bulb there, this one green. On the left is a set of metal spiral stairs leading downward – those must've been added more recently — on the right is a hallway that doubles back. There are nets hanging down from the ceiling, like they've been long forgotten there. Everything else is dark. I hear more rushing, and a couple of someones pass by down below. They're moving fast, the ship creaking beneath them as they go.

I guess everyone wants that million dollars after all. I couldn't have been talking to Cecil that long. Maybe everyone else was quicker to agree when no one was watching. If so, they have a head start. Which means I'm behind. I'm late to the mall late at Christmastime — there may not be any Chums left.

I drop down the spiral stairs as fast as I can — the metal rails are smooth — it's like sliding down a screw. The steps are painted orange and green. Whoever was down there must be rushing after something. My feet hit the floor. They're already gone.

Maybe they were chasing something important, so I decide to follow them. I'm not even sure I'll recognize a Chum when I see it. What if they're really small? This could be like hunting for Easter eggs.

As far as I can tell in the darkness, there's an open doorway to the left, and another further up on the right. Otherwise, the place looks empty.

Something small skitters across the floor in front of my foot. It disappears. It was probably a rat. Gross.

I duck through the doorway on the right. There's a room filled with barrels and rope and some cabinets, with a camera mounted on the ceiling, and a door on the opposite wall. There's a big wheel as tall as I am mounted to the wall, with pegs nailed into the rim. The wheel has sections painted on it like slices of pie. Each slice has a decal pasted on it. Several of the decals are numbers: 100, 700, 1,000 and 99,000. There's also a decal of a rat, a pile of money, and a big yellow smiley face.

I grab one of the pegs and pull slightly. "WELCOME TO FUTURE'S WHEEL!" booms a voice. The whole wheel lights up. Each section has a bright light behind it, except for the yellow smiley face. I'm not sure why, but that seems odd to me, like that slice of the pie must be broken. "Spin to win!" says the voice.

So I do. I pull the wheel down as hard as I can — much harder than average I'm sure — and it spins with a satisfying clack-clack as the pegs click past a small arrow that points toward the decals as they pass.

The wheel spins around a full three times before it finally begins to slow. It creeps over the 100, the 700, a picture of a hot dog, then finally settles on a 50. The lights on the section with the 50 flash. "You've won!" says the voice. The light goes dim under the 50 and a small metal door beneath the wheel flaps open.

I look inside. There's 50 dollar bill behind the door. Not bad. Could've been a 99,000, but not bad. I take the 50, and hold it up to the lights on the wheel. It's got a great big round smiley face in the center, where

Ulysses S. Grant should be. That's odd. "Chum Bucks" it says, written in fine print below the serial numbers. "For exchange to legal tender at the end of the game."

Great. As good as the real thing I guess. I pocket the bill. I'll buy Dad some steaks. He loves steaks.

Now there are two sections of the wheel dimmed. The one I landed on, and the big smiling yellow head. It looks like someone got here before me. They won something, and I have one guess what it is.

I try to spin the wheel one more time, just to see if I can get the 99,000, or even the hot dog, but it locks up. Must be that only one spin's allowed per contestant.

There's nothing else in the room except more toppling stacks of junk. Even the barrels are sealed shut, so I decide to move on. I shove the door open. It gives way, scraping along the floor, and I come out into another hallway.

It's empty too. I wander around for another dozen twists and turns. There's an occasional string of blinking light bulbs. It's dark for the most part and there are more ropes and metal tunnels and cameras, some of them taped to the wall.

I ignore them. It's getting harder to be urgent. I haven't seen anybody or anything as exciting as the wheel. All my dashing and diving is just a waste of energy, when there isn't anything to find. These corridors are endless! I'm surprised at what a titanic this ol' Mayflower is. It didn't look this big from the outside.

I hear the occasional patter of feet on the wooden floors, or creaks in the timbers, but all I see are shadows for at least another half hour. It seems like ages, and I start to get tired of looking.

I step through another doorway into yet another room. This one is full of wooden crates and all sorts of rusty metal machinery with gears and cranks and tubes. It looks like a giant tractor engine, with a tangle of hoses attached and oil dribbling out. None of it is on. It's leaky and wet in here, so it might be a pump.

"Get out!" says a voice. It's a woman. She sounds panicked, terrified. It's coming from the shadows in the corner. "There's nothing in here!" she screeches.

I put up my hands to show I'm harmless. Truthfully, I'm just glad to see another human being. "I don't want anything," I say. That sounds dumb, so I add, "I'm looking for termites."

The shadows shift. I can make out her outline. She's tall, and a bit overweight. She leans forward, and the light catches her curly brown hair and round face and glints off her silver sequined shirt. It's the Glamour Sequin Girl. "You won't find them here!" she says.

Good. At least she's checked. I don't want bugs to chew a hole in the hull. "What is in here, then?" I ask.

She hisses. I'd expect that from a lizard, or maybe a wild cat. I don't think she wants to be my friend.

Something squeaks, like a little girl's talking doll, "I'll be your Chum forever," it says, in a faint robotic whimper. It's coming from behind her, in the shadows.

"Is that a Chum?" I say. I can't see it, but I want to. I need to know what they look like in real life. I didn't think they could talk.

"There's nothing HERE!" she shouts. She holds something big and round up toward me. It's too dark to tell what it is. As she does, an ear-splitting scream rips through my ear drums.

I cover my ears, knowing that if it doesn't stop, my brain will probably bleed.

I don't know whether I should run or curl up into a ball, when the screaming stops. There's no way that could've come from her. It was too loud.

Suddenly she charges me, her club in the air. It bursts into a crackle of light. The whole room flashes white, and her lipstick covered mouth is twisted open like a gargoyle. I'm horrified. She really wants to hurt me. She swings her club at me.

I push off the floor as hard as I can, dodging backward awkwardly. She misses. What'd I ever do to her? "I just want to look…" I say. I'm blinded by the flash. All I can see is white. I have to get out of here, and fast.

She swings again. This time I'm more ready. I duck behind a barrel, then shove it toward her, knocking it over. She stumbles, and that gives me the second I need to make it back out the door. There's wide enough berth now between me and the psycho woman. I put my hand on my club, just in case. "Lunatic!" I say. "No one's trying to take your Chum!"

"I don't care!" she screams. She kicks a box at me. It hits the wall and shatters. "Get out of here!"

"Fine!" I shout, wondering how they ever let a maniac on the show. She seemed so calm and normal when we were up on deck.

I'm a little mad at myself for getting bullied away so easily, but what was I supposed to do? I'm not going to steal her Chum from her.

The screaming starts again, so I beat a retreat down the hall the way I came, trying to put as much distance between me and the active volcano as possible. She wouldn't hesitate to fry me, and I don't want to give her the chance to sneak up from behind. Shakespeare couldn't tame that shrew.

I hope she of all people doesn't win. If she gets famous she'll scare people away, and no one will watch TV anymore. What was that screaming anyway?

She did already find her Chum. She must have won it on the wheel. That's why the smiley face was dim. That was good luck — for her. I didn't know they talked. If only I could have seen it. I'd know better what to look for.

"This is harder than I thought," I grumble to myself. It would be nice to have someone to team up with, or at least talk to. I'm still hungry. And I have to use the bathroom.

I turn the corner and there's a big red lever sticking out of the ground. It's as tall as I am, with a black rubber grip on the end. Mounted on the wall at eye level are a bunch of tiles – each one the size of my head. They're arranged three high and three across, just like a tic-tac-toe board. They're slowly blinking on and off randomly, one at a time. There is a different picture on each of them. A dollar bill, a bottle of ketchup, a purple flower, a spiky bear trap, a fish, a stick of dynamite, and there it is – another big yellow smiley face.

Another chance to win a Chum. I decide to take it. I grab the lever with both hands, and a recorded voice booms "You're playing Pull-A-Prize, where you're a winner every time! Pull to win!"

That sounds good to me. The lights start flashing faster and faster. First a half second per tile, then less, until they're flashing so fast there's no way I can pull the lever in time to get exactly what I want. So I take two breaths, count on luck, and pull hard.

The tiles suddenly stop. One stays lit up, blinking right at me. It's the ketchup bottle. I'm not really sure what kind of prize that is, but it beats a flower I guess.

The tile flips open and a nozzle slides out. It hisses, then sprays ketchup all over my shirt. I feel cool, slimy paste soak through the cotton onto my skin. I hate ketchup.

"Play again?" asks the game show voice.

I consider the bear trap and stick of dynamite. A dark figure runs across the far end of the hall. Someone else is close. I decide to take my chances elsewhere. It's too much of a risk, and besides, Pull-A-Prize is probably rigged anyway. I wipe the ketchup away with my hand, then wipe that on the wood.

I'm starting to get anxious. The clock is ticking, and I haven't seen a single Chum yet. Cecil was counting on me. He said that I could win this. If that's so certain, I'd rather just be at the end of the game now, where I've won it all. Wasn't I made for that? I hate not knowing!

There are more hallways and staircases and ladders — some of them old, some of them new — all wrapped in a dark and musty smell. I decide to make my way back up on deck to take a timeout; I have to go that bad. I climb the next three staircases I can find, which isn't easy to do, with all the twists and turns. I wander for another quarter hour, until I climb a short ladder, open a blue door and come to a stretch of hallway that looks familiar. There's a staircase at the end, with four doors and the glowing green sign that says 'This Way to Chums' at the top. I'm back at the beginning. I'm lucky I found it.

I climb the steps toward the four doors. My club stops humming, then clicks off. There must be a remote that powers them down when they come to the staircase. I click the trigger just to be sure. Nothing happens. No sparks.

There's a fifth door, one I couldn't see before, all the way to the right. It's painted a lovely red and has a sign marked 'Crew'. It looks more modern, since it's not made of rotting wood. It's closed. There's bound to be a bathroom in there, so I shove the door open and go inside.

This hallway is well-lit by round portholes every few feet, which means I'm on the outer part of the ship. All I see is ocean out there. I should be just below the deck, if I remember right. I go through another door that swings on its hinges, and come to a hallway that runs across the ship from side to side. There's a big shiny stainless steel door, and a brass one across from it that's bolted into the wall.

The brass one's dotted with rivets. There's a small glass window at eye level. It looks like a bank vault. I'm not going to pass up a good bathroom when I see one, so I rap my knuckles against it. "Come in," says a muffled voice inside. I pull on the handle and yank on the door. It's so heavy, it only scrapes open halfway.

There's a guy in a white lab coat with a mushroom cloud of black hair staring up at a glass computer monitor. His back is to me.

The monitor shows a map of the Los Angeles coast. Red dots appear on it, one after another, like pimples before the prom. One blue dot pulses on and off. Then the red dots move slowly toward the blue one, almost like they're swarming. They all disappear, then go back to where they started, and swarm again.

A second monitor displays a timer that's counting down. It beeps, and a computer voice whines "Estimated four days, 18 hours until Friend's E-Day".

I don't have to ask – this is not the bathroom. I shouldn't be here.

A second man is hunched over a desk. He's got on a pair of spectacles the size of root beer mugs. There are only a few hairs poking out the top of his head. He looks old, like my science teacher last year.

There's a big round yellow smiling rubber head the size of a cantaloupe on the table next to him. A tangled mess of copper, blue and red wiring spills out of the head onto the table. It's got to be a Chum — or what's left of one. I feel my throat leap a little. I want it.

He's picking at the wires with a pair of tweezers, too focused on his task to notice me. "You're so certain they're our friends, but when they get the chance they'll tear us apart," he says, shining a light into the Chum's head.

The man with the mushroom cloud of hair points up to the timer. "We have to convince them!"

The man with the huge specs turns to face the monitor, "You mean the contestants do…" he says gruffly. "I don't want those deaths on my hands!" He looks right at me. "Hey! How did you get in here?" He sh
He jumps from his chair, spilling papers and circuit boards

I turn and run. I've suddenly got the feeling that I've seen something I shouldn't, and I'm not going to wait to see what they'll do.

"Stop him!" I hear them shout. I look over my shoulder. A sailor comes out of a door at the end of the hall, club in hand.

I can't let him catch me. I sprint down the stairs, jump down the last few steps, swing open door number 1, and barrel off into the darkness. There are shouts behind me, and the pounding of feet. My club surges on as I go, and that's a good thing — if that sailor gets too close, I'll have to fight.

I dive through the first doorway I can find, come to a staircase, and slide down it. I'm running blind through the dark. I shove past what looks like the beanpole skinny guy and Candy #1 in the hall, and double back through another storage room. There are cameras everywhere. I hadn't thought of that. They could track me.

I pass two games along the way, one that looks like a golden pyramid, and another that looks like a giant hamster wheel with letters on it. I'll have to remember those for later.

Finally I see a metal tube in the wall, and dive through it. I burn my knees as I rub across it, and tumble out the other side onto my back. There's a narrow door there, so I throw myself inside and shut it behind me. It's a closet, with a bucket, mop and drain. It's dark. There's only room for me, and no way in but one. I try to slow my breathing. What is going on with this show? I wonder. There are things Cecil and Mr. Director haven't told us. Something about convincing Chums. Something about tearing us apart.

I wait. It's so cramped in here, I can't even lift my arms. The silence is awful. My chest is a giant, iron lung, heaving in and out, clanging in the quiet. I'm scared.

There's no one. I still have to go, and it's getting bad. I wait for what seems like a year, jumping gently up and down. There's no one still. Maybe I gave them the slip. I should stick my head out and take a peak.

Business first. I empty myself out into the drain. It sounds like a thundering avalanche, and it's sure to give me away, but there's nothing I can do. I wait for another year. Silence.

Then there's the scuffling of feet. It's faint. Whoever it is, they must be far away. I grab hold of my club.

I press myself harder into the shadows. The door is shut tight. I can't let them find me. Especially if it's the Captain. Or his first mate Killjoy. Who knows what they would do? Poor Fatman. He knows — or knew.

The scuffling comes closer, but it's moving awfully slow. If it were guards, they would be running.

It's almost a scratching sound, like a rat, or a battery-powered car. Then there's a whir. It must be a machine.

"I'll be your Chum," says a tiny, toy-like voice like a sad puppy's whimper.

My heart gives a start. I crack the door open and peek into the hall. There, plodding back and forth across the floor on two huge plastic feet, is a big, yellow-headed rubber thing no higher than my knee. It's coming toward me, with two big fists and a set of shiny, polished chompers, its thumbs stuck up in the air like a pair of plumpin' sausages.

I open the door and scan the hall. No one's there.

"I'll be your Chum," it whimpers again. What a lost little puppy. I don't know whether to pity it, fear it, or call it creepy. If grandma were here, she'd want to pinch its cheek; she'd say it was adorable.

Whatever it is, it's my ticket to round number two, so I scoop it up and get ready to go. It's like holding a watermelon — heavy and a little bit awkward. "I'll be your Chum forever," it says. It sounds happy. I could almost swear it was looking at me.

I'm kind of glad. I almost feel like a dad, and this little Chum is my adopted puppy. He'll keep me from dying for the day.

I turn him over. Curious. There's a yellow button in the middle of his back. The button has a light bulb logo on it. I press it, and the Chum's eyes light up a like a pair of flashlights, casting a yellow glow all over the hallway. That was unexpected. Chums do things. This could be useful. I switch it off.

There's a doorway at the end of the hall, and a ladder going up to my left. I start toward it — I need to find a place I can hide out until the end of the round — when I hear a familiar voice. "Big B!"

It's Marcus. He must've seen my Chum light up. He's at the end of the hall with Gumbo under the only light bulb for miles. Funny thing is, I'm actually glad to see him. "Marcus!" I shout. We knew each other way back when — before this game turned everything to madness. "I found one!"

"I know. I saw," he says. He's frowning. "You must have a Luminance Chum. There are Banshee ones, Oil Slick ones — all sorts of them. Some of them don't seem to do much. Gumbo here found a Flash Chum."

A Banshee Chum — I'm pretty sure that's just a name Marcus made up for it — but that must've been what Glamour Sequins used to make that screeching sound. "What's a Flash Chum?" I ask.

Marcus doesn't answer. "Do you want to join our alliance?" he asks instead.

Candy #2 — the Candy in the red dress from the front row — steps out from behind Marcus into the faint pool of light. Touchdown — the guy in the football jersey who was putting the moves on her — is with them. He looks tough. He was probably the quarterback.

Touchdown's cradling a Chum under his arm. Candy #2 has one too.

I'm flattered — I've just been invited to the party — but I'm not sure how all that could work. I've got a Chum, and they have two. That's three to split between five, and Chums split in two don't score you points.

"We don't have enough," I say.

Marcus looks at Gumbo. His cousin looks like Paul Bunyan he's so huge.

"That's the point of the alliance," Marcus says. "We'll find more."

It might be nice to work together, then at least I won't be so alone. I meet them halfway down the hall.

"And we can take the rest," says Candy #2.

I stop and look at her sideways. That's not something I'd expect from Candy #2. But then again, I don't even know her.

"Is that where you got that one?" I ask.

Touchdown smiles. "It's like stealing meat from a vegan," he says.

I don't think he knows what he means by that. He's got one arm around Candy #2. She must be his new girlfriend.

"Don't think you can do that," I say.

Marcus shakes his head, "It's part of the game."

"How do you figure?" I ask. It's not like he's played before. Last thing I remembered the game started today.

Marcus rolls his eyes. "The song. He and she and him and her will stab you in the back for sure," he recites. "You were there for the orientation just like the rest of us. It's policy."

Orientation? Policy? That's just something Marcus would say. It's not like we're starting a new job or school or country or something. This guy thinks he's some kind of senator or upper level management.

"We could let people find their own Chums," I say. That just seems fair to me.

Marcus shakes his head. "Have you ever even seen a reality show?" he asks.

Come to think of it, I have. But only twice. Maybe that's how I fell for all this. I won't tell him that, though. It'll just make him proud of himself. I bite my tongue.

"You have to play the full extent of the game, and master the group dynamics," says Marcus.

I think what he means is you have to cheat and manipulate. "I'll go on my own, thanks," I say. I turn to walk away.

Marcus lets out a groan. "Gumbo, go ahead," he says.

My brain does a double take. I don't like the sound of that. I turn — I'm not fast enough — Marcus and the others' hands cover their eyes. Gumbo holds up a Chum. He presses the button on its back and a blinding, white light flashes through the hallway. Everything goes white hot for a split second, then black, and I see white stars burst across my vision like fireworks. I'm blind.

I turn to stumble away, when something jabs me hard in the ribs. There's a pain in my side, like a thousand forks stabbing me all the way through my body. There's a flash and a crackle — my fat's hit the frying pan — everything goes white again. It hurts so bad. I drop to the floor. My head smashes against the wooden ladder as I fall. Everything flashes blue and red, all at the same time.

"I'll be your Chum forever," says a tiny, whimpering voice, and then everything goes black.

▶ CHAPTER 7
HOLLY HOTSTUFF

Everything is black. More like there is nothing. Not even black. I'm not sure how long I've been gone, or where I've been. Not even sure where I am now for that matter. It's like swimming out of a deep dark tunnel.

Then I feel a heavy metal pole digging into my side, like the mast fell on me, and my veins are stretched and my bones ache. I have never been so keenly aware of my own marrow.

My head hurts. Bad.

I remember where I am — lying on the floor — inside some ship — way out to sea. Marcus. That flash. I shouldn't have ... My Chum! I force my eyelids open.

Everything is fuzzy. I blink. I can see dimness in the hall. There's something coming toward me. I try to focus. It's someone.

Got to get out of here. Can't take another attack. Whoever it is comes toward me. Must move my limbs... I'm helpless, exposed.

"You'll never win like that," says a voice. It's pleasant, almost teasing. Holly Hotstuff. Relief washes over me. My eyes manage to put her face in focus.

I'm drooling. She can probably tell. I turn my head to hide the fact.

She touches my face then feels my head. It's kind of energizing. I grunt. She jumps back.

"Are you going to bite?" she asks.

I try to push myself up. Everything wobbles. I manage to sit with my back leaned up against the wall. I shake my head and draw my knees in close. "No, just slobber," I say.

She laughs. I don't know why. I'm just glad I got my mouth to work. It's good she thinks I'm funny though.

"Someone got you pretty good," she says.

"It was Marcus and his cousin."

She gives me a blank look.

"I know them from school. They wanted to form an alliance, but I said no."

"Hmmm," she says. "An elitist, huh?"

I don't get it.

"They shocked me," I say. "And then they stole my Chum."

She lets out a low whistle. "Bandits!" she says. "But what you gonna do?"

I think of the room with the brass door. I'm glad she's here. I have to tell somebody what I saw. Holly seems like someone I can trust. "There's something they're not telling us," I say.

Holly gives me another look. "Like where Atlantis is?" she asks.

This girl is nuts. "No, about a countdown. There's a timer. Something called Friend's E-Day is coming." I tell her as fast as I can everything about the big brass door, and the guys in lab coats, and the monitors, and the swarming dots, and how the sailor chased me.

"Friend's E-Day?" asks Holly. "What's that supposed to be?"

"I dunno," I say, because I don't. "A whole day sponsored by the letter E?"

Holly frowns. "A day when everyone makes friends online?" she says.

That makes a little more sense. They are called Chums after all. Is that what this is all about? Buddies and friendship? Still, I'd like better answers than that. At least it sounds friendly.

There's more to it though. "They're trying to convince the Chums about something," I say. Before they turn on us, I think. But I don't say it. It can't be true.

"But they're just little dolls," she says.

I shake my head. That little guy looked up into my soul. "Have you seen one?"

Holly rolls out her lower lip, looks up at her forehead and sighs, "I've been trying."

"They seem almost … intelligent," I say. Suddenly, I miss my Chum.

"Take me there."

"I don't think that area's part of the show. It's the crew's section of the ship. There weren't any cameras."

"All the more reason to go," she says.

Like I said, she's nuts. At least that makes her easier to talk to. "They won't like that," I say. She gets up.

"How do I get there?"

I shrug. "It's not that easy to find."

She turns to go. "I guess I'll find it myself," she says.

It's crazy, going back. It's like walking into a lions' den. Or I could stay here alone. I don't want that, either.

She ducks her head through the tube in the wall. I decide to go with her and push myself up on my pulsing feet. They're tingly, but working well enough to stand. I hope the electricity gave me powers, because I'm sure I'm gonna need them.

I crawl through the tube. We can look for Chums along the way, and I can always turn back before we get there. Does this mean we're a team or something? That makes it kind of awkward, since I might not know what to say, if it weren't for all this imminent danger, and since she's hot stuff and all.

Maybe she'll think I'm weird. Maybe it won't get to that. We might even split up before we get down the hall. At least she won't find out what a noob I am. "Holly?" I say.

She turns around. "Yeah?" she says.

"I'm glad you're here," I say. She waits, like I'm supposed to say something else. "Because, it's good that we have two spark clubs, so we can um, back each other up. More firepower." Maybe that sounded dumb.

She nods. "Agreed. Glad you mentioned that."

Or maybe it sounded fine. I'm just a person and she's one too. I promise not to think so much. If only she didn't seem to know so much about everything!

I take the lead and she follows me down the hallway. We take a few turns, and climb another flight of stairs, and go down a couple ladders. I wander through all the twists and turns, trying my best to make up the longest route possible to postpone what's certainly trouble. I'm getting there, just taking the long-cut to do it.

I drag my feet and we go up and down a set of spiral stairs. I'm hoping that Holly doesn't notice how I'm stalling, but really, it's for her own good, and mine too. I'm just not sure what we'll do when we get back to that laboratory. I need time to think. As far as plans go, I've got nothing.

"Are you sure you know the way?" asks Holly.

"Kind of," I say. I'm not sure I can stall any longer, and I don't want to look stupid in front of her, when I see one more distraction to help me delay what I hope is not inevitable. "Look!"

There's a dusty old trap door at the foot of the stairs with a single iron ring just big enough to poke my finger through, screwed into the wood.

"That's the way?" she asks, arching one eyebrow at me like a drawbridge rising up.

I didn't even know people could do that with their eyebrows, so I'm a bit flustered. "No, not necessarily."

"Hm," she says. If only she weren't so insistent!

"But it is a trapdoor," I say.

"Point taken," says Holly. She kneels, setting one knee of her long plaid shorts in the dust. She pokes her finger through the iron ring and pulls.

It doesn't budge. "Let me try," I say. I grip the ring with both hands and pull hard. It's stuck fast at first, then breaks free, and I heave the heavy door up an inch. The hinges groan, then squeal. Holly jams her fingers underneath the door and helps me pry it open the rest of the way. Together we drop it onto the stairway with a thud.

Holly's eyes light up. Down below is a dusty crawlway barely tall enough to crouch in. There's a crude smiley face, only as big as my hand, with a gigantic grin and two eyes scratched into the wooden floor below. An arrow, also scratched into the wood, points further back into the crawlspace.

"Chums?" she says.

"Looks like it," I say.

"I'll take a rain-check on that out-of-bounds laboratory."

I'm sure she won't let me forget it.

Holly lowers herself into the crawlspace and scoots on her hands and knees underneath the floor and out of sight. I take one look behind me, just to see if anyone's watching us. I don't want Marcus sneaking up behind me again.

Fortunately, the coast is clear. I reach down below the floor with one sandal until my toe touches bottom. I'm relieved that we're not going to the lab right now. And it's cool that Holly and I found this together. After all, it is a trapdoor.

My hands and knees scrape softly along the wood as I crawl in the direction the arrow pointed. Holly is right in front of me, but all I can see is the seat of her shorts and the soles of her high tops.

It's really dark down here. The only light is soaking in from the trap door behind us, and it isn't enough.

"Can you see anything?" I say quietly. The fact that we're sneaking around down here makes me think I should whisper.

A faint green glow wraps around Holly's red hair from somewhere in front of her face. It lights up the floor and the ceiling above us. "Calculator watch," she says, turning her head around. She holds up her wrist. The green light from a watch with buttons all over its face lights up her teeth. She's grinning. Never mind that a calculator watch is something a grandpa would wear. Now I wonder if I should get one too.

She shines her watch ahead of her and I can see that the crawlspace is wide — maybe even the width of the ship — with wooden beams jutting upward to support the floor every few feet. It feels kind of like the beams are trees, and we're crawling through a haunted forest.

We crawl for what seems like a whole hour. Holly goes straight, sticking to a path between the same row of beams, which is good, because we're far enough from the trap door that I can't see any light coming through it anymore. For the most part, we scoot along in darkness. Holly lights up her watch every once in a while to check our surroundings, but it's mostly the same: wooden floor, wooden beams and darkness. There are machines humming somewhere up ahead. I'm starting to wonder if this is worth it.

"Where are we going?" I ask.

Holly stops. "Here," she says. She shines her watch. We've come to a dead end. There is a wooden wall right in front of her face. The floor is higher here, so I sit up and stretch.

"I guess this was a bust," I say. That was a lot of crawling for nothing.

"Why? They left this trail for a reason," she said. I'm not sure what she's talking about, when she shines her watch down at the floor. There's another palm-sized smiley face scratched into the wood at her feet. An arrow points toward the dead end.

So that's it. She'd been following these smiley Chum faces the whole time. Someone must have carved them, which means we aren't the first to come here. Somebody else had been here before.

She shines her light up. There's a huge smiley face, it looks just like a Chum's head, scratched into the ceiling above us. Its diameter is as wide as I am tall. It's crude, but whoever left it there put a lot of effort into carving it.

It's kind of staring down at me, like it knows how much bigger and more important than me it is. Like it knows what's going on here and I don't. Suddenly I feel small.

"Nice," I say, even though I'm not really sure I like it. There's writing below it, scratched out one pointy letter at a time. It must've taken hours.

The King is First, it says.

"What the…?" says Holly.

That seems odd. The King? What is that all about? King of what? Chums? Is there a giant one we have to find? Is it waiting for us some-where? I wonder if we've just discovered a secret clue about the game, one that only Holly and I know because we were smart enough to find this secret passage, maybe even one that Cecil wanted just us – or me – to find. I'm not sure what it is, but I'm willing to bet it's going to help us win.

"The Chum King," I say.

"Chum King?" asks Holly. Her face is all curled up sideways like bread dough, like she's trying to figure it out. "I think I ordered Chum King at a restaurant once."

I grunt. Even if she doesn't comprehend the magnitude of our discovery, I do. "There has to be more to it than that," I say. "Look how big he is."

"Maybe the King is something we have to find, or defeat," she says.

"Or become," I say. What if one of us is supposed to become the King of all Chums? Does that happen when you win? Or is it something else entirely? Right then I imagine the entire crew setting a crown on my head in a fabulous, fancy ceremony on the island of Betteravia. I could do that.

"The King is First. If you ask Mr. Turing, the King is something we have to wait for," Holly says.

"Mr. Turing?" I ask.

She shines her calculator watch on more letters scratched in the wood below the first line. It's signed: Mr. Turing, 1985.

Mr. Turing. Who is that? And why would he write this message? It seems like with all the arrows pointing to it, he wanted us — or someone — to find it.

"1985," says Holly, "That's when Take On Me was rising up the charts." I don't even know what that song is, it's so old. But of course Holly does. Maybe everybody else does too. Either way, 1985 was a long, long time ago.

That suddenly strikes me as strange — the fact that before I was ever born, someone named Mr. Turing was on this ship, and he knew about Chums. I'm not even sure they had color TV back then, much less reality shows. And didn't Cecil say that we were the first season of Chum? I know I've never seen the show before. "How do you think Mr. Turing got on board the Philanthropist?" I ask Holly.

Her face curls up sideways again, this time to the other side. "I don't know," she says, but I can tell she's thinking about it. "Even if he did, how would he know about Chums?"

I don't have an answer to that. Wish I did.

We turn to go. Holly shuffles past me in the dark, and I start turning around. My fingers jam into something hard. "Shine the light over here," I say.

Holly turns on her calculator watch. The green glow shines on an old leather traveling trunk shoved up against one of the beams. It's like the kind you'd find in an attic, it's covered in dust, and it looks like it's been here for years. "Let's open it," I say, pressing on the brass button clasps. The lid springs open a half inch, and I push it up the rest of the way.

Inside, nestled in a bed of sawdust, are four oversized yellow heads with little bodies: four perfectly intact Chums. A secret stash!

"Jackpot!" says Holly. I couldn't agree more. I grab hold of one with each hand.

"Thank you, Mr. Turing!" I say.

"Wait," says Holly, suddenly hesitating, "Why isn't this part of the show? There isn't anything here to play."

I shake my head. "Sometimes there are just Chums walking around, like the one I found."

"Stray Chums?" she says. She doesn't sound convinced. "These aren't just stray; they've been hidden. Like they're not supposed to be here."

"You want to leave them?" I ask.

"Smiles no!" she says. The way she says it makes me think she's been using that expression for years. She grabs two.

"Wait," I say, handing her one of mine. "Let's take these and save the others for tomorrow, just in case."

Holly nods in agreement. It's a good plan, a safety net in case we aren't so lucky next round. I tuck two of them back in their cozy sawdust beds and shut the lid.

"Holly, turn on your watch," I say. I turn the Chum in my hand over and check the button. It's got a small picture of a life preserver ring on it, like the kind the lifeguard at the pool throws when you're in trouble. I wonder what that does. "What'd you get?" I ask.

"A Chum," says Holly.

"No, I mean what kind of Chum is it?" I ask. She hasn't seen any. Maybe she doesn't know. "Chums do things. They each have a specialty. Look." I point to the button on the back of her Chum. There's a picture of a nose on her Chum's button.

"Bonus!" she says. She presses it. I try to stop her, but I'm too late. You have to be careful with Chums.

There's a faint hissing noise, and a soft puff of air comes out of the Chum's head. "Mmmm," says Holly. It smells like cinnamon.

"You're right. This one definitely is special," she says.

I'm relieved, but a little surprised. A cinnamon smell? That's not very helpful in a fight. Some of them must be higher level Chums.

"Let's press yours," says Holly. She reaches over and jams her finger into the button on my Chum.

There's a burst of air and around the Chum's waist. A little orange life preserver tube blows up around the Chum's waist.

"Charming," says Holly. "I'll trade you."

I'm not sure how useful either of these will be, so I hand her the Life-saver Chum. I was hoping for something more powerful. I guess some Chums are mostly useless, kind of like some baseball cards.

We crawl back to the trapdoor. It's much quicker going back, even with a Chum in one hand. We leave our Chums tucked behind a wooden beam, and peek our heads out before climbing out, just to make sure no one is there waiting to ambush us. The hallway looks empty, so we grab our Chums and close the trapdoor behind us.

Just then, we see two shadows running at the far end of the hall. I almost forgot about my spark club. I reach for it, but the shadows duck down a corridor and disappear. I can't lose this Chum, not like the last one.

We climb the spiral stairs. I wonder if Holly still wants to sneak over to the lab, when a siren sounds. It's so loud, I cover my ears to stop the ringing in my brain. Captain Poursport's voice comes on over the intercom. The weird merry-go-round music echoes through the ship. He's singing:

Did you find your Chum today?
If not then you will have to pay!
Round one is done, so come up and see
Who gets thrown into the sea!

The music stops. My club powers down. It's over. I grip my Chum a little tighter, almost in a hug. I'm sure glad I found him. Today was a long day, but this little guy gives me the right to fight on.

CHAPTER 8

HOLD THE MAYO

Up on top the sun is getting low. It's burning the sky orange and red like a tropical smoothie. It's kind of warm too. The crew has set out long fold up tables, with chairs to go with them. We're all sitting down, with Chums by our side, and suddenly, everybody seems happy. They're relaxed. They're talking; it's like today never happened. A few of them are even exchanging claps on the back. "Great round!" and "Like a boss!" I hear them say.

Marcus comes up to me, his hand in the air. "Big B, high five!" he says. He must have lost his brain lobes. I can still feel the crushing blow my skull absorbed from when his gang shocked me and I fell into the ladder.

"No," I say, and turn away. I don't care if he thinks I'm a jerk — I can't let him think that ambushing me like that was okay.

"How unsportsmanlike," he says, and stalks off, shaking his head like I'm in the wrong. I must be pumped from the win, since I don't care if he blogs about it to his thousands of friends. I won't high five my own concussion.

The crew comes out with platters piled high of hamburgers and I remember how I'm dying of starvation. A sailor sets a burger in front of

68

me. Now that it's three feet from my face, I almost gag. It reeks of pickles so bad, I can taste them with my lips closed. Gross.

Candy #2 looks like she's disgusted too, and raises her hand. "Can I get one without the pickles?" she asks the sailor nearest her.

Captain Poursport laughs. "We don't make 'em any other way!" he says. "The pickles is in the burgers!" He, on the other hand, chomps down on a leg of fried chicken.

"But I'm a vegetarian!" says the skinny beanpole guy I saw earlier in the hall today. I don't think Beanpole gets a choice.

"Minimum is three!" shouts Captain Poursport. The sailors march up right behind us, their clubs sizzling. I know what that means: skipping dinner is not an option.

This is nothing like the video of gourmet food they showed us when we first boarded the ship. I'm getting used to things not being what they seem. It's pretty clear now that the budget for this show isn't what they told us it would be. Still doesn't mean I like it.

I hold my nose and take a bite, since it's either Chumburgers or nothing at all. It's awful. It tastes like it was marinated in pickle juice overnight. Holly coughs next to me. Sounds like she hates it too.

We're not the only ones. People are gagging left and right. Candy #2's picking hers apart with her fingernails, and Pockmark's forcing himself to take a bite. Handlebar is the only one who seems to be enjoying them. He eats seven.

I manage to finish one before I get tapped on the shoulder. I turn around. It's one of the sailors, and he's got a spark club in hand.

"Cecil wants to see you," he says, jerking his head toward the hatch that leads below deck. I wonder if the scientists told Cecil that I saw what they were doing inside the lab. I'm not even sure exactly what all of it meant — the Chums, the countdown — but it seemed important to them, and if it was important to them, it's probably just as important to Cecil.

Holly grabs my arm. "Careful what you say in there," she says. "They'll splice those clips together to make you sound however they want. This isn't live TV."

I nod to her. She's right. I don't know how far my credit with Cecil will go, after going out of bounds today. I might know things that I shouldn't. Maybe no one told him I was up in the lab. Maybe they didn't recognize me. After all, there are a few dozen of us, and it was kind of dim. At least I can hope that.

I go down the stairs toward the four cells where we had our interview at the start of the game. The first door is open. I go inside. The room is identical to room number two. There's a sailor standing guard and Cecil is sitting behind the table.

He doesn't look up. "Sit down," he says. His glasses are on. The guard closes the door behind me. It clicks shut. Now it's just me and Cecil.

He doesn't say anything else after that. He just looks down at his black tablet, like he's reading something. I have to think of a defense. Or I have to play ignorant. I try to remember that last talk we had; he seemed to care.

"You found your Chum today," he says.

It's true, but I play it careful. I have to see what he'll say next. I can't let him know where I got it.

He looks up at me. "Did you encounter any difficulties?" he asks. His face goes soft, like he's genuinely interested.

I'm relieved. It doesn't sound like I'm here to be lectured. "Some," I say, but I'm still keeping my mouth shut.

"Levi," says Cecil warmly, "You've succeeded. We'd like to know what's inside the mind of a champion." He smiles.

Okay, I could talk about that. Maybe this is just a standard recap interview, the kind where they get some footage of the contestants, and hear what's on their mind. So I tell him. "Well, it's not easy to find Chums, especially with everyone running around armed and dangerous like it's a riot or something. I mean, I know that's this city's proud heritage and all, but who are these people anyway?" I say. The rest just spills out of me, in hopes I say something that sounds good. "They're all best friends until a million dollars is on the line, then you better believe they'll gut you when they get the chance. A million dollars isn't even that much nowadays, with inflation and all."

Cecil smiles. I must be saying something good. I don't know why I have to be worried. It's the losers who have to be worried. "And who did you encounter difficulties with?"

"Marcus Earl. He ganged up on me with three of his cronies, and they attacked me and stole my Chum."

"Oh, that is discouraging," says Cecil, shaking his head in pity. "I saw the footage. He betrayed you when your back was turned."

So he knows what I went through! I flush hot. Just thinking about Marcus makes me mad.

"Perhaps the next round you'll get the upper hand. There will be chances for that, you know."

"I'd like that," I say. "That guy's a total idiot." Cecil gets it.

Cecil's grin curls up, plumping out his hippo cheeks. The camera blinks red.

Instantly, I recognize my mistake. Dumb! I shouldn't have said that. It's a perfect sound bite. They'll splice it with some others, make Marcus look like Gandhi, and I'll come off sounding like a terrorist. I played right into their hands.

"I mean, look, we've run into conflicts with each other before, and I don't mean to be so harsh. He's an alright person, just makes your hair stand on end…makes you so frustrated…" I say.

Cecil sits back. His smile widens. Again, I've said the wrong thing. I'm just digging a deeper hole for myself. I should shut my mouth while I can.

"Anything else?" he asks.

I shake my head. My lips are sealed. I can see it now, the way they'll splice the clips together. Me on a tirade. This could end up worse than any online video.

"Can I go now?" I ask.

Cecil' stare bores into me. "I'm hungry," I say. It's true, just not for Chumburgers.

"Good," he says, smiling. "We want you to get your fill." Cecil waves a hand toward the door. It opens. I take that as permission.

I turn and climb back up the steps as quickly as I can. As much as Cecil is on my side, the guy's still weird. I feel like I'm in the principal's office when I talk to him. Then again, everyone who's old feels like a principal to me. I don't understand people with careers or mortgages.

I get back to the table and sit by Holly's side. At least she's still a teenager. "What happened?" she asks.

"He just wanted to know about what happened today," I grumble. I'd rather not talk about it. At least he didn't ask about me trespassing in the lab. He must not know.

Captain Poursport's voice booms over the loudspeaker. All the light bulbs on the ship start blinking at once, flashing on and off at different times – red, blue, yellow – so that it's hard to focus on anything. The music Captain Poursport sang his jingle to earlier starts playing, this time without words. It must be the Chum theme. "Chum check!" he hollers. "Line up!"

The sailors start herding us toward our little orange x's until we're all lined up in neat rows. Nobody seems to regret leaving their dinner, except Handlebar, who's still chewing the last of his eighth Chumburger. Everyone has their Chum in hand.

Holly is lined up on her X in front of me. Candy #1 is on my right. She's got a Chum too. "I found one when I was hiding," she whispers, her glossy pink lips frowning. "Those sparky things scare me." She points to the spark club clipped to my belt.

I nod. I know exactly what she means. I hug my Chum in front of me in both arms. I want to make sure he doesn't get away, or a fall overboard, or vaporize into thin air. Finding a Chum of my own feels as rare and special as finding a dinosaur skull, and I'd hate to drop a winning million dollar lotto ticket like that down the drain.

Captain Poursport paces across the front of the first row of contestants. His arms are clasped behind his back, and his eyes are narrow, searching, panning up and down each contestant as he passes. He's grinning cruelly, his lips pressed close together and curled up slightly on one side. From the looks of it, this is his favorite part of the game.

I grasp my Chum a little tighter. I look to the shore. We're slightly further out than we were this morning, a long stretch of gray water between us and dry land. That makes me nervous. But I can still make out a skyscraper or two in the distance — that gives me comfort. I still think I could swim it if I had to. I look at my smiling Chum. I could if I had to, but it's not going to come to that.

Captain Poursport completes his inspection of the first row, passing slowly by each contestant with a quick, gruff grunt. Killjoy is right behind him. So far, they all have Chums. As near as I can tell, everyone in front of me has one. I don't dare sneak a glance behind me.

The Captain looks over the second row. Holly gives him a big toothy grin, and holds up her Chum to her cheek like she just won it for Best Actress. Don't provoke him… please, I think. I shuffle my feet.

Captain Poursport grunts again. Grunt. Grunt. So far, everyone's a winner. He comes to our row, slinking down it like a drill sergeant, looking for lint on my sleeves. He passes Candy #1, then stops directly in front of me, his face inches from mine. His day-old fish breath wheezes out over his bristly beard right into my airspace, and his eyes lock on my Chum. I wonder for a second if there's something wrong with it. Maybe it had been sitting in that box since 1985. Maybe it wasn't supposed to be in the game at all, or it's defective. What if it doesn't pass inspection?

His eyes lock with mine, but I don't dare look at him. I look down. Twenty million seconds pass, then he grunts and moves on.

My back turns to jelly, and I feel myself melt just a little. I passed. Round One is done.

I look over at Holly. She doesn't even seem to notice how close we came to losing.

Captain Poursport finishes inspecting the row. When they're far enough away, I sneak a glance backward.

"Cheaters! Cheaters!" he roars. He's come to the last contestant, a guy with hair down to his back with a black heavy metal T-shirt. Everyone turns. They're all holding their Chums tightly — every last contestant. Somehow, everyone found a Chum.

No wonder the Captain's so mad. No one lost. That wasn't supposed to happen.

Captain Poursport looks like his head is about to blow up, his face is so red. He looks back over the rows in front, back and forth, desperately searching for a loser he might have missed. "Cheaters!" he cries again. Killjoy is hovering nearby, like he doesn't know what to do.

Captain Poursport turns, and with a powerful grip, clamps his arms around Beanpole, who's standing in the row in front of him.

Cecil is up on the captain's deck whispering to Mr. Director. They look down at the Captain, then back at each other. Cecil leans over to one of the sailors and says something to him that I can't hear. The sailor salutes, then rushes down to the steps toward us.

At the same time, the Captain is dragging Beanpole to the railing. Beanpole drops his Chum. He looks shocked; he's trying to figure out what's going on. "But I found mine!" Beanpole screams.

The sailor Cecil sent steps between Captain Poursport and the railing just as Captain Poursport hoists Beanpole above his head to heave him over the side.

"It looks like it's time for a Who's Your Chum Challenge!" barks Mr. Director into his megaphone.

Captain Poursport stops. He turns away from the railing and drops Beanpole like a sack of bones. A wide grin grows across his face underneath his bristling beard. "My favorite," he snarls.

I don't like the sound of 'Who's Your Chum Challenge'. It's not because I don't know who my chums are, because I do. I'm almost totally positive a few people on this deck would be my chum, if asked. Not that any of them know me, really. But they probably would jump at the chance. What am I even afraid of? I don't even know the rules yet.

The problem is really that anything could happen. It's not fair. I'd already won today!

In seconds, two rows of sailors come marching out on either side of the deck with long wooden planks over their shoulders. They line up beside the railings, drop their planks with a thud, then slide them into fixtures on the deck. There are dozens of planks, each stabbing out over the water like spikes on an urchin.

It looks like there's roughly one plank for each contestant.
Holly glances over at me. She bites her lip. This doesn't look good.

▶ CHAPTER 9
WHO'S YOUR CHUM?

"The rules in the 'Who's Your Chum Challenge' are simple enough," shouts Mr. Director. "Go ahead, everyone take your place at the tip of your planks," he says. The sailors unclip their spark clubs from their belts. I know what that means: we don't have a choice.

The sailor closest to me shoves me over toward the closest plank. Two more shove Holly and Candy #1 to the planks on either side of mine. I hesitate, and he taps me lightly on the back with his club. "Mind your manners," he says. They wouldn't make us all walk the plank, would they?

I step up onto it. It's a wooden board about as wide as my waist. "Out you go," says the sailor gruffly. I shuffle out a few feet, keeping low so I can keep my balance. The plank bends and wobbles under my weight. The sea is tumbling and churning past, far beneath me as the ship cuts through it.

I feel exposed, like I'm hanging from a cliff without my shorts on. It's colder here too. The water gives off a salty chill when you're standing over it. I stop shuffling. My toes are dangerously close to the end.

I'm still holding my Chum. Everyone else is too, as if to prove they shouldn't have to do this. Touchdown is crouched down on his plank, his knuckles white from holding on so tight. I can't say I blame him. I try to focus. I have to keep my balance.

"Okay, that's far enough," shouts Mr. Director. "Go ahead, turn around. Face the ship." I do what he says. It's better that way; I can keep an eye on the sailor. "Captain, you know what to do," he says.

Captain Poursport opens a wooden chest at the base of the mast. He pulls out an armful of metal saws with rows of tiny teeth on their edges and tosses the saws, one by one, to his sailors. A few moments later every single plank has a sailor with a hungry saw standing over it.

The sailor at the base of my plank cocks his head and smiles at me. I don't think he meant that smile to be nice.

"Now, we'll randomly select one of you contestants to answer the following question:" says Mr. Director. He reads from a sheet of paper, "Who was the leading actress in last year's hit soap opera, Love Trap?"

So it's a question and answer game? A dramatic bass note thrums in the background. A sailor holds a glass fish bowl full of tiny papers up to Cecil. Cecil reaches in without looking and draws out a slip. He points to a woman with short grape-purple hair who's standing three planks over.

She looks startled. "Me?" she says, her voice cracking. "I'd have to say… well I'm not really sure. I don't watch Soaps, only the news and sports mostly. I know I've heard of that show though. It's in the tabloids sometimes. Pouty Lippmore?"

BBbbbbzzzzzZZZ!

A buzzer goes off, grating the inside my skull. "I'm sorry, you are incorrect," says Mr. Director. "Pouty Lippmore is actually the star of The Desperation Game, a prime-time drama for teens full of pointless relationships and name-brand fashion!"

The sailor standing near the woman with grape-purple hair kneels down and begins to saw her plank at its base where it connects to the ship.

"No! Wait, I can answer another one! Please!" cries Grape-head, tears falling down her face. Her plank bows as the saw cuts into it. She's clinging to her Chum like it's a life preserver.

I feel sorry for her, and a little afraid. If Cecil had pulled my name out of that bowl, there is no way I could have answered that question.

"Please, just give me one more chance?" sobs Grape-head.

"And so you shall!" cries Mr. Director. "Everyone gets two." The sailor stops sawing. He's halfway through. There's an almost audible sigh from the contestants. I let out a long breath myself.

Mr. Director glances at his sheet of questions. "Next question: in which city did the third episode of Ballistic Bad Bros take place?'

Cecil reaches into the bowl again. He pulls out another slip, reads it, then points to Pockmark.

Pockmark does a fist pump. He looks like he knows this one. "Detroit," he says.

Bbbbbiiiiinnnnnnnng!

A chime goes off. "You are correct!" shouts Mr. Director. "This is where the fun comes in. Sir, please choose another contestant's plank to saw."

Pockmark looks delighted. This is exactly the kind of thing I would expect him to love. I glance over at Holly. She's cool as a cucumber over there. Candy #1 looks frightened.

"Him!" growls Pockmark. I look up. He's pointing at me.

My jugular ties itself in a knot and my stomach flattens. What did I ever do to him? He's had it in for me ever since we left the shore. I don't know why.

Captain Poursport smiles again — I can tell he loves this — and the sailor next to me kneels down and saws into my plank.

The metal teeth make horrible zipping sounds as they tear into the grain. The wood splinters under my weight, and I'm sure it's going to crack. I reach down and grab the board with one hand as it bows lower.

The waves are boiling and foaming up at me from below. If this plank breaks, I'm going to have to keep clear of the ship so I don't hit the water close to the hull. I don't want to get sucked underneath. I try very hard to keep myself from screaming.

The sailor finishes, and the horrible sawing sound stops. My plank is bending, but not broken. I try to keep from wobbling.

"Next question," says Mr. Director. He drones on. I don't hear the rest. If even one more person gets a question right and chooses my plank, I'm deep-sixed. If I get one wrong, same deal. There's a loser each round, right? Why wouldn't they want to saw me, just to save their own skin? They could send me to Davy Jones's locker and they'd be safe.

Suddenly I hear Mr. Director say the word Panzerfaust. What was that? I'm all ears now. I should have been paying attention, and for a second, it feels like a surge of strength comes from within.

Cecil is pointing at me. Me? All eyes turn toward me.

"I… uh…" I say. This is either some really bad luck, or Destiny is reaching out her long and slender hand. "Can you repeat the question?"

Mr. Director does. "In the campy melodrama Pirates of Panzerfaust, what was the name of the ship's security officer who suffered a tragic death in the first season by the Tribe of Manafawasiki?"

Suddenly, I stand up straight and tall. I just might have watched that episode 2 to 33 times, and so I could have the answer for him, if I knew, but the more important question at hand is what does he mean by 'campy melodrama?' Is that supposed to be some kind of low blow or something? "Hans!" I shout, not because he deserves to know, but because I want to live.

Then I feel all eyes on me and my self-conscious epidermis turns it up a few degrees Fahrenheit. I glare hard at them. "So what if I watch that show?" I almost say, but I don't. Holly gives me a salute.

I hear someone snort. I can't be sure, but I think I hear him mutter "gumpalo" underneath his breath.

Bbbbbiiinggggggg!

"You are correct!" says Mr. Director.

Duh. Of course I am, but I still feel relieved when he says it. What if Destiny is on my side today?

"Sir, please choose a plank to saw," says Mr. Director.

Which of these contestants do I want to send overboard? I hadn't thought far enough ahead to consider this. The logical choice would be Grape-head. Nothing against her, but if she goes down, we'll all be safe. I've already got one strike against me.

I don't know if I can do it though. She was crying like Niagara. She watches just about as many soaps as I do. We could even be friends someday.

"Ummm. Him," I say, pointing to Marcus. It's just one cut. It won't kill him.

"What?" he says. His fists ball up and he looks like he's about to leap off his plank at me, though he's on the other side of the ship.

I shrug, and mouth "sorry" at him, but it doesn't seem to do any good.

His eyes narrow as the sailor saws his plank, and I have to admit, that did feel kind of good.

The next question goes to a heavy metal dude with hair down to his waist and a skull on his jacket. He gets it wrong. After that, there's another question, this time about who directed Shiny Sorenson in her debut film. It's Glamour Sequins who gets picked, and she knows the answer right away. "Franklin Bubblehoff!" she says and before the chime even goes off she points to Heavy Metal Dude to get his plank sawed off.

"No! You can't!" Heavy Metal Dude screams. "I found my Chum!" His plank is bending sickeningly low. He starts for the boat.

Captain Poursport shoves him back, then heaves a heavy mallet into the air over his head, and brings it smashing down on what's left of Heavy Metal's plank with a crack.

Heavy Metal's eyes grow wide, his plank breaks, and he goes tumbling down, legs kicking wildly as he disappears over the side of ship. I hear a dull splash, and everyone on my side of the boat races over to his side of the deck to see. I go too. The sailors don't stop us. I think they want us to see. They want us to remember.

I wish there was something I could do. I look to the jet skis again, and the sailor behind me taps his palm with his club. They would stop me before I even got started.

Heavy Metal is spluttering. His head bobs up. "But I won! You can't! I won!" he cries as he drifts away and the ship sails on. He removes his shoes and starts his arms turning, swimming toward the shore. And that's it. He's gone.

"He'll make it," I say silently to myself. I hope he does anyway. He has to. This is all part of the show, right? Instinctively, I play back the scenario in my head, trying to figure out how I could've escaped the Captain if I were in Heavy Metal Dude's place. There has to be a way out. There always is.

Captain Poursport turns back to the rest of us. He's breathing heavily, his chest going up and down. "There's always a loser," he mutters. He stalks off to the captain's deck.

"And that's the 'Who's Your Chum Challenge!'" shouts Mr. Director. He applauds, but no one else joins him.

***

Two hours later the sailors bring out bedrolls and blankets. They throw one into my arms. They've taken all our Chums away to get ready for tomorrow.

I'm not feeling so great about Holly and I tricking the system and finding those extra Chums now that Heavy Metal Dude's been forced to walk the plank. There's not really much to feel good about.

No one else seems to care too much though. They all start comparing prizes. Pockmark face guy pulls out a tablet computer and shows it off with a double pump of his eyebrows to Beanpole. He must have won it in one of the games. Glamour Sequins sprays herself with a bottle of perfume labeled "Deep Space." It's the size of her head.

"Sleep!" barks Killjoy, stalking onto the deck with six armed sailors on either side. They've got us surrounded. Maybe they're afraid we'll attack. They're probably not taking any chances after throwing two of us overboard. Everyone gets quiet pretty fast.

I unroll my blanket and settle down next to the port side of the ship. Some luxurious accommodations these turned out to be. Nothing like the video. At least there are bathrooms below, and water to drink.

Holly's sitting with her knees drawn up to her chin a few feet away. A few contestants are still comparing prizes. There are some huddled around Marcus and Gumbo muttering between themselves.

In another hour the sun is down. I'm dead tired, and I'm trying to sort out in my head everything that happened today. It takes me another two hours after that until I finally fall asleep. At least I've lived through today, I think as I drift off. Tomorrow . . . well, tomorrow is another story.

● CHAPTER 10
WINNER

I wake up to screaming. Or shouting. My eyes fly open, but my body and brain are still foggy. The sun is just peeking out over the horizon over a faint and hazy strip of land in the far, far distance. The water is gray, and there's a lot more of it than before. Something doesn't seem right.

And suddenly I realize what's happening. Land. We're too far out; double, triple or quadruple the distance we were the night before. Maybe more.

"What happened to the shore?" Touchdown screams. He must have been the one who woke me up. He's looking up toward the captain's deck.

Holly is already standing at the railing, staring back toward the land. Her face is like stone.

"Round Two," sneers Captain Poursport. He's enjoying this.

I start to multiply numbers in my head. Two miles? That's 140 laps, but this might be ten miles. 700 laps. Or is it twelve miles? That would be — it doesn't matter. I can't be sure how far out we are anyway. All I know is, whoever goes overboard might as well be swimming to the moon, with nothing but black space between them and shore.

I have to win today.

Everyone else must be thinking the same thing, since they're already up and standing ready, eyes fixed on the stairs that lead to the decks below, spark clubs in hand.

We don't even get a second to think about it. Captain Poursport blows a whistle, and the doors fly open. The contestants charge toward the stairs all at once, like a stampede, shoving and elbowing to be first.

I'm stuck in the back of the herd. Holly's next to me. She gives me a look and I know what it means: we're going back to our stash.

I get prodded in the small of my back by a club, which, thankfully won't be switched on until we get below, but will probably leave a bruise anyway. I hear everyone's clubs power on at the bottom of the stairs.

We're forced into a single file line as we squeeze into the narrow hallway, which is probably the only thing keeping a sizzling spark club battle from breaking out. I hear several clubs crackling, but surprisingly, I don't hear anyone fall.

I push my back up against the wall and hold my club out in front of me. The herd's thinned and stretched out some as contestants siphon through the three doors at the end of the hall. The contestant in front of me pulls her trigger and her club starts sizzling, so I keep my distance. The contestant behind me is Holly.

I slip sideways through the yellow Door Number 3. Holly's follows me.

We slide down the ladder, just like before, and land in the hall. A couple of dark figures run off toward the other end, and someone else is climbing down after us. We turn left, run as fast as we can, then take another turn.

I stop to catch my breath. "The land…" I say. Holly nods. That's all I need to say. This changes everything. Yesterday it was just a game. Today the game's turned dangerous.

"Good thing we've got backups," Holly says, panting.

I'm glad Holly decided we were still teammates today. Or that I decided that, whichever. We never talked about it. She's just . . . here.

We creep through the ship's hallways, trying to retrace our path. It takes much longer than yesterday to find it. There are shadows darting down the ends of the halls, and voices around corners. We don't want to meet any other contestants. Not now. It would be a bad time for a fight.

It only takes a few more minutes to find the top of the spiral staircase. I'm more than relieved when we do.

"Oh," says Holly when she gets to the bottom. I follow her gaze. A heavy wooden plank has been nailed down over the trap door.

I feel my hopes explode. Our chums were in there. This is bad.

"Now you have to take me to the lab!" Holly smiles.

Or we could find some Chums. But Holly's not waiting. She climbs the steps, brushing past me as she goes.

"You coming?" she asks.

I don't want to play the game alone. I already know how that feels. So I follow her up the stairs.

When we round the corner, I hear a muffled voice from somewhere down the end of the hall. "The more of us there are, the easier it will be," it says. I'm pretty sure I recognize it.

I put my finger to my lips to quiet Holly, and creep closer to the far corner. It sounds like Marcus, but I want to be sure.

It is. He's standing in a huddle with Gumbo, Touchdown and Candy #2. There are three more contestants with him that I don't recognize in the dim light. I duck back into our hall and push Holly in the opposite direction. They're just far enough away that I don't think they saw me.

"Go," I whisper. Thankfully Holly doesn't argue this time, and I follow after her. We duck into a short passage just a few feet away. Once we're inside, I bump into Holly. She's not moving. I realize our mistake. It's a dead end.

"Wrong way," she says. She turns. I move to step back out into the hall so we can dart away, when I hear footsteps and voices again. This time they're only an arm's length away. I freeze at the corner.

"What we've decided is that we can use you as scanner. You'll move out ahead of us, flushing out any Chums or opponents before the rest of us get there," Marcus says. He's talking to a short, square-shaped guy. They must have broken their huddle; they'd moved surprisingly fast in our direction. Marcus is so close, if I jumped, I could punch him. I catch my breath and hold it. I feel Holly tense up behind me too. He must not see us in the shadows.

Gumbo turns and looks right at me, or at least in my direction. He wrinkles his forehead, like he's thinking hard about something. He sniffs the air, then keeps walking.

Six heartbeats and they've passed us.

"The more of us we can commit to the alliance, the more we can dominate." Marcus's voice trails off as their little team continues down the hall.

Holly nudges me in the back with her elbow. "Their squadron is growing," she whispers.

I nod. I'm not sure they're far enough away yet that we should speak out loud. I wait for a few heartbeats more, then finally let out a breath. My lungs were starting to burn.

"Let's wait here until they're gone," I say. My head still aches from yesterday, and I know that even with Holly on my side, we don't stand a chance going up against Gumbo and Touchdown again. Besides, I doubt Holly and her smiley face earrings are the fighting type.

We huddle back as far as we can into the corners of the dead end. Holly even slides down onto the ground and hugs her knees. I press my back into wall, and we wait.

It feels like a whole hour before the muffled voices are finally gone. We stay hidden for just a few minutes more, then Holly peeks her head out really close to the floor, like a burglar.

She motions for me to follow her. "Coast is clear," she says, and we creep out of our hiding place. Luckily, no one's there.

We take a few turns, and climb another flight of stairs. I can't help shake the feeling that we should be forming alliances too, not looking for more trouble back at that laboratory. If I want to win, I've got to keep Cecil happy.

It doesn't take long for us to find our way back to the stairs with the four doors at the top. Luckily, we don't meet any contestants along the way. I feel my spark-club power down at the bottom of the stairs.

"You mean the lab's back here at the beginning?" Holly asks. She seems disappointed. "I could've found it if you'd just told me."

Which is exactly the reason I didn't. I'm still not sure this is the right place for anyone to go. I shrug.

She smiles. "Ah, well, show me the way."

She lets me go ahead. I can't believe I'm doing this again. It feels like such a bad idea.

I put my finger over my lips to signal for her to be quiet.

We tip toe to the top of the steps and sneak up to the red door. I hesitate. She reaches over me and pushes it open a crack.

I put my eye up to the crack and peer through. The coast is clear. I push it open carefully, slowly, so that it won't creak, and Holly and I go through it. I motion for her to stop so I can peer around the corner.

The brass door is shut tight and this time Killjoy's there, standing guard. He's so tall, he could probably dunk without jumping; he's such a skyscraper. And he's got those weird silver teeth. I don't want to mess with him. I turn back to Holly and mouth the word "guard" silently. She nods.

I can't see the timer, but I hear it beep, just like before. The computer voice whines "Three days, seven hours until Friend's E-Day." There it is again. That count down timer. I don't like it. Whatever it's counting down to, I'll bet it's not BBQ chicken pizza coming out of the oven.

Suddenly the door behind us opens. The two scientists from before — Specs and Mushroom Cloud — come walking through. "You!" says the one with the mushroom cloud hair.

"Run!" says Holly. She shoves me toward the big brass door. Killjoy spots us right away. He goes for his club.

There's no time to think. I run straight past him and heave myself against the stainless steel metal door opposite the brass one. It gives way, and Holly falls in behind me. I shove myself up against the inside of the door, hoping I can block him from coming in. We're in a stainless steel kitchen. The whole place reeks so strongly of pickles, I think I'm going to faint.

Killjoy slams against the door. It bounces me back. I recover, and shove my shoulder up against it, closing it again. There's a little metal hook hanging from the doorframe. I slide it into an eyelet on the door, just as Killjoy rams the door again.

The door holds, but only barely. Holly's shoving a table over to me; it scrapes across the floor. I leave the door and help wedge it up against the wall and a counter, barricading the door. Killjoy rams the door again. It doesn't budge. We hear an angry, muffled shout, and a thud. He probably fell on his butt.

He'll get back up soon, and we've got no way out. There are no windows. No other doors. Our clubs are disarmed. We're trapped. They might just throw us overboard, and not even wait until the end of the round.

"In here," says Holly. She's lifted up a small metal door in the wall. There's a shaft behind it.

"Where does that go?" I ask.

She knocks on the metal. It vibrates like a gong. "It's going to make us answer that question ourselves, I think," she says.

"I'll go," I say. I swing both legs into the hole, then carefully lower myself into the shaft flat on my back. It's angled downward and I start to slide. I keep my feet up and my hands out, so I can brake against the sides. It only works for a moment before gravity breaks my grip and yanks me down by the lungs.

I'm falling. My skin is hot on the steel, and I can't brake anymore without burning my hands off. It's like a square water slide, or maybe a ventilation shaft. It's so dark, and I can't see, and there's nothing I can do about anything.

I wonder just how far this shaft will go, or if it will dump me into the ocean, when suddenly I splash down into a pool of something chunky, wet, and sticky.

I'm glad to be alive; I've landed on my butt chest-deep in what feels like half-digested slime chunks inside somebody's gut. Only it's really cold in here. The smell is awful. Like clams. And maybe blood.

I hear a crashing up above. I dive out of the way, and Holly splashes down right next to me — almost lands on my head.

"Uhh," she says, disgusted. She dry heaves. "Where are we?" she manages to sputter, wiping her mouth on her shoulder.

It's dim, so I squint real hard. We're in some kind of holding tank. It's about as long as a school bus. There's a low red light barely glowing on the opposite side of the chamber. It's cold, like a refrigerator. The walls curve down and inward. My best guess is that we're in the very bottom center of the ship, just above the keel. Either that or we're in the belly of a whale.

"We're in the entrailed bowels of the underbelly," I say, though it doesn't make any sense. It sounded good though.

"I think you're right," says Holly. That makes me feel good. I like saying things that are right. "Plus we're swimming in fish guts," she says. She's right too.

"It could be the ship's dump tank. That was the kitchen up above, so they must toss all the rot down the hole into this chamber," I say.

"We slid through a garbage chute. How awful," says Holly, "but believable, considering everything else."

I push myself up onto my feet, then turn to help Holly, since I heard that's what gentlemen do. Now that I'm standing the fish guts come up to the tops of my thighs.

"Your club," she says. "It's gone." I reach down. Sure enough, my belt is empty. I need that club. I don't want to be left unarmed.

"It must've fallen off in the goop." I plunge my hands down into the garbage and feel around. I start to worry. I touch something that feels like spiny little ribs. Something wiggles past my leg. Gross.

That's it, I'm through. I pull my hands out. It's like cleaning a public toilet. I can't do it, no matter how bad I need that club. "We'll leave it."

Holly taps her baton lightly on my arm. The trigger is off. "Good thing we're allies," she says. She winks at me.

I see her point. I don't think she'd actually fry me. I guess that means we really are friends.

There's a doorway at the far end of the sludge tank, so I paddle my way through the stew of goo, sloshing as delicately as I can.

Something sloshes in the water. It sounds like a fish jumping, or something sliding through the goo. I look back at Holly. She heard it too.

I try to move as quickly as I can, without disturbing the slime. Everything is tinted red because of the colored light bulb. I don't like not knowing what's beneath me, it makes me feel — exposed.

I wade to end of the tank, just under the red bulb. Just a few steps more to get out. There's a splash on my right. It startles me. "Holly, let's go," I hiss.

There's a whimper and a stirring near the far corner, to the right. "I'lll be your chmmmm…." says a small voice out of the darkness. It's barely audible.

Holly looks at me, and we both know what it is. A Chum. "Go get it," she says. I trudge my way as quick as I can to the corner, splashing up bloody slime as I go.

Floating near the edge of the tank, its face covered in guts, is a bright big yellow head. It struggles to move; its legs kick uselessly, gummed up by the slime.

I pick it up. I wipe its face off, and it seems to smile at me. "I'll be your Chum!" it says. It makes me want to hug it, just like the last one did.

"He must have fallen down the chute," I say.

"And we've rescued him." Holly cradles its head in her hand. "He's adorable," she says. She puts her hand on her baton, then smiles mischievously. "We'll have to share."

I don't know how that'll work, but I concur. I can't just leave Holly without one. It's our only way to keep from drowning in the depths of the sea. We have to find one more, or one of us will get thrown overboard.

We pull the Chum over to doorway at the end of the guts-pit. I check the button on its back. There's a tiny picture of a key. "What kind is it?" she asks.

"Not sure," I say. "A Key Chum, I guess." I press the button, but nothing happens. I shake it. There's a clinking inside, like something's loose. "It must be broken."

I let Holly climb out first, then hand her the Chum. She doesn't shock me as I pull myself up, so I'm pretty sure now about that friendship thing.

Holly gives it back to me. "I wonder if this is all leading up to a bait and switch?" she says.

"What do you mean?"

"A lot of these shows — they start out with a false premise. They tell you that you're playing for one thing, then they switch the game halfway. The audience is usually in on it, but the contestants are not. It adds to the drama."

"But what's the bait?" I say.

"The Chums," says Holly. "Maybe there's more to them than they're letting on."

I think of what the guys in the lab coats said. They'll tear us apart. I shake my head. I can't believe it. "Cecil would have told me," I say.

"Why?" she asks.

"He just would," I decide that I can't tell her. It would only complicate things if she knew he had picked me to win.

So I change the subject. "You sure know a lot about reality TV," I say.

"Yep."

"You watch a lot?"

"No, but I read as much as I could about it on the internet before I came. I wanted to be ready. It was like ingesting several seasons worth without having to actually watch any of that drivel."

I'm puzzled. "If you don't care about these shows, then what are you doing on one?"

She smiles. "Sailing," she says. "I'm absolutely terrified of open water, and I'm here to face it. Sometimes, you have to force yourself to do things that you don't know how to do."

"And that's it? You don't care if you win? Or who will see you?"

"Nah. I'm in it for the experience. I want to live, so when I look back, I can spend my time remembering instead of wishing."

I have to admit, that's pretty cool. Just like I thought, she's a girl with principles, no matter how weird they may be.

"Who knows? Next summer, after I get my license, I'm going to buy a scooter and drive it up the coast to Oregon."

"How long will that take?"

"I dunno. A week. Maybe two. I'll eat honey packets and ketchup from fast food joints, and camp out in baseball dugouts along the way."

"And that'll work?" I ask. I've never heard of anyone doing that before. She winks at me. "Of course. I've got my lucky bumblebee." She reaches into her shirt and pulls out a shiny, golden bumblebee necklace with crystal wings the size of my thumb. At first I want to laugh. It looks like something a grandma would wear.

I try to picture it, Holly Hotstuff riding along with her red and blue plaid highwaters, bumblebee necklace blowing in the wind, and for some reason, I add a blue wizard's hat covered in silver moons.

I think of myself, back in the locker room, covered in toilet paper, thrashing for my life.

"Aren't you ever worried people will think you're a little weird?" I ask.

Holly looks at me like that had never occurred to her before. "But I am," she says.

That's hits me kind of hard. I don't know what to say. I'm quiet. There's a puzzle here, but the pieces are all jumbled, and there's this new one that's really big that doesn't fit in anyplace.

"Don't you go to Palms?" she asks.

I nod.

"Good" she says," I go to Culver City. Maybe I'll see you at football games or something."

It's funny that she would bring that up now, while we're in the middle of the sea, not knowing if we'll ever make it back to land, or if the crew will electrocute us. Still, it's nice that she lives close by, or that she'd even want to meet again. One can still hope for perfection in the world.

And suddenly, in the middle of all this, I have a moment of realization: I've been electrocuted, chased down a garbage chute, and adopted by a talking yellow ball-head, all aboard a ramshackle ol' pirate ship, and I can't believe any of this is real. It's one of those things that people tell me doesn't happen. One of those things I always daydream about, or watched on my favorite shows, or read about in books. It's exactly the kind of thing Dad or kids at school told me wasn't real, and now I'm living it, only in my mind, I wasn't covered in guts.

Maybe, since something like this is real, I can't really blame myself for dreaming up all those daydreams I dream of. They aren't any crazier than what's already happened to me today.

We go through the doorway into a short hall. There are sealed buckets stacked up on either side. A clear plastic curtain hangs from the ceiling. We push it aside. The air is so much fresher and warmer here, like we just got out of a cold meat locker.

I take a big gulp of clean air. I'd been holding my breath. My clothes are still soaked in fish guts, but at least I can breathe now.

There's a narrow passage. We go up three steps, and Holly's club powers up. "I guess we're back on the field," I say. I put my hand on my belt, wishing mine were there.

"I'll have to keep an eye on you," she says. I smile. "Especially since, the most troubling thing about all this is that I never learned to swim," she says.

I'm floored. Holly can't swim? "What?" I ask. I almost can't believe her. "If you lose, you'll drown for sure." She's crazy to come out here, not just weird. Crazy.

She shrugs, "Guess we'll have to find me another Chum," she says, and pushes open a set of double doors.

I concur. We'll have to do that — or something to get her out of this mess. No wonder she wanted that Lifesaver Chum. Too bad she couldn't keep it. But if I win, I guess that means that Holly — well, she'll lose. I try not to think about that.

Behind the doors is a small room, no bigger than a closet. On the opposite side is a blank wall with a flickering black screen with green letters on it. It looks like my grandpa's computer. There's even a green block cursor blinking at the end of the line of letters. Below the monitor is a doorknob locked away behind a small glass door. I look for a keyhole. There isn't one.

"Welcome to Logic's Quest," read the letters on the screen.

The words disappear. A new sentence appears. "What is the color of silence?" it says.

Holly looks at me sideways. "Another game," she says. "Your turn."

Great. I'm pretty sure I don't like these, but if it means winning a Chum, I've got no choice. Besides, we're at a dead end. It looks like we have to answer the question to get out of here.

There are three spinning rollers at the bottom of the terminal, kind of like the rollers on a slot machine. They slow down and lock into place, one by one.

From left to right they read:

fear   nachos   yellow

I read the question again. "What is the color of silence?" it says.

How can I answer that? This seems like a trick question. Only one of the choices is even a color. I turn to Holly. She's wrinkling her nose, staring at the answers. I don't think she knows either.

"You can't see silence," she says. I know I've never seen it. Smelled it once, but never seen it.

"It sounds like a typo," I say.

"No, it's got to be one of those brain teasers; we're supposed to figure it out."

"Silence. If you can't see it, how can it be a color? Fear sounds right, since that's a feeling. Nachos are too crunchy to be silent."

Fear. Nachos. Yellow. I remember hearing in science class that colors have frequencies. So does black have no frequency? Then I'd guess black – if it were an option.

I press a button below the word "fear".

The computer buzzes harshly in my ears. Wrong answer. I brace myself, waiting for some kind of hammer to swing down on us from the ceiling or a trap door to open.

Several moments pass by. Nothing happens. It's quiet.

"Please try again," says the computer in a tinny voice. I relax. Holly lets out a breath.

"I would've guessed nachos," she says.

A new question blinks onto the screen. "Which is better, snow on the grass or pastrami sandwiches?"

The three wheels start spinning again. They slow down and lock into place:

black   1,000,000   quadruplicate

This question's not any easier. I don't even think that quadruplicate is a word. "Your turn Holly," I say.

Holly scrunches her nose and stares at the screen. "Snow or pastrami?" she asks out loud. "Those should be the options. The question doesn't even seem related to the answers."

She thinks for a minute, then smashes the "quadruplicate" button.

The computer buzzes loudly again. It feels like it's scratching my eardrums. "Please try again," says the computer.

Another question blinks onto the screen. "How many infinities in zero?" The answers spin into place:

wormhole   truculence   pants

I feel my frustration double inside me. None of those make sense. There must be something we're missing. "There's something odd about these games," I say.

"Like when they make you balance encyclopedias on your head while dodging tiny zombies?" says Holly.

I glare at her, not sure if she's making it up or not. She doesn't seem as frustrated by this as I am. Maybe she doesn't care. No, that can't be it. She has more to lose than anyone. It's something else.

"I guess you haven't played that one," she says, shrugging. "Don't worry. Not worth it. I didn't win."

"No, I mean something strange with all of them. Like they don't fit in with the rest of the ship somehow. Like they're an afterthought to this whole show."

Holly scrunches up her nose again. I think that means she's thinking. "Well the cameras only show you the sets they want you to see. It's like those old west towns they built for those cowboy shows. The buildings were just facades."

She's right, but there's something more to it – something at the back of my mind that I just can't quite put into words.

"Like they're a distraction," I say. As soon as the words come out the thought becomes real and immediately I know I'm right. A distraction. From whatever is really going on in this game.

I wonder again if I should tell her what I know about the Chums. I decide against it. The truth is, I don't even really know what's going on with the Chums. They'll tear them apart, he'd said. How could they? They're just little things. I look down at the one cradled under my arm. Not him. No way.

"Mmmm hmm," says Holly. "A distraction sounds about right. Like I said: the bait and switch."

We go through several more questions, the nonsensical answers spinning into place and new questions blinking onto the screen every time we get one wrong. Holly and I both look for some kind of pattern, but there doesn't seem to be any logic to it. It feels like hours have dragged by — precious hours where everyone else is finding Chums and winning at the game while we're stuck here behind this stupid door with no way out. Plus, that buzzer is really starting to hurt my ears.

In between questions, Holly and I talk about Friend's E-Day and Mr. Turing's strange message about the King. We don't come up with any answers, but at least I get to wonder out loud.

The next question blinks onto the screen:

"Why are you here?"

"That's what I want to know," says Holly. It must be getting to her now too. Three answers lock into place:

yes   no   maybe

"Who named this game Logic's Quest anyway?" says Holly. "It's probably the worst possible name." She kicks the wall with her toe. "There are no answers to these questions!"

Something clicks. She might be right. That's the best idea yet — to link them together — the pattern is that there are no answers at all.

Last semester in English we learned about this famous knot called the Gordian Knot. It was supposed to be so complicated, it was impossible to untie. Many people tried it, but no one could figure out how to find the ends. One day Alexander the Great came to the city where it was tied. He was determined to be the first to untie it. It didn't take him long to realize it was impossible, so he sliced it in two. That was it. He'd untied the impossible knot. Maybe Logic's Quest is a Gordian Knot.

"I know the answer," I say. Holly looks at me like she desperately wants to know what it is.

I pick up our Chum and smash his feet like a battering ram into the little glass door. It cracks. The Chum's plastic feet are sturdy. I smash the glass again, then two more times, and it finally shatters.

"The answer is brute force?" asks Holly. She smiles. "You're a barbarian Levi, and I like it."

I reach inside and twist the doorknob. The wall swings open.

It opens up to a room with a strobe light. My eyes try to adjust. Several cameras train on us as we enter. There's at least a dozen, maybe more, contestants there, all with spark clubs in hand, positioned near the walls. There's a vaulted ceiling, supported by several wooden beams. In the middle, hanging from the ceiling like a chandelier, or a bunch of yellow grapes, is a net full of oversized yellow heads with big plodding feet, and sausage- like thumbs attached to plastic fists: all the Chums we'll ever need, just out of reach.

Handlebar mustache guy is standing on our left, his club in hand, with Glamour Sequins Girl in her shiny shirt at his side, and Pockmark right behind them. Marcus, Touchdown, Gumbo, and Candy #2 are on the right, along with a few others. There's a dude in jeans twitching on the floor, he must have just been shocked. There's a woman sitting with her back to the wall on the left, her head between her knees. Altogether there's enough voltage between them all to fry a dinosaur.

Holly steps in front of me blocking me from their view. "Don't let them see your Chum," she whispers. I hide it behind my back as best as I can. I can't lose this one. Not like last time. She pulls out her spark club.

The doors close behind us. Suddenly all eyes are on us, and we're on center stage.

"Hi," says Holly.

Gumbo takes a threatening step toward us. He raises his club. "You sure you want to do that son?" says Handlebar, moving in as well. He aims his club at Gumbo.

Holly pushes me back. "Why don't you take the ones up there?" she says. Pointing to the net of Chums.

"Can't. They're locked," says Handlebar. There's a rusty iron chain running from the net over a metal hook on the ceiling and down to a handful of padlocks anchoring it down. It looks like someone doesn't want these Chums set free. It's Mr. Director and the Captain's idea of a joke.

My Key Chum. I press the button again. Still nothing happens.

"Genius over there tried to break the lock with his club, but that didn't work," says Marcus. He's pointing to the skinny beanpole guy, whose club is shattered at the hilt. Beanpole doesn't look up.

"Enough!" says Handlebar. He advances to the center of the room. His toes are touching enemy lines.

Touchdown pulls out his baton. Gumbo steps in front of Marcus. "Hold on!" says Holly. It's too late. Gumbo swings his baton at Handlebar, who ducks and kicks him in the shin. Glamour Sequins screams. Touchdown heaves himself at Pockmark, and the two go down. There's a burst of electricity, and a buzz.

I don't want to get involved, but I can't let them kill each other either. If I get that chain loose, I can dump the net full of Chums on the crowd. That should stop the fight. I'm going to climb it.

I take my Chum and make a dash for the pile-up. I wish I had my club with me. I leap over Touchdown who's getting a gut full of amps from Pockmark who's just been punched by Candy #2, who threw herself over some person I've never seen before, when an unknown someone's arm breaks out of the tangled mass and catches me by the leg, tripping me up.

I go down hard. My ribs crush against the floor and the air shoots out my lungs like a whoopee cushion. My Chum drops out from under my arm and rolls over, just out of reach. I kick my leg, and whoever caught me screams out in pain. Serves them right.

I pull myself up to my knees, and scramble after my Chum without even getting to my feet. There's no time. I grab hold of his leg, just as Marcus leaps over and locks both hands around its head.

He pulls. It feels like my Chum will split in two, but I'm not letting go, no matter what. "I'll be your Chum forever," it says. It's slipping out of my grip. Marcus looks at me, with his polished boy band face, his blond hair plastered to the right, and I'm hit with a sudden urge to shave his sickening little skull. Instead I swing my other arm around, grab the Chum by its second leg and yank for all I'm worth.

There's a Pop! and it's head comes off in Marcus's hands. He looks at it, surprised, like it was his own leg or something. I'm surprised too – and I even feel bad for it. A small, metal piece clanks to the ground. "You broke it," he screams. Marcus's eyes go slanted; he looks like he just ate the devil.

Then I see it. The metal shard -- it's a key. Of course, the Chum is a Key Chum. I bet the key fits the padlock. All this time, hidden inside this Chum, and we had to break it to get it out. Oh, clever, clever Cecil, you riddling sphinx!

I may never get to see the key up close. Marcus reaches for his club and pulls it back to strike. I look up. I'm defenseless, and all I can do is move, but he's already on his feet.

There's a whoosh, and a splat, and Holly jabs her club into Marcus's side. He goes down in a smashing heap of techno-hipness.

Holly. She saved me. I grab the key and shove it into a lock. It doesn't fit. There are four more locks to try. Holly presses her back up against me, and swings her spark club out like a sword, with sizzle enough to light the sky. She's acting as my shield. I get the key to fit in the second lock, turn it, and it falls open. One down. I toss the lock aside.

We need four more keys. I shake my headless Chum. There's a jangle inside. It has to be the others. I have to get them out. I press the key button on its back ten more times with a rapid-fire finger, but nothing happens. It's broken, and there may be only one way to get them out.

I look at my Chum's happy, round, disembodied head on the floor. It's smiling at me. Like it knows what I have to do, even though it's afraid, because it's going to hurt him bad. And I hope for his sake, and for Holly's, that this works, because this round can't last much longer.

So I lift its plastic body high and smash it to the ground.

It shatters. I hate that I did that, but it had to be done. I pull the arms off, and there's a mess of gears and circuit boards. In the wreckage, just as I hoped, are four more keys. "Help me," I say to Holly. She drops her club and scrambles for the keys. I grab two, and shove the first into a lock. It doesn't fit. Two more tries with two more keys and I get a match. I twist, and the padlock falls open. I tear it from the chain.

I fumble with the other key, while Holly finds one that fits one of the locks, first try. Wow, she's smart. I find the final key. The fourth one's easy, since it's the last one left. I fit the key in the lock and turn.

"You broke it!" Marcus says, staring at the mutilated Chum. He's pushing himself up from the ground. Holly's got her club aimed at him, so he doesn't make any sudden moves.

I put my weight on the chain to take the tension off, then pop the last lock off the chain, and let go. The whole net full of Chums comes crashing to the ground, right on top of the mass of tangled fighting people limbs. There are cries of pain and rage. And more struggling. "I'll be your Chum," say the little yellow heads in chorus as soon as they hit the ground.

Glamour Sequins is the first to notice what's fallen on her head. She squeals in delight, snatches the closest Chum by the foot, and stumbles to her feet. She must have had hers stolen. She takes one look at the melee in front of her and bolts for a door at the far end of the room, Chum tucked under her arm like a football.

It only takes about two seconds before everyone else in the pileup notices what's going on. Gumbo shoves Handlebar off his back and swipes one Chum, then another. Pockmark grabs Gumbo's second Chum by the arm and pulls. He yanks it free, and rolls out of the pile. Gumbo grabs another one, and tosses it to Marcus. There's got to be more than enough Chums in there, but no one seems to notice. They're too intent on fighting.

Candy #2 sneaks out the door with the Chum she already had. It's not long before everyone has a Chum, and starts to figure out how many there are. They filter out the door, some of them running, some of them sneaking, one by one, probably to go and hide somewhere. Handlebar gives one to Beanpole, then he turns to me, "Smart moves, kid," he says. He runs out the door.

Now it's just me and Holly left, and four little Chums stranded on their backs, legs kicking in the air like toppled tortoises. "You are the new awesome!" she says, and jabs my chest with her finger.

I've got to admit, that was pretty rad. I just stopped everyone from killing each other, gave them Chums, and saved them from getting thrown overboard for today. I look around to make sure that all the cameras in the room can see me. Sure enough, they're all aimed on yours truly. Prime time just got primal, and I'm the caveman star.

Holly and I grab a Chum each. I set the three that are left up on their feet – can't bear to see them struggle like that — and we head for the door. I take one last look at the poor, defenseless Chum I smashed to bits, his pieces scattered across the floor. They're just toys, I remind myself, but I can't be quite so sure.

"Let's go," says Holly. We run up some stairs. A woman with hot pink hair and pierced lips comes down the stairs with a short dude wearing sagging pants.

"There's more in there. One for each of you," I say pointing back to the room. They must have heard the commotion.

A minute later a siren blares from somewhere up above. Holly's club powers down, and Mr. Director's voice sounds over a loudspeaker. "Round One is complete! Report to the deck for judging!" he says.

We find the stairs and go up on deck. I collapse on the ground and sigh, relieved. It's over. We've won the right to stay aboard for one more day.

▶ CHAPTER 11
LOSER

It's not more than a minute after dinner and I'm called into the tiny interview chamber again. Killjoy leads me down the steps, just like last time. He doesn't try to intimidate me like he did before, though I can tell he wants to. It's like he got yelled at by someone with more clout than him. He just waves me down the stairs with the club, his lip pouting out in front of his silver teeth.

Cecil is inside waiting for me. I can only imagine what hot water I'm in now. I sit.

Cecil presses some buttons on his tiny black handheld computer. He seems disinterested. "You solved my riddle today," he says. He gives a faint chuckle. "There was more than one Key Chum, but you were the only one brave enough to break yours and find the four keys! Brilliant! And then you won the Chums for everyone!"

"So you're…" I say. Not mad? I don't finish my sentence. I don't want to give him any ideas. But I'm confused. Does this mean he doesn't want to talk to me about the lab? Killjoy had to recognize me. There's no doubt about that. But if Cecil didn't call me in here to talk about that, then what does he want?

It's strange. Cecil doesn't seem to care about the rules very much. Does he even care about the game at all? Maybe not if he's decided I'm champ.

At least I've been taken off the cross-examination stand. I relax a little. "Yes, I did win all those Chums," I say. "It was easy once I knew how to do it."

"You were brave, to sacrifice your Chum like you did," says Cecil.

The poor little guy. He was just a kid. Couldn't have been more than two years old. "It was worth it; I got more," I say.

Cecil looks up at me intently, his hands gripping the tabletop. "Yes, you did! And you saved everyone else!" he says eagerly. His voice is loud.

I'm taken aback. I didn't expect him to react like that. I don't know what I said. I must have struck some kind of chord. He reaches over and clicks off the camera. The red light goes out.

I sigh and sit back in my chair. It's a relief to have that thing off.

"Levi. Levi," he says his good hand massaging his temples. "That riddle was made by me for you."

Just for me? I'm flattered, I guess.

"Do you know what an allegory is?"

I do. They're like metaphors. I learned about them in English last year. I nod, but I can't tell what he's getting at.

"Levi, sometimes, no matter how painful it is, we have to do things we don't want to do. Tell me, did you want to sacrifice that Chum?" he asks.

I shake my head. Of course I didn't. Its dismembered body's probably still lying there, torn apart by the people who were supposed to protect him.

"So you understand! You know what it means to give up one for the sake of many!" Cecil rips off his glasses. His pale blue eyes are cold, but storming. I'm not sure what he's trying to tell me. "Would you do it again?"

I suddenly feel like there's more to what he's asking. "I think so. If it will save everyone from being thrown to sea." I don't know why I told him that. He's the one who's behind all this anyway.

He cradles his head in his hands. "That is why I must do so too," he says. He whimpers. I think he's sobbing.

Now I know I don't know what's going on. When people get emotional, I don't know what to do. "There, there?" I say. Maybe that's what he's expecting. Something's going on in there inside his adult head, under that slicked black hair — something important that I need to know — and I wish I could put my finger on it.

"Then you won't hold this against me?" he asks, looking up from his hands. His eyes are glistening. His cheeks are wet.

I don't know what 'this' means. Holding us captive aboard his ship? Throwing us overboard? "I don't see what good it will do," I say, since he's got all the cards, anyway. He's going to do what he wants, regardless of what I say.

He shakes a plastic coated finger at me. "I knew I picked the right one to win," he says. He stands. The door behind me opens, filling the white room with the last rays of sunlight streaming down the hatch. "Thank you," he says.

I stand and turn to go. The whole interview has muddled with my mind. I'm most indefinitely not unconfused since everything's murkier than mud. What does he want from me?

"Cecil," I say. There's something I've got to ask him before I go. Something I can't believe is real, and I have to know. "The Chums, they wouldn't turn on us, would they?" I say.

Cecil looks confused. Or at least he's not letting on what he knows. "Metaphorically, or literally?" he asks.

"Either," I say.

"I wouldn't try," he says. He puts his glasses on. That didn't make much sense. I'm as confused as ever.

Killjoy pulls me out of the room by the arm and shoves me up the stairs. The door closes behind me. "Next time I won't go so easy on you," he hisses in my ear, shoving me away. He must feel like he can do that now that no one is looking.

For the most part, I ignore him. My mind's too busy trying to sort out what just happened. Something about sacrificing one in favor of the many. Cecil thinks I understand him, or desperately wants me to.

"What happened?" asks Holly when I get back to the table.

"I don't quite know," I say. I have to chew on it. I need time to think it out.

I stare out to sea. The sun is touching the water in the west, painting a glowing trail of orange between us. The rest of the water is dark.

Way out to the east is land — I have to peer hard to find it — it's just a skinny strip of faded dirt now, miles beyond the horizon. My stomach drops in a sickening way. Things are even worse now than they were when we woke up this morning — they've been getting worse by the minute. Yards and yards of water stretching out between us and safety . . . We've been headed straight out to sea the entire day.

I try to calm myself. I don't have to swim it. I don't. I won. I don't know if I could swim it now that we're this far out. I have to stay aboard. I have to make it to Betteravia.

Captain Poursport comes to the front of the captain's deck, and bends his knees and turns up his elbows like a marionette. He looks funny and awkward. The merry-go-round music starts playing again, and he starts to sing.

You tested all your wit and might,
But there were some who didn't fight,
And now you'll find out what they did,
Because they merely ran and hid!
Not everyone is clever 'nuff,
To win this game when things get rough,
And so we show you on this night
The one who lost and serves her right....

The music stops. There's a scuffle and a sob. I look to the front of the ship. Candy #1 is standing there, in her skinny pink dress, her bleached blonde hair askew. Her mascara's running down her cheeks. There are two sailors on either side, holding her hostage by her arms; her wrists are bound with tape. Sailors pour out on deck on either side of the tables, their clubs buzzing with volts. They have us surrounded.

"What's going on?" I ask.

"She didn't find her Chum," says the sailor next to me. "There weren't none left."

"Like we said, there were enough for all but one of you," says the sailor next to him. He laughs. I think of the one I destroyed.

They set me up. There was no way out. They knew we had to break one.

And now we're much too far out for Candy #1 to make it back alive.

The two sailors next to Candy #1 march her past us. "Candy!" I say. She looks over at me. "I'm sorry," I say.

I want her to scream at me, to tell me how I did this to her. This is my fault. Instead she looks at me with innocent eyes. "For what?" she asks.

My eyes burn. The tears break out. I shove one of the guards. I have to set her free. He punches me in the ear. I stumble. A sailor catches me from behind and puts me in a headlock.

"It's okay," she says to me. She looks proud, dignified. "I want to go."
I don't understand. She'll die out there. She can't want that.

"When it's your turn, you will too!" shouts Captain Poursport. His crooked teeth are bared underneath his bristly beard.

They march Candy #1 to the back of the ship and perch her on the edge. Captain Poursport cuts the tape with his dagger, mutters a few words to her that I can't hear, then shoves her over the back of the ship. He's cackling. She screams as she falls out of sight into the sea.

▶ CHAPTER 12
QUITTER

Two hours later the sun is down. The sailors have us surrounded, six on each side of the ship. They've been standing careful watch over us, ever since they pushed Candy #1 overboard.

They've handed out the bedrolls again, and the contestants are starting to set up little camps across the deck. Handlebar's camped out near the mast, where he's tied a makeshift lean-to with his blanket to the scaffolding for the lights. Beanpole and Glamour Sequins and a half a dozen others have unrolled their beds right next to him, like they're part of the same platoon.

Marcus and Gumbo's followers are bedded down near the port side. Their faction is larger than Handlebar's, and it looks like they have the stronger fighters. There are a few stragglers that haven't chosen a side yet. They're camped somewhere in between.

If I were to join a side, it'd be Handlebar's, but I don't feel much like being around anyone right now. Holly sits down next to me, but I don't have much to say.

No one's happy or talking much like they were at dinner. Candy going overboard changed all that.

It's warm, like daytime, except there's a mild breeze. The sky is clear and the night is inky blue. The stars are brighter out here, than they are in the city, but that's little comfort.

I try to sleep. I'm so tired, after everything that's happened today, but the haunting image of Candy's final march is too fresh on my mind for me to close my eyes. She was the first person I met on this boat. She was nice to me. All she wanted was to be a movie star.

I don't care what Cecil's little black computer might say. We're too far out now. Candy's not going to make it back to land. I look around the ship. I doubt any one of them can. And we're getting further. The stakes are getting higher every day.

I try to make it all seem better in my head. She knew the rules. She was fighting for a Chum, just like everybody else. I passed her in the hallway. She was searching for one too. I got mine stolen away the first round, then I broke my second one today. I fought hard for my third. I earned my right to stay, as much as anybody else. If I hadn't, they would've tossed me into the depths.

But my Chum could've been hers. I didn't steal it from her, but I took one that she could've had. We all did. I know it's the game, and those are the rules, and that's what we were fighting for, but every person who takes a Chum is slowly killing someone else. Someone has to get thrown into the sea.

And where does all this go? What will happen seven rounds from now? Or a dozen? Where will the alliances be then? There can only be a single winner, standing on Betteravia, a sea of floating bodies in his wake.

I turn. The deck is hard beneath my meager pad.

I should've given her my Chum. Or found a way to get the keys, without breaking it apart. Like the Captain said, there were enough for all but one of us to find one. I didn't know I was being forced to destroy the one that should have spared Candy's life.

This whole Game of Chum, it's just like Logic's Quest: pointless. No way to win. A Gordian Knot.

Maybe that's what Candy figured out, why she didn't try to fight. She said that she wanted to go. But why? She looked like she really meant it.

Who could I endure to see thrown into the bottomless waters tomorrow, to struggle and paddle for all that they're worth, for hours, maybe even days, until they've got nothing left, and they sink under the waves, never to breathe again, after all is said and done? Pockmark? Touchdown? Beanpole? Not even Marcus, doesn't matter what he's done.

Holly. Please, don't let it be Holly. I want her to live through this.

And what about you, Destiny? Didn't you promise to get me to Betteravia, and that I'd make it to the end, victorious, famous? I'm supposed to be something! You didn't tell me it was going to be like this!

Holly — she doesn't care if she ever makes the silver screen, or flat one, or any one for that matter. She's fine with doing what she does, and doesn't need anyone to tell her when her awesome meter's reached tip-top. Why can't I be like that? Why can't I have . . . such freedom?

I know Cecil wants to see me on that island. He wants to see me make it big. He knows I'm going places. But this — this isn't worth any amount of fame or glory — I don't care what people back at home might think.

Right then I realize what to do. It hits me hard. The puzzle in my head fits together. It all makes sense.

It's inevitable, when I think about it. I can't stand idly by while someone else is executed. Tomorrow, I'm going to turn my back on Destiny. I'm going to forfeit the game.

▶ CHAPTER 13
THE TRUTH ABOUT CHUM

I wake up with the sun hot on my neck. The sky is white. The water's blue again. It goes on forever, nothing but more and more of the same. If only there were a landmark!

There are a few people stirring. The crew comes out with paper bags full of breakfast. More Chumburgers. I wolf two down, trying to ignore the horrid pickle taste. I need as much food in me as I can get.

I haven't told Holly what I'm going to do. I'm afraid if I do, she'll try to stop me. I'm not so sure I could explain myself anyway.

Mr. Director comes out atop the captain's deck and squeals through his nasty megaphone, "Everybody up! It's time for round three in the gleefully glorious Game of Chum!"

Handlebar groans. All the people sleeping at his feet stir, then they wake up too.

It's not long before all the bedding is taken away by the crew, and everyone is forced to eat at least one Chumburger.

One of the sailors hands me a baton. I take it, but I won't need it.

"I'm happy to report we captured some excellent footage yesterday," says Mr. Director. "The drama's at an all-time high! You people are all show business naturals!" and yada, yada, fraud-cakes. I can't even hear what he says, I'm so far checked out of the game.

Captain Poursport shoots a gun, and everyone's off, dashing for the hatch, like bulls stampeding through a bottleneck. Only Holly pauses. She notices I'm not moving.

"Go," I say. "Help them. We've got to find a way out of this."

She stares at me, like she can read the pages on my brain. "I can't stop you, can I?" she says. She must know what I'm about to do.

I shake my head. "No, you can't."

She narrows her eyes. I think it's in determination. "Someone needs to tell them your Chum is up for grabs. There will be enough. It will give us a chance to call a truce," she says. Brilliant, brilliant Holly. I hardly know what she's thinking, but it sounds like she's hatching her own type of plan. She pauses. I don't know what else to say. "Good luck," she whispers.

She turns and disappears below.

I'm there, on deck, alone in the hot sun, with nothing left to think about but the miles that lie ahead. The sailors notice me, but say nothing. The hours pass. I find some shade below the mainsail and try get more rest.

I've swam one mile at a time, but never more. I don't know how far in me I've got. The land is just a strip of brown, a sliver and nothing more. The whole world might as well be water, for all that I'm concerned.

So one mile. After that I'll do a second. Then after that one more. I wonder what it'll feel like, with the waves lapping at my face. I'm sure it will taste like salt. How far off is that splendid, handsome sliver of brown and solid dirt? Twenty? Thirty miles? If I make it to the beach, a day or two from now, I'll call for help. Maybe the police will come — if I can get them to believe a story mad as this.

More hours pass. The sun has passed its peak. The breeze is pleasant, refreshing. But with each ticking moment, the land gets further still. There's so much water! The world's so big. I wish I were in the mountains.

Finally, the day begins to cool. Killjoy approaches me, two of his sailors by his side. "We don't need the siren to tell us who the loser is today," he says. "Took all the fight out of you, did we?"

I smile. He jerks his head, and the two sailors grab me by the arms. They tape my wrists so tight with duct tape I can hardly get my elbows apart.

"Cecil will want to see you for your final interview," says Killjoy, bearing his silver fangs.

"It's probably about your teeth," I say. "He said I could buy them for a nickel." As long as I'm going to do this, I might as well tell them what I think of them.

Killjoy is not amused. He slams me in the gut with his elbow. I double over, gasping for air. My plan might be insane, but I'm still proud of the fact I've got one.

Killjoy leads me down the hatch, where door number four is already open. Cecil is inside the white cell, waiting, his sunglasses on, his hands folded. Killjoy closes the door. We're alone. The siren wails.

"You disappoint me, Levi," says Cecil. Ouch. That's something Dad would say.

I take a seat in the silver chair. I'm going to make myself comfortable while I can. Cecil grabs his plastic hand by the wrist, twists it, and pops it off his arm. There's nothing but a smooth, bald stump left.

I scoot back in my chair. "Hey! What are you doing?" I say. That was weird, and gross. Way worse than taking out your dentures in a restaurant. And now I know for sure it's fake.

"I assure you it's quite normal when you get used to it," he says, in his poker-smooth voice. He holds his plastic hand up to the light, admiring it.

Maybe I was rude, but I really can't care.

"Don't you want to know what happened?" he says. Of course I do, but I'm not going to ask. I don't think you're supposed to do that. I nod.

"My hand was mangled by piranhas, in the Amazon when I was twelve. The river was flooded with my own blood, and the pain was beyond compare. Imagine. A hundred tiny shovels digging out your skin, morsel by morsel," he says, and sets his hand upright on the table. He's oh so calm and detached for such macabre words. "I nearly bled to death. The doctors couldn't save it. There was little left to save."

Piranhas. How awful. What should I say? Words of advice are little comfort. The deed is already done. "I'm sorry," I say.

Cecil explodes, "Sorry doesn't keep history from repeating itself!" He's angry. He's boiling. "I resolved to do something, while I was lying in my pain. I couldn't let this happen ever again, not to anyone else."

This isn't my fault. He's being stupid. Why does he bring this up now? All his interviews – he's talking around some point – like he's afraid to tell me what it is. "What do you want me to do?" I ask.

He smiles. "I'll show you."

He stands up. The door behind him opens, and two sailor-thugs enter the cell. They grab me by the arms, pulling me out of the chair. "Come with us," says Cecil. Like I have a choice.

They drag me down the hall, through the red door, then to the brass one. Cecil opens it, and motions for me to go inside. "I don't think I'm allowed," I say. "People get angry when I go in there." I smile, making sure to show as many teeth as I can. The sailors shove me through the doorway anyway.

The two technicians are there, both wearing lab coats, one with round spectacles on his head, the other with a mushroom cloud of hair. The screen on the wall — the one with the map of the Los Angeles coastline — is swarming with blinking dots again. There are at least twice as many as before, and they're closing in on a single blue one. There's the same countdown timer as before.

A sailor steps in and aims a camera at me. "I love getting this part on tape," he says.

Cecil pushes him aside. "I want to explain things to you Mr. Middleworth, so that you'll understand why we are doing what we have to do," says Cecil. He's choked up again, almost sad.

There's a rack full of half-assembled Chums under the desk on the left wall. I'm fairly certain I know what I heard now. Those Chums are going to betray us. "I know the twist," I say. "The Chums are meant to tear us apart."

The man in the lab coat with the round specs atop his head looks grave. "No," says Specs. He looks very serious. "Believe me, it's not the Chums."

I don't understand. Then what were they talking about?

Cecil lowers his chin and glares at me over the top of his glasses. "You know the feeling Levi — everybody does," he says, his voice low and dreadful, "You hesitate before getting in the ocean, because you wonder what's waiting there. You look behind you in the water, because something tells you you're being watched. You worry about your toes, since they're trailing behind you, exposed. Then you suddenly scramble for shore as fast as you can, because you don't know why, but you're sure you have to get out of the waves, because if you don't, your life might be in danger. Well there is a reason, Levi. It's them. And you're afraid because the only thing standing between you and them is the thing that they only think they know — that you're probably not worth eating."

Specs reaches over and flips a switch on a third monitor. It flickers on. A shark's silhouette flashes across the screen. Then another, larger one. Then another. I was wrong. My gut fills with molten lead.

Sharks.

That's what they were talking about, when they said they'd tear us apart. The things below you cannot see. I feel faint.

"Why do you look so afraid?" says the technician with the mushroom cloud hair. "I assure you! They are shy, gentle creatures!"

I can't believe he's saying that. "Tell that to the people they've eaten!" I shout. I'm not falling for those lies.

Mushroom Cloud's hands tremble. "No! Don't be fooled by media sensationalism!" he cries. "Listen to science! Those were flukes! Mere accidents! Surfers who looked like seals from below. They test things with their mouths. It's not their faults! Everyone will tell you — sharks don't like the taste of human flesh!"

He's mad. I struck a chord. It seems like he's had this argument before.

"On this point my colleague and I beg to differ," says Specs.

I'm not listening. I don't care what either of them say. "Don't like the taste of human flesh? Why don't you tell that to the sharks!" I shout. I think of the stories, the attacks I've seen on the news.

Mushroom Cloud laughs. Specs steps in front of him. "In a manner of speaking," says Specs, "we're about to."

I stare him down. If I concentrate hard enough, maybe I can shoot a laser out of my eye and melt his face.

"Sharks are indeed highly intelligent creatures," says Specs. "They don't eat humans — for the most part — because sharks don't like the way we taste – and the sharks remember what they've eaten. And the reason we taste awful is, well…"

He sets a plate with a Chumburger on it in front of me.

So that's it. Chumburgers. They've been force-feeding them to us for a reason — not just to be cruel.

"It's the pickles in the bloodstream. Sharks hate it," says Specs.

I feel like a beef cow who's been fattened up for the kill. "Then why throw us overboard?" I ask. I'm afraid I know what he's going to say.

"To remind the ones who've forgotten. To let the young ones know who've never tried," says Specs. "You're awfully yucky to a shark when you're full of pickled Chumburger. They don't forget a meal like that for at least a year."

So we're all just human sacrifices. That's all it's been all along.

He turns and types furiously into a keyboard and tiny skulls appear, dotting the Los Angeles coastline. There must be hundreds, maybe even thousands of them. "See, here is an extrapolation of the attacks that would occur, with the current rate of human water sports, and the current shark population."

I can only assume that each one of those skulls represents a human life. It's a gruesome thought, and I'm suddenly very aware of the blood crawling through my veins.

Specs hits another key. "Because of this ship and its crew, and crews who took on the responsibility long before us, the projected deaths have been drastically reduced." The skulls disappear one by one, until there are only 4 or 5 left. "The ones that slip through the cracks are the ones that make the news."

"You've heard that odds are you're more likely to get struck by lightning than be attacked by a shark?" says Specs. "That's mostly true thanks to the Philanthropist. It's been setting sail for more than a hundred years." Cecil's lips curve upward slightly. I think he's allowed himself a grin.

This is all too much. I go overboard. A shark eats me. Humanity is saved. So that's what Candy knew. Maybe that's why she was so willing to go. "Then the show, the Game of Chum — it's never going to be on TV is it?" I ask.

Cecil shakes his head. "Nor has it ever been," he says.

And none of the contestants ever find out because they all . . . I'm horrified. I came for nothing. "And the Chums?" I ask.

Specs picks one up from his workbench. He holds it up and opens up a panel in the back. It's just a bunch of wiring. "There's about as much technology in here as your average electronic toy robot," he says. "It's nothing more than a walking, talking doll."

Holly was right about there being a bait and switch. Only it's something she never would have guessed. "Then why the ruse?" I demand.

"Would you have come any other way?" asks Cecil.

I look down at my sandals. He's right. I bought it all, hook, line and sinker. They should've called the show Chump. Now I'm going to die. I snatch the Chumburger from the plate and take a bite. It's hard to hold it while my wrists are bound.

The countdown timer beeps. "Two days, three hours until Frenzy Day," whines the computer voice. Suddenly, I hear it differently than before. How could I have missed this?

I smack my forehead. There is no day of electronic friendship, nor celebration of the letter E. All my theories about Friend's E-Day were wrong. Because I'd heard it wrong. I'd heard what I wanted to hear — what I hoped was true. There is no Friend's E-Day coming. Instead, something much more horrible is about to happen. Frenzy Day. I whisper it out loud. It's Frenzy Day.

"You can prevent it, Levi," says Cecil.

I look up at him. He is sincere.

"Leave us," says Cecil. Everyone clears the room, one by one. Specs goes out last. He shuts the door behind him. Now it's just Cecil and me.

"Remember what I said about sacrifice?" says Cecil. "Sometimes, we have to give up the one for the good of the many."

Maybe he's right. All they're trying to do is save human lives. But I don't want to die. Was that what all his talk about allegories and sacrificing Chums was about? Now it makes sense. He was trying to hint at something. He was preparing me for this.

"There is no Betteravia either, is there?" I ask.

Cecil shakes his head. "I didn't think so," I say, chewing on the rest of my Chumburger. I really wanted there to be an island, but such a wonderful place — now I know it's too good to be real.

I finish the Chumburger. In a weird way, I savor every bite, since they're actually my last. Who am I to upset their plan to save the beaches? The problem with their whole plan is that it actually makes sense. I told myself I wasn't going to let anyone else go overboard, that I was going to try to make it home. One thing hasn't changed — I can't let anyone take my place. The other thing — making it home — that's what I'm not convinced of anymore.

"Then let's go," I say.

Cecil calls in the guards. They take me by the arms and march me up the stairs, out of the hatch, and onto the deck. Everyone's there. They all have Chums. They look happy.

"Goodbye," I say to Holly as we pass. I don't know what to tell her. Everything's changed since they took me to the room with the brass door. Everything is different. I know I have to go.

They march me up the stairs to the captain's deck at the back of the ship. Captain Poursport slides away a section of the railing. He's laughing, like this is some sort of game to him. He pulls his dagger from its sheath and cuts my bonds.

I'm going to be thrown overboard. This is it. I'll never be ready, but it's not like I have a choice. Still, there's one more thing I need to know. "Cecil," I say. He looks at me. "You thought I was going to win . . ."

Cecil is grave. His face betrays no emotion.

"You fell for that?" barks the Captain. I look at him, stunned. What does Captain Poursport know about Cecil's hopes for me?

"He tells that to everybody!" cries Captain Poursport, then stabs me in the forearm with his dagger. It breaks the skin; it cuts into my muscle. It's stinging, blinding, awful. I wince in pain, refusing to let myself scream. Then there's a splash of warm blood — it must be mine. I'm muddled, confused by what Captain Poursport said. That's not possible. Cecil said I was the one. That was my Destiny. O, it hurts so bad!

The pain! Tears burst out of my eyes. I'm too hurt to fight. I can barely stand. I feel two gnarly hands grab my arms — it's the Captain — he shoves me backwards hard, and I fall headlong over the side of the boat into the Pacific.

▶ CHAPTER 14
SHARK BAIT

I splash down head first — it feels like I dived through concrete, especially on the sore spot where I hit the ladder. The water's cold, and it shocks me back into reality. I sputter to the surface, tiny bubbles tumbling up around me.

I catch my breath and look around and try to get my bearings. The sun's gone down, but it's still light. I'm somewhere in the blue Pacific, the Philanthropist sailing away from me fast, with my arm bleeding out bait at a gallon a minute, so they're sure to come, and when they do, I know it'll be for me.

First things first: I take off my clothes – all except my undies. It's easier to swim that way. Then I tear my shirt and try to bandage my arm. It's hard, because I have to tie the knot with my teeth, and I'm bobbing up and down on gentle, swelling waves. Problem is, I've lost enough blood already — they'll be able to smell it. They'll know where to find me.

There's a gurgle and a burp from the back of the Philanthropist. She spews out something warm and dark — it flows past me, mixing with the dark blue sea. It stinks of clams. It's a bowel-full of bloody fish guts — her parting present — a blaring red announcement to anything with teeth that dinner has been served. So that's what all that slime was for in the bottom of her hold. It's Captain Poursport's way of making sure I'm as good as dead. I hate that man.

A minute or two more, and the Philanthropist is gone — she's just a thimble on the horizon; there's no way she's coming back. Cecil — he betrayed me. I changed my mind. I don't care how noble their pursuit is. I don't want to die.

I spy land. It's a faint bump of brown — maybe a hundred miles off. It looks even further since I'm only one head off the water, a floating speck in endless blue. I've got such a long way to go.

I get started. I kick my legs, opening them up like a pair of scissors, then snapping them together, and reaching out my right arm. I glide. Then I do it again. Kick, glide, pull. It could take days, but time is of the essence.

I fight the urge to swim freestyle. It's fast, but it'd burn up all my energy. I've got to stick to sidestroke; it's more efficient. If necessary, I can switch to elementary backstroke. Or breaststroke. I'll swim a mile. Then when I finish that, I'll swim a mile more. I'll do it over and over, and maybe raw determination will be enough to get me to the shore.

Kick. Glide. Pull. Kick, glide, pull. How many kicks will it take to get to land? A million? Maybe more.

Kick, glide, pull.

The water swirls at my feet. It's hard to tell, in the undulating waves, what's an ocean current and what's something that could be worse. I can pretend they won't come, but I can't help it; I'm an ostrich with his head in the sand, only this world is upside down, and I'm the visitor here.

I have to keep swimming. Kick, glide, pull. Kick, glide, pull. I start to get a rhythm. It feels good, to be on the move at least. It's all I can do. Must keep going.

Land is hard to see over the waves. So I stop and put my head up. I want to make sure I'm aiming in the right direction. I turn a few degrees to the right, then start to stroke again. Kick, glide, pull.

I feel something bump me again, this time, on my leg. Be still, my pounding heart. There's nothing you can do. There are a hundred miles of cold water between you and the ocean bottom. Who cares that a million hungry teeth-machines are revving their engines at the smell of your blood?

Up, out, together. Glide. Up, out, together, glide. I get back in a rhythm. I have to keep on going. I have to save my energy, no matter how bad I want to sprint. I know guys have swum the English Channel. How long did that take them? Twenty hours? It must be thirty miles wide. I'll have to do my best.

Something bumps my other leg. It could've been a log, or a buoy. It felt like a hard fat worm.

I didn't think they'd come so soon! Is this Destiny's revenge because I turned my back on you? Or was this your cruel plan from the start?

I put my head down. And turn my arms like windmills. I'm going for a full on sprint. It burns. I can't last long like this — it saps my energy — but I have to get away!

There's another bump, this time on my left side. It's twice as big as I am. Crap.

I spin around. There's a fin, all dagger-like, the thing I didn't want to see, cutting through the gray water. It disappears beneath the waves. I only hope the sunlight holds.

Oh crap. Crap. Oh crap.

I ball my fists up. Time to make a stand. Am I supposed to strike the eyes or gills? They say to hit its weak points. I put my head under water. I have to see them if I'm going to fight.

The water's dark and blurry and filled with tiny grains of white silt. Below me though, the water gets deeper and darker and goes on forever, and I get a sudden feeling of panic, since there's a whole world beneath me I cannot see.

A shadow flicks in front of me. There he is. A grayish mass whips its tail and circles round to face me. Everything about him stabs — his grayish fins, his endless teeth — oh, those awful teeth — his lifeless, lightless eyes. The beast that God let Satan make.

"Hungry," says the shark.

I pull my head out. I swear it spoke to me. That was a shark, and those were words. Funny, the things you find out right before you die.

I take a breath and dive below. He looks me in the face with gleaming teeth and swollen gums. "Hungry," he says again. It's real. Though his lips don't move, it echoes through the sea.

"Kill you," says another voice. I look around. A second shark's behind me, stalking me through water. He's wider than the first and a little bit less blue. He joins the circling too, and then I know that what Mushroom Cloud said about 'shy and harmless creatures' can't be true, since a shark just told me otherwise himself. He wants me good and dead.

Dad, I think. He has no idea where I am right now, and probably won't find out. And what about Venice High? Or kissing a girl someday? I need air; I force myself to the surface. For that second I'm like a blind kid in a killer's house, so I dive again, and look down at the endless, midnight blue.

"Kill you. Kill you. Kill you," says the second. It comes from all around.

"Hungry," says the first.

They circle around me once. Twice. I change my mind. I'll swim for it. I put my head down and kick up a storm as furious as can be.

"Hungry. Pinky."

I stop again. I changed my mind. I have to be able to see them. I dive below.

Their circle's getting tighter.

Maybe since they can talk, they'll listen. I've got reasons for which to live. "I have friends!" I plead, though it's barely true. My words are garbled bubbles; the sharks don't seem to care.

They fire off like missiles. Their jaws fly open. The one in front of me comes first. There's a hole inside him long enough for all my bloody meat-bits. I don't want to die.

A third one snaps through the water. I dodge to the right, but it can't do any good. I'm no match for them: they're too fast.

I brace for impact, when something hits my bare feet from the bottom, and I'm pressed upward in an explosion of bubbles.

I wince, but no pain comes. There are three echoes and a thud, like an underwater gong.

Whatever's below me is flat, and pressing me upward like an elevator. The faint outline of a shark wiggles off through the bubbles. The platform pushes harder, until my head and neck rise out of the sea. I'm not floating anymore. I'm completely out of the water. I fall down on my butt. My heart is pounding.

And then I look down between my naked, folded legs. There are green, rough hexagons, like a turtle's shell, right below my tighty-whities. I'm either crazy, or there's a giant sea tortoise underneath me. The shell rises up, breaking the surface until the water spills away, and my limbs — they've just been pulled out of the cobra's den — every last one of them remains unsevered.

There's hissing and gurgling and splashes all around. I look behind me. A metal tower's surfaced. It's taller than a house, with rails and poles and cables, all welded on in nooks and crannies like a high-tech metal skyscraper.

And then it occurs to me: I'm either dead, or I'm sitting atop a submarine.

A metal crank spins on top of a cylindrical hatch on top of the tower. The lid is pushed open from the inside, and a man's square head with a bushel of long, black curls barfing out of a gold-trimmed skipper's cap peeks out from the hole. He grins enormously, like his teeth were stars in a Broadway show, and throws one stout arm, then another, out of the hatch.

He manages to squeeze the rest of him out, which doesn't look easy, since he seems just a bit too big for this world, until finally he's standing on deck. He's a square — nearly as tall as he is wide — a slick gray double-breasted, knee-length coat buttoned all around him, a pair of binoculars slung around his neck, a golden smiling skull with crossed bazookas fastened on his cap. His face is baby smooth.

I recognize him instantly, which makes me sure I'm dead. I turn the rest of myself around so I can meet him.

"Welcome to the Torqueod!" he booms. "You've just been saved from certain death by none other than the Pirates of Panzerfaust!"

▶ CHAPTER 15
THE TURTLE'S BACK

Now I'm utterly confused. Standing before me in the middle of the Pacific on the deck of a magnificent submarine painted like a turtle's shell is the exact man that I once idolized, and then imitated, and then denied that I knew. What he's doing here, I can't say, except making my childhood turn real.

"I'm Captain Bombardigo," he shouts, extending a thick gloved hand.

"I know," I say. I try to shake it. I'm trembling. I was so close to being dead. "Sharks," I sputter. "You saved me."

"Indeed!" says Captain Bombardigo, gripping my hand for me. "In the jolly nick of time too!" He slaps me on the shoulder and laughs. "They almost tore you limb from limb, then swallowed all your shredded guts!"

I'd rather he hadn't put it like that. "And this, it's the Torqueod?" I say. I can't believe it. It's got the same green shell, just like the submarine in the show, only as far as I can tell, it's shaped like a regular old sub instead of a turtle. The best part about it is that I'm actually on board. I'm alive, and I am happier than I could ever be.

"This is the Torqueod," confirms Captain Bombardigo.

"And you're with the Pirates of Panzerfaust?"

"I'm in command of the Pirates of Panzerfaust," he says gripping his lapels with both fists proudly. I love the way he says that.

"And you're Captain Bombardigo?" I ask again. This is the man I wanted to be. Accept no substitute. I have to be sure it's him.

"And I am Captain Bombardigo!" says the One and Only, bowing.

"And this is the Torqueod?" I ask. I could do this all day, since every time he answers yes, I marvel at the news.

"I think we covered that."

I shake my head like I'm trying to jostle loose the truth. It's real. It's all real. I should be happier than a bluebird. Yet, there's something not quite right; never mind that I'm in my undies.

Captain Bombardigo turns toward the hatch. "I do hope you'll come aboard," he says.

Wait. I don't understand how the submarine from the TV show I used to watch is right beneath my feet. "How is this possible?" I ask.

"Come aboard and see."

This is crazy. I have to know. I follow him.

He stops at the hatch and points inside. "You first."

There's a ladder going down a narrow tube. I swing my legs over and climb inside. I hold tight to the metal rail and am careful to duck my head in close, so I don't hit the side of the shaft. I go down, rung by rung, until I can't see the sea anymore. It's cramped inside — even more cramped than below deck on the Philanthropist. There are pipes and gauges everywhere. Captain Bombardigo closes the hatch above us with a clang and screws down a small wheel until the hatch is sealed shut.

This can't be real. I must be dreaming, or hallucinating.

It's dim. My feet hit bottom, and I'm standing in a small rectangular chamber. Everything is gray in here, except for a maze of color-coded red, blue, and green valves and handwheels snaking all over the walls and squeezing in on what little space is left. At least five men are at different controls, wearing loose-fitting, navy-colored sailors' shirts, with belts and daggers strapped to their legs and scuffed black leather boots. They're dressed in the standard crew uniform, just like I remember them.

Two of the sailors look up at me and whisper to each other — maybe it's because I'm not wearing any pants. "Guten Tag!" says a third.

There are a couple of vertical tubes behind me, with a viewer in each. They must be the periscopes. I follow Captain Bombardigo down one more ladder. There's a circular hatch in the wall in front of me, which looks like it leads toward the bow of the submarine.

Captain Bombardigo squeezes past me and the men, then with some difficulty sticks a leg through the circular hatch in front of us. "This way," he says. I duck through the hatch. We pass a curtain on our left and an array of sound and radio equipment blinking with lights on our right, duck through a low door, and come into a small but comfortable room with two cushioned benches.

Inside, seated or leaning against the wall, are a group of men who are all very, very familiar to me. There's a bald one in the corner with an eye patch. He's torn his sleeves off, so that his gigantic arms are bare. I recognize him. He's the ship's gunner. "You're Albrecht," I say. He nods.

And then there's another man, skinny and short, with plastered red hair and a freckled face. He's wearing a stained white apron. "Friedhelm, the cook," I say. He smiles.

The sailor with the two crossed bandoliers is Hugo, and the one with a blonde buzz cut is Dieter. There's only one man I don't recognize. This doesn't seem possible, yet they're all here — everyone from the TV show, with all the same uniforms and weapons and even their hair; it's all just as it should be. I'm dumbfounded — and somewhat confused. "It really is you, the Pirates of Panzerfaust," I say.

Albrecht shoves Friedhelm, and Dieter gets to his feet. "Ya!" They all say, and stomp the ground in unison. It's something they used to do, when they were all in agreement about something.

"But how did all of you get here, on this submarine?" I ask.

Captain Bombardigo squeezes himself to the center and raises a finger for silence. "I shall tell you. We were there in the shipyards of Hamburg, commissioned by Der Fuehrer to join his thundering war machine, when I and my faithful crewmen intercepted a code not intended for us, and learned of Der Fuehrer's heinous plots against humanity; tearing the swastikas from our sleeves, we turned our back on the Fatherland, and set sail for a noble course, seeking adventure beneath the waves! To right the wrongs that befall mankind, wherever they be found!"

I recognize his speech immediately. It's the opening voice over at the beginning of each episode. Albrecht and Hugo hum the theme song.

It's all so real and tangible. I never thought I would see them or be in the same room. I reach out to touch the Torqueod's walls, and then a thought strikes me, and I realize what's making me mad. I turn to Captain Bombardigo. "Why didn't you come before?"

"We found you way out here, in the water," says Captain Bombardigo. "We surfaced like lightning as soon as we saw you. Zounds lad! You weren't harmed, were you?"

That's not what I meant. I mean six months ago, on land, when I was put to shame for being him. If he'd shown himself then, the people on the internet, they would've known he was real — they couldn't have laughed at me. I don't know how to explain all that to him. It sounds stupid.

I point my finger instead. I'm hot, and frustrated. "No, I mean, you can't really be Germans. You're speaking English. And World War II was more than half a century ago!" It comes out tense, a little angry. Maybe I would've believed them when I was small, but I'm practically an eighth grader. Now I know too much.

Captain Bombardigo raises his finger again. "Are we not on a U-boat? Did we not pass from the Atlantic through the perilous straits of Magellan to our new Pacific home? We are at your service, lad."

"No! I mean how did a full TV show suddenly come to life?" I shout. Maybe I am dead.

Albrecht lifts his eye patch. His eye underneath is perfectly fine. "Trillionaire loony tycoon, Mr. Pengerwist. He bought us a submarine," he says. His voice is deep, rumbling, and distinctly American.

"What?" I ask. At least it sounds like an honest answer.

"They can explain," says Captain Bombardigo. He jabs a thumb back behind him. "The Captain is needed in the control room!" he says loudly, and maneuvers his way around me, then dashes out the circular hatch we came through as best as he can.

I stare after him. It's like his pants suddenly caught fire, he's gone so fast.

"Don doesn't like talkin' about production stuff," explains Friedhelm. "He thinks it breaks character. He can't help it. He's an actor, through and through, every moment of every day."

"Don?" I ask.

Friedhelm points to the hatch where Captain Bombardigo went. "Captain Bombardigo, as he's known on Tuesday nights at 7pm Central."

"I don't get this," I say.

"It's kind of a lot to get. The crazy trillionaire hired all of us to be pirates full-time," says Albrecht.

"So the sub's not exactly shaped like a tortoise?" I ask.

"That'd be hydro-dynamically impractical," says the man I don't recognize. He's seated, but he looks like he'd be tall and slender when standing; he's got a hawk-like nose and a pair of wire-rimmed glasses.

"And who are you supposed to be?" I say.

"Um, that'd be Doctor Wissenschaft, I guess," he says. Doctor Wissenschaft was the ship's scientist, and engineer. This guy looks nothing like him. Nor does he have an accent like he should. He's not dressed in any particularly remarkable clothes — just a striped, collared shirt and a pair of slacks. For some reason, his voice sounds familiar and dangerous.

"You don't look like Doctor Wissenschaft," I say.

"That's because I'm a real live engineer and scientist," says the guy. He rises. He is tall, even taller than Captain Bombardigo. "The real Doctor Wissenschaft — or the actor who plays him in the show I mean — refused to sign on when he got another gig on a soap opera. He's playing some guy in a coma. Which worked out well, since they needed someone like me on board to run things."

So that's why I don't recognize him. This Doctor Wissenschaft is a stand-in.

"A few years ago we — I mean they — were approached by their — our — investor, Mr. Pengerwist," says Doctor Wissenschaft. "He's an old Silicon Valley guy who'd managed to pull out all his money right before the dotcoms went bust. He had enough to spare, and he was maybe the only one to make it out of that downturn alive. Then he put it all into social media a few years after that, and now he's living fat and happy — if not a little senile — in a mansion on the hill. He divorced his wife, sold his kids, and decided he was going to do something with his money — he was going to make a difference."

"That's when he approached the Pirates, or I mean, the cast," Albrecht grumbles. Hugo coughs.

Doctor Wissenschaft ignores them. "Look, the show was getting cancelled anyway, and these guys, well, he offered to pay a boat-load of cash, and all they had to do was sign on for a couple of years, and go save people and stuff."

I'm trying to process it all, but it's like chewing on Styrofoam — it's just so hard to swallow. "Then you're vigilantes?" I ask.

Albrecht sighs. Doctor Wissenschaft shrugs. "We would be, if we had anyone to fight. Instead we do scientific research, mostly," says Albrecht.

"Sounds like real tough pirates to me," I grumble. Albrecht looks taken aback. I don't mean to be rude. But I guess I am being just that. It's just that these guys have been hiding out all these years, kind of like they abandoned me, and now they just come waltzing up, and expect me to let them back in my life, like nothing ever happened?

I slump down onto the bench. "I'm sorry. It's just that I was attacked by sharks today." But that wasn't the worst or strangest part. I'm not even sure I want to tell the rest. It scares me just to think about it. "And . . . and they spoke to me," I say. I put my head in my hands. I'm so tired.

No one says a word. I look up at them. Doctor Wissenschaft — the new one — looks a little sheepish. "Oh, um, my fault. Sorry about that," he says.

"What do you mean?" I ask. He's pulling at his hair. He looks guilty.

"Heeeee," he says. I don't think that's really a word. He gets up and inches toward the bow of the ship. His head almost hits the ceiling. "I'll show you." He ducks through a door.

Friedhelm and Hugo let me pass. I think I hear Dieter chuckle behind me. I squeeze through the door too, and I follow him through a tiny kitchen, not more than two and a half feet wide, with a couple of small burners on top of a narrow stove.

"This is the galley," says Wissenschaft, continuing down the length of the sub into the next room. "And here are the officers' quarters." There are a couple of bunks folded up near the ceiling, and another row beneath them near the floor. It looks like it would be hard to get a good night's sleep on such narrow beds. Almost everything is painted a dull gray. It's all metal in here.

"And below us," Wissenschaft says, thumping on the floor with his foot, "are the batteries. They run the electrical systems. We have to run up top sometimes in order to keep them charged."

He takes me through another circular hatch, and we come into the longest, most spacious room yet. Its walls are curved toward the front, just like I imagine the outside of the sub's nose would be. The far end of the wall is flat, with two big holes in it.

Everything is brightly lit, unlike the Philanthropist. There are a few more metal bunks with flimsy mattresses on the right and on the left, a bunch of blinking lights, three monitors and a pair of computers spread across a table, with circuits and red, blue, and green wiring. Pipes and parts no bigger than my finger spill out all over the table. It looks like somebody took apart their microwave and didn't clean it up. A magnifying lamp on a swing arm is bolted to the desk. There's a pile of yellow notepads strewn across the floor, and a pair of charts with a bunch of formulas and diagrams and lots of exponents scrawled all over them in pencil tacked to the wall. It must be a laboratory. It's a mess. "Here," he says.

He switches on a speaker. It crackles. "Hungry . . . hungry . . . hungry," growls a voice.

"See!" I say. I'm not crazy. "That's them. Outside the sub. You can hear them too!"

"I can."

It's even stranger now that I'm hearing it from someone else. It proves I didn't imagine it. "They told me they were going to kill me. It was like they looked into my soul."

"Again, my fault. Sorry," says Wissenschaft.

I don't understand. Is he the one who put them up to this? If so, I don't feel safe. He flips on one of the monitors. An image of a shark's nose flickers onto the screen.

"I've been researching sharks for the past decade — did my postdoc at Scripps," he says proudly. "My emphasis was on the ampullae of Lorenzini."

"Italian Renaissance art?" I ask.

"Not quite," he says.

Maybe it's a planet I haven't heard about. One to take Pluto's place. "I give up," I say.

He points to thousands of tiny pores on the shark's nose. "That's what those dots are. You'll find them in every species of shark. They're tiny jelly-filled sensing organs — electroreceptors. They can actually detect magnetic fields."

I'd heard of that on nature shows. I usually change the channel when it comes to shark shows though.

"See, the pores are sensitive enough to detect voltage differences in the water — down to 5 one-billionth of a volt!" shrills Wissenschaft. He's talking furiously. "They use that to detect the minute electrical fields given off by muscle contractions in their prey."

That's why thrashing animals get eaten first. At least that's what I'd heard. "So you swim, you die," I say.

"It's even better than that!" says Wissenschaft. "They're so sensitive, you don't even have to move. They'll still find you! Such remarkable, beautiful creatures!"

Oh great. Here we go again, another hippy-scientist telling me how wonderful sharks are. Then why doesn't he just be one? "Next you're going to say they don't like the taste of human flesh," I grumble.

"Oh no!" he says, grinning. "They do. They really do."

That kind of scares me. Is this guy mad? He is a scientist.

"Most of my colleagues in the scientific community will disagree. But that is perhaps because they've never bothered to ask the sharks what they think." He types something on the keyboard, and a new display pops up.

This time, it's a simple animated diagram of a shark seen from overhead. He's swimming, and a there are concentric rings pulsing from his body.

"Look, have you heard about how sharks hunt alone? Okay, most of the time that's true — very solitary creatures. But then sometimes it's not. They've been documented hunting together, working as teams! Coordinating their efforts to move prey into just the right location, right before they feast!" he snatches one hand with the other.

Now he's lost me. "What does this have to do with whether or not they like to eat human beings?" I really want to know. I need the vindication.

"Okay, so my research, what I've been working on since my post-doc, it's about body language. You know how 80 percent of what you communicate comes from your posture, your stance, not your words? It's easy to tell if you're angry, because your fists are all balled up, and your shoulders are scrunched together. Same with sharks, but on a more subtle level. You can tell from their behavior when they're angry, or content, or hungry."

"Well yeah," I say, "because it's bitten off your arm." It's just hard for me to sympathize, after what happened and all.

"Most humans can't distinguish the differences between these creatures' moods, because as they say, 'It's all shark to me.'"

I grimace. I think that was a science joke.

"But I can," he says.

"How?" I ask.

He plays a video of a shark swimming through a reef. "Hours and hours, even years of observation! Terabytes of recorded video. It's all there — there are subtleties between species of course — but it's all there! I've seen enough body language in the same scenarios to establish a strong correlation. The same patterns when they're tired, or when they're going to mate, or right before they attack."

He puts his fingers together, and takes a somber tone. "But I found the real key to understanding the meaning behind each shark's pose or posture when I built this!" He points to a white box with a metal wire coiled around it.

"A lunchbox?" I ask.

He adjusts his glasses. "No, it's an electroreceptor — my very own ampullae of Lorenzini. There's one exactly like this, attached to the Torqueod's hull. Sharks have muscles too. When they move, they send off signals of their own! Each muscle combination has its own unique signature. I've been building a database of shark muscle actions and their corresponding signals."

That kind of makes sense to me. "So they can talk to us, sort of like dolphins do?" I ask. I don't know whether that makes me feel better or worse, knowing that the things that tried to eat me were smart enough to know what they were doing. Worse. Actually, it makes me feel worse.

"Well with this device, I can find out what they're saying. I've attached meanings to the signals. I'm building a dictionary." He presses a key.

"Yummy," says the computer. He presses it again. "Yummy."

He presses another key. "Kill you," it says.

The voice sounds familiar, like I've heard it somewhere else, but not while in the sea. "Why does that voice remind me of someone?" I ask.

Doctor Wissenschaft looks embarrassed. "That's because it's mine," he says. "Bad recording, sorry. I was gathering data when we found you today, and had the sub's loudspeakers on. I projected the translations into the sea."

"So those words, they were yours?" I ask. It's all beginning to make more sense.

"Well, yes. They were my actual words, triggered by an automated mechanism — sharks can't talk of course — but I assure you, they very much meant what was said."

I feel kind of sick to my stomach now. I was so close to being dead. I think of the others. Fatman. Candy. Whatever happened to them?

"The beauty of it is that the database works on fuzzy logic," says Doctor Wissenschaft. "It's more than a simple one to one correlation. The algorithm I've developed to correlate the electrical impulses to the words is able to make connections based on statistical analysis." His eyes start to widen with excitement. I'm not sure I understand it all.

"The more data we collect, the more we can interpret body language we have never even seen. We're well on our way to having a universal shark translator!" Doctor Wissenschaft nearly screams the last word with excitement.

Great. Now we'll be able to invite them to parties. I frown.

"It's miraculous, isn't it?" booms a voice from behind me. It's Captain Bombardigo, standing in the doorway. He comes toward the machine. "To think! Our very own Doctor Wissenschaft is the first to hear a shark of the deep speak! Truly, a feat only possible by a Pirate of Panzerfaust!"

Doctor Wissenschaft shifts on his feet. He looks like he's not sure how to respond. "It is what it is," says Doctor Wissenschaft, suddenly humble. It strikes me as odd how quickly he went quiet when the Captain entered the room.

"No! It is genius! And I'm certain that someday the scientific community will finally recognize your work!" says the Captain. Doctor Wissenschaft frowns. That seems to have hit a sore spot.

He turns to me. "And you! My boy! You're a man of infinite pluck and grit, to survive out there like you did. If only I had the strength you do!"

That hardly seems fitting coming from someone as large as he is. He's built like a dump truck. It makes me feel small by comparison. I'll assume that was a compliment, I guess.

It makes me think of the others — they probably weren't so lucky.

Candy — she looked so sad, but resolved. Now that I know what was waiting for her, it makes things even worse. "Captain Bombardigo, have you picked up anyone else? Maybe yesterday?"

The Captain turns, his big curly locks swinging across his chest. "No indeed, honored guest. There aren't usually people floating in the sea."

My stomach twists inside itself. So they didn't find her. She must have died out there, torn to bits by . . . . My eyes start to sting. Part of the blame is mine. I should've given up the game of Chum the day before — or as soon as it got started. I wonder what Holly's doing right now.

"Speaking of that," says Doctor Wissenschaft, "what were you doing swimming forty miles from shore?"

Forty miles? There's no way I could've swum all the way back. That leaves little hope for anyone else, regardless of the sharks. "I was thrown overboard — fed to the sharks because I lost the Game of Chum. There's a ship called the Philanthropist. Her crew is executing passengers, one by one, until all of them are dead."

Captain Bombardigo's limbs explode in a flailing flurry. "What!" he exclaims. "That's heinous! Why didn't you say as much? We can't stand idly by! We'll rescue them!"

I'm glad that Captain Bombardigo sees the gravity of things. Perhaps I'd judged him too harshly before.

"Why would you even get on board a ship like that?" asks Doctor Wissenschaft. He's calmer than the Captain.

I explain about Cecil and Captain Poursport, and the TV show, and the promise of a million dollars and how great Betteravia was supposed to be. Doctor Wissenschaft takes it all in. I can tell he's thinking. The Captain looks thoughtful too.

"We'll arm the torpedoes!" yells Captain Bombardigo. He's pacing back and forth. "And we'll blow up that foul Philanthropist! Send them all to Kingdom Come!" Captain Bombardigo is practically boiling in his boots. He looks like he's going to smash something, or break the bunks next to him in two.

Doctor Wissenschaft cowers behind him, his arms up just in case. Perhaps that's not the reaction I was looking for.

"Captain, we can't blow up the ship. We'll kill everyone aboard," I say.

"Well, whatever! We'll blow a hole in her side the size of Greenland then!" he says. "I can't have people drowned at sea! Not in my Pacific. Not on my watch!"

He turns and yells down the corridor so loud, it echoes off the steel, and leaves a ringing in my ears. "Pirates of Panzerfaust! On the morrow, we go to battle stations!"

EXPLODE

I sleep fitfully that night. I toss and turn on a bunk Doctor Wissenschaft was kind enough to give me next to his equipment in the forward torpedo room. It's cramped, but comfortable enough, especially since I'm not sleeping out on deck of the Philanthropist. I need the sleep.

I think of Holly. I hope she survives tomorrow's round. Handlebar too. He stood up to Captain Poursport, when no one else would. I hope we can get to them before it ends. If we do — what a surprise for Poursport that will be! I can almost see him turn purple with rage.

But what if someone is hurt — or worse? Captain Bombardigo doesn't seem worried about that — about blowing up a ship full of innocent people. I can't live with myself if it fails. Just how good at firing torpedoes are these guys anyway? Dieter and Hugo are only actors. Who's going to press the button?

I turn over onto my front. I might be asleep, but I'm not really sure. I see Candy's face. It's cold, blue, and lifeless. Her eyes are closed, and her mouth is open. There are bubbles dripping out. A ball of acid hardens inside my gut and burns me in the throat. I have to set things right.

I gulp back tears. There is no Destiny. I am alone.

When I wake, I am stiff. I don't know how long I've actually slept. There are no windows, so I can't tell if it's day or night.

Hugo and Albrecht are sleeping in the bunks next to mine. Albrecht is snoring. He looks so peaceful, with his mouth wide open, his nose aimed skyward. His bullet bandolier is hanging from the bedpost. For a second, he doesn't look like the actor I'd seen on TV, and I try to remember if I ever knew his real name.

I slip as quietly as I can down to ground level, landing on my tip toes. I pull on the gray pair of shorts and submarine shirt that Albrecht laid out for me the night before. I'm dressed like a Pirate of Panzerfaust now. I still don't have any shoes.

I duck through the circular hatch and go through the room with all the bunks, most of which are stuffed with familiar, sleeping pirates. The sub is quiet. I go through the kitchen; I'm hungry, but I'll have to get something later. I find a small bathroom. It's just as small as the ones you find on an airplane, if not smaller. When I finish my business, I hear someone shuffling about in the room next door, so I poke my head through the hole to see who it is.

Doctor Wissenschaft is sitting at a big black box that's fixed to the side of the sub. He's staring into a pale green screen, that echoes a ping at regular intervals.

"Sonar," I whisper.

Doctor Wissenschaft raises his head. "Shhhh," he says, putting his finger to his lips. "We've been tailing the Philanthropist for hours now." He points to a blinking dot on the screen. "We started looking for it from the point where we picked you up. We're pretty sure that's them, but we need you to give us a visual identification once the sun rises so we don't go blowing up some innocent cruise ship or fishing boat."

I sit down at a chair next to him. I'm glad we found it. "Doctor, if we really fire torpedoes on this ship, won't it kill everyone aboard?" I ask. My nightmares are still fresh in my mind.

He looks at me sternly through his metal-rimmed spectacles. There are dark bags under his tiny eyes, and he's still wearing the same clothes from the night before. He's tired. "We'll fire them into her rudder, so they can't steer her. Then when she's adrift, we'll board her and take over. We'll be careful. Your friends will be alright," he says.

He doesn't sound quite sure, but at least we're not going to blow the whole thing up, which makes me feel a little better. Then I think of Captain Poursport and his thugs. "There's a whole crew of armed sailors on board, and they'll be more than ready to fight," I say. I look through the hatch back toward the main bunk I just passed through. There are at most twenty men onboard the Torqueod. There's got to be at least that many fighting men, plus ten more aboard the Philanthropist. And the Pirates of Panzerfaust are just actors. Captain Poursport's men have had practice being brutal.

Doctor Wissenschaft shrugs. "I suppose we'll do what we can. We have weapons, at least," he says. There's an open cupboard stuffed with swords that are long and curved, with bright brass hilts.

"Are we ready to blow that tugboat to the land of Smithereens?" booms a voice from behind us. Captain Bombardigo squeezes himself through the hatch, his binoculars dangling from his neck.

Doctor Wissenschaft looks uneasy. "Yes. We'll handle all the actual aiming and . . .

um . . . firing of the torpedoes of course. It's very complicated, you see," he stammers. "But we'll wait for your command."

Doctor Wissenschaft gives me a stern look, almost shaking his head with his eyes. I get the feeling that Doctor Wissenschaft hasn't told the

Captain that they're aiming for the rudder. He probably doesn't tell the Captain a lot of things. I seal my lips.

"Good then!" shouts Captain Bombardigo. "We've never fired the Torqueod's torpedoes before. We've got to make the first time a momentous explosion!" he says, slapping me on the back so hard that I almost smash into the sonar display.

I wonder how concerned Captain Bombardigo really is about this rescue. "But don't we want to save them?" I ask.

"Of course!" he says, "And we'll do it with gusto!"

Doctor Wissenschaft sends me over to the kitchen, where Friedhelm is cooking up some scrambled eggs. I squeeze onto a narrow bench next to Albrecht and Hugo and wolf down a plate full. I was hungrier than I thought.

After breakfast the Pirates take to their submarine duties: tightening handwheels, checking valves, cleaning up after themselves. Most of the real work seems to be done by the guys in the gray sailor uniforms. They're busy scurrying about the engine room pulling levers and yelling instructions to each other. I ask Albrecht about it.

"Yeah, well these guys were all Navy trained," he says. "They've actually been on submarines, so they know how to work one. It's not very easy to do, with all the ginormous apparatuses involved, not like driving a car."

"So you didn't actually fire your own revolver into the ballast tank to spring a leak and take the sub down faster so you could escape those cannibalistic bombers on Micronesia?" I ask. That was one of my favorite episodes. Albrecht had saved the entire crew, all in the nick of time.

Albrecht laughs, jiggling his gigantic arms. "Don't think that would actually work. That probably would've killed us." He points to the rear torpedo room where all the engines are. "I'm trying to learn how to do my part so I can help out. Luckily those guys have been patient enough to teach me."

An hour later I hear Doctor Wissenschaft's voice over the loudspeaker. "Levi, please report to the control room in the conning tower."

The nearest crew member points the way, and I pass through the hatches until I get to the main control room with the maze of color-coded valves and pipes, where I first entered the sub. Doctor Wissenschaft is up above, so I climb the ladder up through a hatch to meet him. We're standing in the small room inside the Torqueod's tower where the hatch to the outside is.

"It's first light now," says Doctor Wissenschaft. "We're close enough to the ship, you should be able to identify it." He unfolds two levers on either side of the periscope — it's a long vertical tube fixed to the ceiling — then turns the viewer toward me.

I put my face up to it, and try to focus my eyes. The viewing field is narrow, but I can tell that it's early morning, the sky is pale blue, and the water is a deeper blue. There's a tall ship with three masts and orange and blue siding sailing away from us: the Philanthropist.

"That's it," I tell Doctor Wissenschaft.

He turns and, pressing a button, speaks into a microphone. "We have a positive ID," he says.

Captain Bombardigo's voice comes back through the loudspeaker. "Roger that!" he says. There's a click and a whir, as sirens start to blare and the lights turn a dull red. A second later Captain Bombardigo pokes his gigantic head up through the hatch below like a gopher. "Pirates of Panzerfaust, battle stations!" he booms so loudly, it practically shakes the sub. I cover my ears.

Captain Bombardigo hoists himself up through the hatch into the tower room with Doctor Wissenschaft and me. Pirates pour through the hatch after him, throwing themselves at levers here or cranking on gears or flipping switches over there. Captain Bombardigo pushes me out of the way and stuffs his face into the periscope's viewer. "We've got to pour on the speed," he says, "catch up to 'em, then come around broadside."

One of the pirates in gray takes a look through the second periscope. He signals to another pirate, who speaks into the microphone. "Engine room, take us up to twenty-five knots. Target is tacking. We can intercept when they come around."

Captain Bombardigo shoves the pirate at the microphone out of the way. "Take us up to twenty-five knots so we can intercept!" he barks.

"They're zigzagging against the wind," Doctor Wissenschaft says to me. I steal a glance through the periscope. We're closer now, and the Philanthropist has turned so that its left side is facing us.

The sailor in gray leans over, trying to get around the Captain so he can use the microphone. "A quarter mile to intercept," he says.

"A quarter mile to intercept!" booms Captain Bombardigo.

"Prep the torpedoes," says the sailor.

"Arming torpedoes," comes the voice through the speaker.

I peer through the periscope again. I wonder if I'll be able to see anyone on deck. Like Holly, or Marcus. Captain Poursport is in for a treat. He won't know what hit him.

"Torpedoes armed," says the voice from the speaker.

"The torpedoes are ready to go," says Captain Bombardigo to the sailor in gray.

"Prepare to fire," says the sailor.

"Say hello to the vengeance from the deep!" cries Captain Bombardigo. He jumps feet first down the hatch, slides down the ladder, and pounds off toward the forward torpedo room.

"What's he doing?" cries Doctor Wissenschaft. He looks scared.

Two sailors scramble down the ladder after him. A second later, Captain Bombardigo's voice echoes through the sub's PA system. "FIRE!"

There's a clanking sound. Then a hissing, and an explosive gurgle. "He's fired the torpedoes," echoes a surprised voice through the metal hatches.

"You'll pay for your crimes you nautical naves!" crackles Captain Bombardigo's voice through the speakers.

I swing the periscope around and peer through it. There's a streak of rippling water shooting out of the Torqueod. It disappears, then the dead center of the Philanthropist explodes in a burst of splintered wood and flame. A direct hit. A half second later a shockwave hits the Torqueod, rocking it on its axis.

I'm knocked off my feet. I steady myself as soon as I can, and swing the periscope back around until I have the Philanthropist — or what's left of it — back in my sights. The Captain was right; the ship's been split in two, and its bow is dipping into the ocean. He blew the whole thing to Kingdom Come, just like he said he would.

▶ CHAPTER 17
THE RESCUE

"You'll kill them all!" I scream, but Captain Bombardigo isn't there to hear me. Suddenly, the siren in the sub is ringing through me, like it's pulsing out of my chest. It was a direct hit. They're all as good as dead. We've got to get up there. We've got to do something.

The pirate in gray next to me yells into the microphone, "Blow out the tanks and bring her up to the surface!" Two of the pirates slide down the ladder and bolt back toward the engine room.

In a moment, there's a grinding sound, and a gurgle, and the Torqueod starts to accelerate upward, just like an elevator.

"Prepare a rescue team!" cries the pirate in gray into the microphone. Some more pirates in gray come up the ladder, with yellow life preservers strapped on and orange-and-white striped lifesaving rings under their arms. Albrecht comes up the ladder after them. He has a life preserver strapped on as well. It's crowded in the tower now, but I'm happy they're going to help.

There's a splash, and then I hear the sound of the waves lapping up against the tower. "Go!" shouts the pirate in gray, and one of the pirates climbs the ladder to the top hatch, cranks the wheel and pops the hatch open.

There's a rush of air and a weird sucking in my ears as the pressure in my skull subsides. I can taste the sea air again, and I'm anxious to get outside.

Pirate after pirate climbs up the higher ladder and shimmies out the hatch, until Albrecht goes, and then it's my turn. I grab hold of the rails and scramble up, banging my left shin on the rungs by accident. It hurts, but there's no time to think about that. I stick my head out of the hatch into the sunlight. It's bright, and the fresh air breathes up against my cheeks.

I blink in the sun until I can see. The pirates have brought the Torqueod up right between the two halves of the Philanthropist. The sailing ship's bow and stern are both tilting upward dangerously on either side of us as they sink, like the two halves of a drawbridge. The front of the bow is completely submerged and it's turned over on its side so I can see the whole deck. It's taking on water fast — there's no telling how long until she's completely sunk.

The main mast is on the rear half of the ship. It teeters, then falls, crashing into the water alongside the submarine like a felled redwood, the sail drifting down, then going limp like a ghost sinking back to the grave.

The tank at the hull is broken in two, spilling fresh, bloody chunks of fish meat into the water. It won't be long before the sharks come.

There's mass panic on board. The contestants — the people I fought for and with — are screaming and crying, scrambling to get to higher ground, like rats clawing to the top to stay dry.

I scan the ship for Holly. I see Handlebar and Touchdown near the top, holding on to what's left of the mast, hoisting people up the steep deck face, fighting to keep them out of the water. There's Beanpole and that Glamour Sequins girl, but still no sign of Holly. She's got to be there somewhere.

Captain Poursport and his sailors are at the back of the ship, where the captain's deck is sinking below the surface at a half a foot per second. There's a bunch of bulky things — probably half a dozen of them — I can't tell what they are — each covered in a white tarp, struggling to stay afloat at the back of the ship. He tears the tarp away from one of them: there's a jet ski underneath. He pulls his sword from its sheath, hacks at a rope anchoring the jet ski to the ship, and cuts it free. He grabs a red plastic gas can in one hand, and leaps aboard the craft. He straps the can onto a metal rack attached to the back of the jet ski, and cinches it down. He grabs another can, this one green, does the same, then starts the engine. Another sailor leaps aboard, straddling the seat behind Captain Poursport.

"Go ahead and have the ship, you scamps. You'll all be bloody shark steak anyway!" cries Captain Poursport, gunning the engine. It makes a high-pitched whine as he jets off through the waves toward the distant shore.

A dozen more of Captain Poursport's sailors tear back the other tarps, then strap can after can onto the remaining jet skis before piling onto them — two or three to a boat — and jet away after Captain Poursport like a school of demons, leaving all the contestants behind to scramble for their lives.

"Those were the only lifeboats!" cries Touchdown.

The pirates in gray charge across the Torqueod's deck toward the wreckage. "Quickly! Lower yourself into the water and come aboard!" cries Albrecht toward the sinking ship. He throws the lifesaver ring like a discus into the water. It lands near the Philanthropist's stern. There's at least twenty feet of gurgling, churning, bubbling boils of sea between the Torqueod and the Philanthropist.

Marcus and Gumbo are nearest the ring. Gumbo grabs hold of Marcus and leaps from the ship's railing. He lands, crashing into the bloody water and disappearing beneath it. After a moment he finally surfaces and pulls Marcus out from the depths, shoving the ring under his arms. He struggles through the water, splashing and thrashing through the waves.

The sailors throw ring after ring, and Beanpole follows Gumbo, leaping into the water after him.

"Get down to that submarine! And get clear of this ship!" cries Handlebar, and starts to lower Glamour Sequins down the swiftly tilting deck. The captain's deck is now completely underwater, and the front half of the ship is worse off still, with only bare guts and its torn and shattered ribs peeking out from beneath the sea.

I swing both legs out of the hatch and climb down the tower onto the deck. Gumbo and Marcus reach the Torqueod as I get to the edge. Albrecht gives them a hand and hoists them out of the water. Candy #2 and Pockmark and the rest are all jumping one by one into the ocean. There are plenty of lifesaver rings to go around. Handlebar makes sure everyone gets down to the water, then he jumps for it. So far, there's still no sign of the sharks. There's a whole school of humans paddling their way through the water. It looks like every last contestant is on their way. Every last contestant, except for one.

Then I see her, below deck in the forward half of the Philanthropist, on the broken edge of a room, waving for help. It's Holly, and she's trapped.

"I'm coming!" I say, and I strip off my shirt as I run to the tip of the Torqueod and dive head first into the bloody water.

I turn my arms as fast as I can. It's the most important sprint of my life — the water's cloudy below, a murky mass of blood and woodchip soup, but I can't stop now. Pull. Breathe. Pull. I kick hard, stretching myself long and thin like a torpedo, slicing through the water as best as I can. Ten feet. Twenty.

The sea is full of bubbles and rough water. It's not like the pool. The current is strong. My hand hits a large, splintered board — shrapnel from the explosion. I dive beneath it — there could be nails — and come out on the other side. I dodge another large chunk of the ship, this one curved and bigger than a bathtub. Thirty feet. Thirty-five. Finally I reach the shattered front half of the Philanthropist.

It's dipped onto its side, its hollow guts almost completely below the surface. There's one hallway still exposed, broken, splintered wood jutting out from it like knives. I swim over, between the pointy shards, and feel around with my feet until I touch a solid floor a foot below the surface. The floor is steeply slanted, with nowhere to get a good grip. I manage to wedge myself up against the wall. The water's up to the middle of my shin.

"Holly!" I call out.

"I'm here," says a quiet voice. It sounds like she's above me.

I look up. There's a room — it would've been next to the hallway I'm standing on, were the ship still upright. It's been cracked open like a walnut, and now it's just a shell, with Holly dangling on the edge.

"Jump!" I say.

"I still can't swim," she says. She's sobbing. If we weren't about to drown, it might have been a joke.

I hold on to an exposed pipe and lean myself out away from the ship. I can see her now. She's about ten feet up, her face streaked with tears. Even if she jumped in, I'm not sure how deep she'd go. It'd be hard to find her underwater. I need another way, but the ship is sinking fast. The water's already up past my knees.

There's a mostly submerged white wooden door down the hall under the water. It's about two body lengths below me, at an angle. "Meet me at the door!" I say, and point back into the ship. Holly nods.

I push off the floor with my back and glide feet first into the hall-way. I've heard that sinking ships can suck you down, which just makes matters worse, so I'll have to work fast. At least two-thirds of the door is underwater. I reach down and feel around for a knob. Nothing. I take a deep breath, then dive under. There's the latch — I grab it with my right hand and yank it hard. It doesn't budge.

There's no way to pull the door open with all that ocean water pressing up against it. So I go up for another breath, then dive again. This time I put my back against the opposite wall and kick out with both my legs, hitting it as hard as I can. My bare feet sting from the impact, but it works. The door pops inward, away from me. I surface, gasping for air. Water pours out of the room onto my head and face.

"Holly!" I shout.

She leans her face over the side of the door jam, her smiley face earrings oblivious to the emergency at hand. "Let's go," I say.

She turns over on her stomach and slides feet first down toward me. I grab her by the hand and scramble up the hallway until we get to the edge. She plugs her nose and jumps into the sea, without waiting for me. I dive after her, and find her a foot or so underneath the water. I throw my arm around her front and grab her by the armpit. I kick us up to the surface, take a deep breath, stretch out into sidestroke position, then pull-glide as fast as I can away from the sinking wreckage.

The Philanthropist lets out a booming burp, then sinks down another foot. A huge chunk of shattered timber breaks free from the side and plummets into the sea behind us.

Only twenty more feet to go, and we'll be back on board the Torqueod. Holly tries to kick, but it just gets in the way. "Hold still," I say. Holly's weight makes swimming awkward, and my head goes under.

"Hungry," I hear something say.

No. Not now. Not this. Not when we're so close. I kick as hard as I can. "Mine. Mine."

Fifteen feet to go. Stretch. Pull. Glide. Stretch. Pull. Glide.

"Hungry."

Something splashes in the water in front of me. I think it's the shark. My body locks up, then I see what it is. It's a lifesaving ring, and it's attached to a rope.

"Grab hold!" shouts Albrecht. He's on the submarine's deck, and he's holding the other end of the rope.

I hook my free elbow around the ring and hold on tight to Holly with the other hand. Holly turns and grabs hold of the ring too. Albrecht pulls, and we're dragged through the water like water skiers behind a boat.

He yanks us all the way to the deck. "Get out of the water as fast as you can," I say to Holly. She scrambles up onto the deck on her stomach and pulls her feet out of the water. Albrecht offers me a hand. I take it, plant my foot on the submarine's green metal hull, and nearly leap out of the sea. I don't stop until I'm safely away from the edge, with solid metal underneath my feet.

A single fin rises up and out of the ocean near the Philanthropist, then sinks back beneath the waves and is gone.

That's enough to shiver my timbers. It was way too close.

I sit down and lean on my knees and try to catch my breath. My lungs feel like they're made of iron, they're clanking so hard and heavy.

Holly turns to me. She's lying on the deck, soaking wet, her red hair plastered to her face, trying to catch her breath too. "You're a good sport, you know that?" she says.

I smile. At least we're both alive. "I think I'll move to someplace nice and dry, like Nevada," I say.

Holly laughs, then punches me in the arm. That's good. That means she's probably okay.

I scan the deck. Now that Holly's aboard, they're all here — every innocent contestant is safe. We even saved Mushroom Cloud and Specs.

However crazy Captain Bombardigo is, it worked. The Game of Chum is finished.

"Who are you?" Handlebar asks Albrecht. Handlebar's hands are propped on his knees. He's catching his breath.

"We're the Pirates of Panzerfaust. We're here to rescue you," Albrecht replies. He smiles a big grin.

"But you attacked us," says Beanpole. He looks mad.

"Oh, yeah, sorry about that. We had to get you off that boat somehow." Albrecht points at me. "We picked up your friend in the water. He told us you were being thrown overboard, one by one."

Beanpole, Touchdown, and Candy #2 stare at me. I thought it would be with awe or gratitude. Instead their eyes are icy. I'm surprised. I thought they would be grateful. I'm not sure what I did to them.

The pirates haul up a huge piece of wreckage as big as a lifeboat on the other side of the submarine. "Get him up here," says one. They prop the wooden timbers up, then yank a limp body in a tattered, trim green suit by its arms onto the turtle-shell metal deck.

Cecil. I turn around so I can get a better look. Whatever reservations I had about blowing up the Philanthropist melt away in an instant. The very sight of that man makes me burn up inside. I hate him. I'm glad his ship is gone for good.

He rolls onto his front and shaking, props himself up on his arms. His prosthetic hand is missing. All that's left is the rounded stump. "You fools! You've ruined it! You've ruined everything!"

"Yes sir!" shouts Albrecht proudly. "We certainly did!"

"No, the innocent lives — the people on shore! Look at this blood," Cecil waves his stump at the spreading cloud of red water. "The tides will take it to the beach! The sharks — now how will they know to despise the taste of human flesh, having never tasted it themselves? Who will tell them what they do not like to eat?"

I gather my legs beneath me so I can look him in the face. I don't want to believe him. I shouldn't. He's lied to me so many times before.

He takes courage and rises to his knees. "You know what I'm talking about," he says, looking me in the eye. "You've seen the data we've spent our lives collecting. Now the beasts below will muster; they'll remain unchecked! They'll seek to quench their blood thirst. If not today, then tomorrow — Frenzy Day is upon us!"

I can't reply. The way he says it freezes the words in my throat. Frenzy Day. The room behind the big brass door, the maps, the skulls, the way Specs and Mushroom Cloud talked. Even the things Doctor Wissenschaft said when we were in his lab — it was easy to doubt Cecil, but Doctor Wissenschaft is convinced the sharks are out to get us too. Suddenly Frenzy Day sounds so frighteningly real.

There's a hollow thud on the green deck behind us. Captain Bombardigo has just leapt down from the control tower. He raises his sword and addresses the contestants. "Welcome to the Torqueod!" he shouts. "You have the pleasure of being rescued from your suffering and inevitable doom by none other than the Pirates of Panzerfaust!"

I've heard this speech. Everyone else looks surprised, as confused as I was just the day before, and maybe a little bit frightened too.

Cecil stands. "You bring a greater doom upon the innocent people who dare step foot in the ocean in the days ahead! A slaughter that they shall remember for centuries! And all because of you!" he shouts, pointing at Captain Bombardigo.

Captain Bombardigo sheaths his sword and strides forward, looking Cecil straight in the eye. He's bristling. "I'll hear no such rabble-babble on board this vessel, you floating scrap! I am Captain Bombardigo!" he cries, spit shooting off his lips, his smooth face flushing. "And this is my submarine."

"Then the coming deaths are on your head," says Cecil. "You will be remembered as —"

Captain Bombardigo doesn't wait for him to finish. He cocks back his arm and smashes Cecil in the face with an iron fist. Cecil drops to the deck, knocked out cold, his sunglasses scuttled in two.

I can only hope to heaven that Cecil B.D. Somethington is wrong.

⏵ CHAPTER 18
THE CAPTAIN'S COMPANY

Frenzy Day. I won't believe him. I can't. Cecil has lied to me too many times already.

The only difference is, now I've seen the sharks for myself. I've heard them speak to me.

I can't say if Frenzy Day is real, or even what it is exactly or how it works, but I know this: if what I saw behind the big brass door on the Philanthropist is true, it's going to involve a lot of sharks, and a lot of people are going to die.

I need to talk to Cecil, to get him to tell the truth. But right now, he's unconscious. They've taken him down below.

The pirates help the contestants up the ladder to the top of the conning tower, then down into the hatch, one by one. Everybody is shaky — they were nearly blown to bits.

"You don't have to play the game anymore," I say absent-mindedly as the last few contestants descend the ladder to come inside. My mind is elsewhere, but I want them to know. Albrecht seals the hatch behind me.

Glamour Sequins sneers at me through muddy makeup tire tracks smeared all down her face. "Just because you already lost doesn't mean the rest of us are giving up." She looks angry, even caustic, the way her eyes are narrowed down to vicious slants.

I'm surprised. The game is over. It's through. "You don't actually still think you are on a TV show, do you?" I ask.

She looks up at me, her eyes burning. "That million dollars is mine," she says.

She doesn't get it. Of course not. She never went down to the room behind the big brass door. She didn't have an exit interview with Cecil or Mushroom Cloud like I did. None of them did. Up until the moments right before I got thrown overboard, I thought it was all a show — albeit a sadistic one — as well. I wouldn't have believed me either.

Handlebar pushes past Glamour Sequins and claps me on the shoulder. "Thanks kid. We owe you our lives," he says. I look up past his big huge 'stache into his hardened face. It's sincere, even kind.

"You're welcome," I say, and can't help but smile, just for one second. At least he understands. He slides down the ladder into the control room below.

I go to follow, when Holly grabs me by the shirt. "What happened to you?" she asks. I turn to face her. I'm glad she's okay.

"The Pirates saved me," I say. I tell her everything I heard behind the big brass door — about Cecil and the show, and how the attacks are going to get worse. She takes it all in. I can tell she's eager for me to explain the details, so I do. It feels good to get it off my chest, especially since she was on board the Philanthropist. She knows what it was like.

When I'm finished, she tells me what happened to her. "We were planning a mutiny," she says. "After you decided to forfeit, that gave us a round where we all knew we would be alive at the end of the day, so we didn't have to fight each other. It gave us a chance to talk things over peacefully.

Most of us didn't want to play anymore — the stakes were too high, and nobody wanted to get thrown overboard. So I suggested we rebel. Almost everybody was willing to play along, the guy with the mustache, even your friend Marcus and his big cousin."

I'm impressed. Maybe I was wrong about Marcus.

"It was that girl in the sequin shirt and the ugly-face growler guy that we had a hard time convincing." She must mean Glamour Sequins and Pockmark. "But even they decided to join the mutiny when they saw they were outnumbered."

Or at least pretended to, I think.

"We were all scared, since we were going to have to go up against Captain Poursport and his crew, and they're such good fighters. We figured though, that if we stayed down below the next day, we'd at least have our volt-clubs. And then we'd find a way to battle it out from there. You giving yourself up really inspired everyone," she says.

It's hard to believe they would even notice me. I don't know what to say. "Thanks," I guess.

"And then before we could hatch our plan, the ship blew up."

I cringe. I didn't try to stop it, and it was so close to being deadly. "Not everyone seems happy about this rescue," I say.

Holly shrugs. "I don't know. Maybe they think they still had a chance at winning, even with the mutiny."

"Or maybe, they were going to rat you out so they could eliminate the competition."

Holly frowns. "That's possible. It was a fragile alliance at best."

I try to take it all in. It seems like as brutal as the Game of Chum had become, some of the players still wanted to win.

Regardless, there are greater things at stake now. "Did you hear what Cecil said on the deck?" I ask. "About Frenzy Day?"

Holly nods. "I don't know what it is though."

"It sounds like a massive shark attack to me. If what Cecil told me is true, without the Philanthropist feeding people to the sharks, they'll go after everyone that sets foot in the water."

Holly looks horrified. "It's Fourth of July weekend. The beaches will be packed."

A thought hits me. Dad will be there.

"I just don't know though — I can't tell if Cecil is telling the truth."

Holly screws up her mouth and bends one eyebrow. "Can we take the chance that he isn't?" she asks.

She's right. I know what those sharks were saying. And Doctor Wissenschaft confirmed what Specs and Mushroom Cloud told me in their lab.

"We have to talk to Captain Bombardigo," I say. I have to explain exactly what's at stake here — just how urgent all this is. I stick my legs through the hole onto the lowest ladder and slide down.

When I get down to the main control room, everyone's there: Marcus, Gumbo, Touchdown, Candy #2 and all the rest. Everyone who can't fit is staring through the hatches from the adjacent rooms at the fore and aft. Mr. Director is there too. He looks a bit groggy. Two pirates hold him tight by the arms on either side. He's been handcuffed at the wrists. They must have picked him up in all the confusion outside. Friedhelm is handing out towels, since everyone is soaking wet. They're all shouting at each other.

Holly and I slide in between two pressure gauges.

"What is going on here?" demands Touchdown.

"Isn't it obvious?" yells Pockmark. "We've been kidnapped."

"Are we still on the show?" asks Glamour Sequins.

Captain Bombardigo throws up his arms. "Enough!" he shouts. He is standing in the center, his eyes as wide as cupcakes. He's so big, he takes up the whole room. Everyone goes quiet.

"Just yesterday," he says, staring them all down, "I and my crew received a distress signal and were given the location of your ship. Of course then it was our sworn duty to enter the battle, no matter what the costs, since your innocent lives were at stake!"

A distress signal? That's a funny way to look at it. Captain Bombardigo wouldn't have known about them if it weren't for me.

"You must fear for your safety no longer! You are in the courageous hands of the Pirates of Panzerfaust!"

Glamour Sequins looks like she's eating all this up. She raises her hand. "And what about our reward — we won, right? Do we get the million dollars? Do we get to go to Betteravia?"

I snort. She still actually believes it.

Mr. Director raises his head. "You idiots!" he says. "There is no million dollars! There is no Betteravia! There was never any TV show! When will you realize it was all a trick to get you on board the Philanthropist?"

Finally. The truth.

Glamour Sequins gasps. "You're lying!" shouts Beanpole.

"Then what are we doing here?" asks another. Everyone looks confused, angry, or both. Some are yelling at Mr. Director. Pockmark and Gumbo look like they're about to kill him.

"You —" starts Mr. Director. Without even turning around, Captain Bombardigo swings his fist back at Mr. Director, smashing him in the face. Mr. Director crumples, then falls to the floor unconscious.

The contestants go silent. I'm all too happy to see him go down. Perhaps that was the drama Mr. Director had been looking for.

"Now," says Captain Bombardigo, "your foes are vanquished. All is repaired. Let's see what the seas have in store for us."

Beanpole raises his hand. "Can't we just go back to land? I want to go home." There's a murmur of agreement.

Home. It might be just what we need. We could alert the Coast Guard, clear the beaches — we could do something.

"We were supposed to see an exotic island!" whines Glamour Sequins. She's crying. Candy #2 nods.

The Captain holds his hands up for silence again. "Hold on a tattered second. I hear all this talk about how Betteravia doesn't exist." He points to Mr. Director's limp body. "That poor, poor fellow. He's no sub boat captain. He's a faker and a charlatan."

"He can say there's no Betteravia, but he doesn't have this —" he pulls a rolled up map from inside his coat, and unfurls it. It's weathered and brown, with the Southern California coastline printed on it.

Captain Bombardigo points to a small brown speck some distance out from the shore. It's labeled in bold, flowing calligraphy, like it was penned by Columbus himself, "Betteravia."

There's a couple of gallons of ooh's and ahh's. He shows the map around the room, so all can see.

"I knew it! It is real!" cries Glamour Sequins. She starts clapping. Candy #2 looks happier than ever.

I'm all twisted around. Where did the Captain get that? I believed in that island when Cecil told me about it in the first place, until I found out he was lying, but if that map is the genuine article, then Betteravia does exist. It's too weird.

Captain Bombardigo stabs a finger into the air. "Take heart!" says Captain Bombardigo, "And I'll make all your dreams come true." He's beaming. "In Betteravia, the root beer flows like rain, and there are two mermaids for every man." He claps Touchdown on the back.

"Mermaids?" says Touchdown. He smiles.

"And what a celebration we'll have! The Pirates of Panzerfaust, in honor of their first victory!" says Captain Bombardigo. He puts his arm around Candy #2. "Just wait until you see it — an island paradise, where you can live out your dreams!" She giggles. There's more applause; it's louder this time.

None of this seems right. First, because Cecil himself told me that island doesn't exist. Second, and even more important, there are sharks out there waiting to eat the whole human race, and we're headed off to an island paradise?

"It's settled then! All of you—make yourselves at home," says Captain Bombardigo. "My submarine is yours—except for you and you and you." He points to Mr. Director and Specs and Mushroom Cloud. "Take the prisoners away and lock them up with the other one." Dieter and Hugo are holding Mr. Director's limp body up by the arms. They drag him through the circular pressure hatch toward the forward torpedo room.

Captain Bombardigo climbs through the forward hatch and disappears into his cabin. The remaining pirates start to usher all the contestants toward the forward quarters. Pretty soon it's just Holly and me in the empty control room, alone.

"I don't get it," I say to Holly. "Betteravia doesn't exist. Cecil told me so himself." It seems strange too, that Captain Bombardigo didn't bat an eyelash at the coming Frenzy Day. If anything, he's ignoring it. But how could anyone ignore the warning Cecil gave on the Torqueod's deck? It was dripping with death and doom.

"We have to get the Captain's help," I say.

"There's no time like right now," says Holly.

I climb through the hatch to the radio room, where the metal door Captain Bombardigo went through just a minute ago is shut fast. Holly's right behind me.

A sudden burst of muffled, heavy music blares through the door. I put my ear up to the metal. It's an electric guitar—it sounds like the Captain is wailing out a riff or two.

I knock. He keeps on wailing. It's getting louder.

I pound both hands on the door. "Captain Bombardigo! We need your help!"

The wailing stops for a brief second, then starts back up. There's no answer. Just more wailing. I'm no musician, but it sounds like he's repeating the same three chords over and over again.

Albrecht sticks his head through the hatch. "You'll never get him to open up while he's jamming. Captain takes his rockin' time very seriously," he says, then disappears again.

I cock back my fist so I can smash the door with a good hard knock.

Holly puts a hand on me. "Wait," she says. "Let me try."

She puts her mouth up to the door. "Egad! Viceicknick has fired a volley of ballistic crabs at the tender heart of the Torqueod!" she shouts.

The guitar goes silent immediately. Captain Bombardigo's door pops open and Captain Bombardigo bursts out into the radio room. "What? He's here?" he shouts.

"Oh, hello," says Holly.

Captain Bombardigo looks left, then right, then left again. "Ho there! That's not the least bit funny," he says.

Holly squeezes past him into his chamber. "What? You, what do you want?" he says, following her inside. I get in before he closes the door. His quarters are narrow—just barely large enough for a bed and an amplifier.

"Captain, we need your help. No, in fact, all of humanity needs your help," says Holly. I've got to admire her pluck.

"Indeed! That's what the Pirates are for!" he says.

"You remember what I said about the sharks?" I ask. I'm hopeful.

He nods, "Of course."

I've got to impress on him how important all this is. It must be my fault that it escaped him before. I do my best to explain it all from the beginning. I tell him about the pickled Chumburgers, and how sharks hate the taste when people eat them, and Cecil's plan, and how now that's all gone awry. I can't help but feel a little guilty. If it weren't for me, Captain Bombardigo never would've blown up the Philanthropist.

Captain Bombardigo paces the room, six feet in either direction. He tugs on his curly black locks.

"So what I'm saying Captain, is we've got to go back. We have to find a way to help everyone on shore."

Captain Bombardigo stands with his back to me. He's silent. I wish I could tell what he was thinking.

"Captain, you can save them!" says Holly.

Suddenly, the Captain spins around, and smashes his fist into his hand. "And we will!" he cries. His eyes are wide; his hair nearly stands up on end. "We'll give a pickle to every person on the sand! We'll get a cage for every shark! We'll save the citizens of the shore, and then they'll be free! We have to do this! We have to be their heroes!"

I'm nearly floored by his reaction. I don't know what to say. I'm grateful, and happy that he'd be so set on saving them. I'm relieved, to say the least.

"But how will all that work?" asks Holly. I'm not sure why, but she seems skeptical.

Captain Bombardigo flails his arms in the air. "We can talk about that later! You have to begin with the end in mind! You have to visualize your victory first, then execute what you've imagined. We're the Pirates of Panzerfaust!" he cries. "There is no other option! We must and we will!"

He takes up his guitar again, and slashes his hand across the metal guitar strings, blasting a chord out of the amp like a shockwave. It stings my ears. "Shark slayers!" he sings, his tongue sticking way out, and attacks the strings in a jarring riff that rocks across the Richter scale.

He doesn't stop for a full minute, the Captain is so pumped. After what seems like an hour, he waggles the whammy bar, warping the chords into a frenzy. Then he goes quiet.

CHUM

"Tomorrow, we take back our oceans," he says. I couldn't be happier about that.

● CHAPTER 19
ALPHA SHARKS

After dinner I take Holly to the forward torpedo room so she can see Doctor Wissenschaft's lab. It feels good knowing that Captain Bombardigo is on our side. He'll be able to come up with a plan. He always does.

The door to the torpedo room is closed. I push on it, swinging it open. Doctor Wissenschaft is inside. He's sitting on a swivel chair, wedged between all his messy wiring and parts. He's got a yellow notepad on one knee. Mr. Director, Mushroom Cloud, and Specs are all sitting on the bunk bed opposite him, handcuffed to the wall. Cecil is there too. His leg is handcuffed to the bedpost, probably since he's missing a hand.

Mr. Director is sleeping, or just ignoring everyone. The scientists are deep in conversation. Doctor Wissenschaft is showing them something on his monitors. "See! If what you say is true, my data supports it!" he says.

Specs nods. "It's remarkable," he says. "The social patterns! The complex communication. It's not too far off from dolphins. You're not the first to hypothesize it, but you've actually proven just how intelligent they are! The language of the sharks—translated into English!"

I hate for these guys to get too buddy-buddy. I don't want Doctor Wissenschaft getting pulled in by their schemes. I clear my throat loudly.

"Ah, Levi. Come in," says Doctor Wissenschaft. "You've met everyone here before, I trust."

I narrow my eyes at them. Mushroom Cloud looks even less happy to see me than I am to see him. "I want you to tell me everything you can about Frenzy Day," I say.

Mushroom Cloud spits. "Why? You've already ruined everything! You've destroyed years of research and work!" says Mushroom Cloud. "We can't get that back."

Cecil sits up. Besides his missing hand, his glasses are gone, and his suit is torn at the sleeves and in the pant legs. He's looked better. "No. Let him hear the truth. He has to know what he did," he says.

Why do I feel like I'm the one who's on trial here? "I blew up the Philanthropist and saved everyone from being fed to the sharks. I won't deny that. And now all of humanity who ever goes in the ocean is in danger. Okay. I get that. But if there's something else I need to know about Frenzy Day, now's your chance to tell me."

Cecil looks at Mushroom Cloud. Mushroom Cloud raises his head. "Once a year at the end of summer, the currents, tides, and winds are just right to spark a mass migration of sharks toward the shore. The ones we've tracked all do it. They're moving in to hunt, and they're doing it in coordinated waves."

"Why hasn't anybody heard about this before?" I ask.

"They have. It's just that so long as the Philanthropist has sailed, we've been holding back the tide. Without it, the dam would break, and every shark in this part of the Pacific would follow his instincts, make his way to shore, and eat the first man, woman, or child he could get his teeth on. Their electroreceptors are very keen, so we're easy to find, and humans are soft and pink—no scales, horns, spines, nothing—the gummy bear of the sea," says Mushroom Cloud with relish.

I shake my head. "That doesn't make sense. I thought this was Chum's first season," I say. "People have been surfing and diving for a hundred years. If what you're saying is true, every time they set foot in the water, they'd be eaten in seconds."

"Think about it," says Specs. "SCUBA diving wasn't invented until late 1930, and it didn't become available for recreation until the 1950s. Surfing became popular around the same time. Before that, there just weren't that many people in the water."

"Okay fine. But that was more than fifty years ago. Why hasn't there been a major attack since then? Thousands of people go in the water every day."

Cecil looks grimly at me. "Mr. Middleworth, the Philanthropist first set sail over a hundred years ago. It's been staving off Frenzy Day every year since then," he says. "This is the first summer that the west coast will have to go without."

"But reality TV has existed for a decade or two at the most," says Holly.

Cecil nods. "Before that Chum was a game show. Before that we'd call passengers and tell them they'd won a cruise. Before that, they'd hire them as treasure hunters. Each generation has its own fixation."

I clench my hands. I know Cecil told me before how long this had been going on, but now it really hits me. That ship's been saving everyone on the shore for a century—and suddenly, thanks to me, it's gone. A familiar guilt wells up inside me. If only there were something I could do.

Specs reaches for a pad of yellow paper, but his handcuffs stop him short. "Doctor?" he asks, and Doctor Wissenschaft hands it to him, along with his pen. "As near as we can tell, there's some kind of signal, either environmental or behavioral, that triggers Frenzy Day." He draws the crude outline of a shark on the yellow paper, then an arrow pointing to the outline of another shark, then a third arrow to another one. "It's works like a chain reaction. Once the first domino falls, the rest follow soon afterward."

Doctor Wissenschaft snatches the paper out of his hand. "Mine," he says.

Specs lets him have it. "Sorry," he says.

Doctor Wissenschaft shakes his head. "No. That's not what I mean. Mine. It's one of the signals they use to communicate. Its closest English translation is mine. Every time there's competition for prey between two sharks, they'll exhibit similar behaviors: swimming parallel to each other, swimming in a circle, or even splashing each other with their tails. It's how they compare size and establish rank. The higher-ranking shark gets hunting rights."

"So . . ." says Specs excitedly, "they could be waiting for the dominant shark to take his turn."

"Precisely!" says Doctor Wissenschaft. He checks off the shark at the head of the chain in the drawing, then checks off the next shark, then the next one. "There's your chain reaction."

Mushroom Cloud reaches for the paper like it's a candy bar. Doctor Wissenschaft snatches it away. "Wait, there's something else too." He draws several more sharks on the page, this time in a pyramid shape. Then he draws arrows from them to the other sharks below. "What if there's a hierarchy, just like in wolves?"

"You mean like an Alpha Male?" asks Specs.

"Exactly like an Alpha Male, but even more powerful. There's plenty of evidence for a social structure in the species."

Cecil's jaw drops. "No. It can't be," he says.

Mushroom Cloud and Specs look at him. "What?" asks Specs.

Cecil's eyes turn icy. "There's a legend that's been passed down, from one owner of the Philanthropist to the next," he says.

Mushroom Cloud rolls his eyes, but Cecil ignores him. I can tell Cecil is serious. It doesn't mean I'll believe him.

"It's a tale of an enormous blue shark with eyes like the blackest night and fins like swords," he says. Specs seems to want to listen. So do I, since the way Cecil says it makes my hair stand on end. "It is said that his body is big enough to swallow a lifeboat whole. Once, a sailor claimed to see him swimming alongside the ship, his nose at the bow, his tail reaching so far back that it could touch the stern. There were a hundred sharks following behind him, a school of death."

"And you think he might be real?" asks Specs.

Cecil nods. "The sailor who saw him died of fright the very next day. I know he's real."

"Impossible," mutters Mushroom Cloud "If such a shark exists, he'd be the Alpha Male and every other shark would have to give him preferential hunting rights. He'd outrank everybody." He's wringing his hands.

"No, more than an Alpha Male," says Cecil gravely. "As the sailors tell it, he commands all sharks. He's not just dominant, he is their king. The King of the Sharks. The Shark King."

The way he says it sends shudders down my toes. I almost have to believe him, since his hippo cheeks are filled with fear, his pale blue eyes distant and afraid. And then I remember it—the message scrawled into the wood in that narrow crawlspace: The King is First. Was that referring to the Shark King? "Mr. Turing!" I say.

Doctor Wissenschaft and Specs look at me strangely. They don't seem to know what I'm talking about. My cheeks flush hot. I know what I saw there. What if Mr. Turing—whoever he was—knew about the Shark King?

"But how can it be real . . . ?" says Mushroom Cloud, trailing off.

No one looks at him. They're quiet. I can't tell if they are buying all this, since they're avoiding each other's eyes. Then Doctor Wissenschaft takes a thick black pen and circles the shark at the peak of the pyramid. He tosses the pad of paper on his desk, then smears his hands down his cheeks, pulling down his lower eyelids.

"How I'd love to record what he would say," he says almost inaudibly.

"You can't be serious," says Specs.

"Why not?" asks Doctor Wissenschaft. "He can't be as big as the stories claim—those are just old maritime rumors—but the existence of a gigantic, dominant shark is entirely possible given the facts."

The very idea of a Shark King—some killer of the deep who commands all things—it makes me cold inside. I hope I never see him.

"Good thing Captain Bombardigo has a plan," says Holly. "He'll know how to deal with this."

Doctor Wissenschaft looks at Holly sideways. He seems confused. "The Captain? A plan?" he says.

"Yes. We spoke with him. We're going to shore to stop the Frenzy Day," Holly says.

Cecil shakes his head. "That was what the Philanthropist was for. There's no time for that now."

Again, the Philanthropist. It's all my fault. I saved everyone aboard, but what about everyone on shore? They'll die because of me. "We'll find a way!" I say. "I'll kill the Shark King if I have to."

Doctor Wissenschaft frowns. "And then what?" he asks. "Another will take his place. There has to be an Alpha Shark."

"Then I'll kill him too," I shout. "I'll kill them all!"

"You would drive an entire species to extinction?" Doctor Wissenschaft asks.

"That's what they would do to us!" I cry. I look down at my feet. I feel ashamed. I know I couldn't do that. I know I wouldn't. It's just not right. But there has to be something I can do.

"It's not as if mere mortals have a choice," says Cecil. "I've never seen the Shark King. Not in all my days. You couldn't find him. And if you could, you couldn't kill him. The watery depths are his realm. He comes and goes in secret, wherever and whenever he pleases. From the trenches below to the sands above, he reigns supreme."

Doctor Wissenschaft shakes his head. "You'd never be able to hit a shark with the torpedoes we have aboard the Torqueod anyway. Sharks are too agile."

So there's nothing we can do. Is that really what they're saying? I've never felt so helpless before in my life. Captain Bombardigo is our only hope. It's reassuring, knowing that he'll find a plan. At least we have that.

The Torqueod jerks upward slightly, and I stumble to regain my footing. A clang echoes through the sub. Suddenly I'm alert. We may have been hit.

Albrecht sticks his head in the door behind us. "Come on up top," he says. "We're here."

▶ CHAPTER 20
BETTERAVIA

Holly and I make our way through the sub toward the conning tower. I'm surprised we were able to get back to shore so quickly. The Torque-od must be faster than I thought. This is good. We have little time to spare, so the sooner the better.

The contestants are backed up at the first ladder, all waiting their turn to go up, like shoppers at the checkout. Two of the Pirates are standing by to help. There's no light coming down the open hatch, so it must be night already. The Captain is nowhere in sight.

Marcus and Gumbo go through the hatch, followed by Glamour Sequins and Candy #2. I hear them squealing with delight. "It can't be real! We're actually here!" says Glamour Sequins.

"It's better than I imagined," says Candy #2 as she climbs out of sight.

Holly looks at me crosswise, and I wrinkle my eyebrows. That's not the reaction I'd expect. There's something funny going on up there.

We wait our turn as voices filter down into the submarine, and feet pound across its metal deck, until finally it's our turn to go up top. Touchdown climbs out right in front of us. "No way! It's all just like he said!"

I have a feeling I'm not going to like what I see.

I grab the ladder and hoist myself up. I stick my head out through the hatch. It's dark, and as near as I can tell, we're in some kind of cave. The Torqueod is docked in a shimmering lagoon that's lit up by thousands of glowing blue starfish, each casting its light up to the ceiling, where it bounces and dazzles its way across the domed rock. At the far end of the cavern is a giant white wooden wheel, its spokes radiating out from a central hub like a spider's web. Smaller shacks of all sorts and colors, blues, yellows, and reds, are hidden in the shadows under the cavern wall, and great big pointy white cylinders stab at all angles into the sky.

Touchdown is running across the deck. He pounds up a metal gangplank onto the rocky ground. I'm floored, because I can't believe what I see. There, at the end of the gangplank are two women with fish tails sitting on a rock, waving to Touchdown—actual real live mermaids.

Where are we, anyway? This doesn't look like any port I know of. For the second time in the last two days, I wonder if I'm dead. "Holly, you'd better see this," I say.

She scrambles up the ladder and pokes her head out of the hatch next to me. "Cool but creepy," she says. "What is this place?"

"I don't know," I say. Wherever it is, it's not home.

The giant wooden wheel lights up with white and yellow lights. It begins to turn slowly, like it's waking from a nap. A pipe organ hidden somewhere in the cave strikes up a bouncing carnival tune that echoes across the walls.

Now that it's bright enough to see, I can make out baskets hanging from the wooden wheel's spokes—it's a Ferris wheel.

The shacks on the walls of the cave are lit up too. They look like leftovers from a deserted amusement park: there's a booth filled with giant pink stuffed animals, a hammer game with the bell on top to test your strength, and a bunch of white and yellow painted clowns with holes in their big red lips for throwing balls. The pointed cylinders look like missiles. Rusty oil drums are stacked up in pyramids scattered all about. There are dozens of mermaids lining the lagoon.

It feels all wrong. I can't tell if I'm in a carnival or a warehouse. And I've always hated clowns.

"I don't know which is more gross, the clowns or the mer-mechs," says Holly. She's making a face like she just ate stinky cheese.

"Mer-mechs?" I say. I have no idea what that is.

"Those," she says. She points to the mermaids. Touchdown has got his arm around one, but the mermaid doesn't seem to notice. She's still waving to the submarine, her tail flipping at the air. I wipe my eyes.

In the light, it's easier to see: the mermaids are mechanical, animatronic mannequins, like the kind you'd find at a funhouse. Their joints must be powered by little motors. I feel a sense of relief, since it means I'm not crazy after all.

A microphone squeals with feedback. Captain Bombardigo is standing under the Ferris wheel, holding a stick of pink cotton candy.

"Welcome to Betteravia!" he shouts. It echoes off the walls. "Make yourselves happy here! You've suffered too much. Now it's time to enjoy your reward!"

The contestants cheer. Betteravia? This isn't the island paradise Cecil described. It's a cave. The worst part is, we're not on shore at all then. How could he do this? We spoke to him just hours ago.

"Captain Bombardigo gave his word!" I say. I boil up inside. I feel betrayed. Why all that talk of being heroes then?

I swing my legs out of the hatch and slide down the ladder on the outside of the tower, then run across the turtle-shell top of the submarine. Holly follows me, and we both go up the gangplank; it's wobbly. When we get to the top, Touchdown is sitting on one of the mer-mech's laps. "I don't think she's interested," says Holly as we run past.

There's a hoot and holler from the Ferris wheel. Candy #2 is riding the first seat to the top. A couple more contestants have filled up the other seats. Two more are throwing darts at one of the booths and Pockmark is tearing the limbs off the stuffed animals in another.

We wind between two tall boulders, and pass down the row of booths. When we get to the Ferris wheel, Captain Bombardigo is already gone.

"Hey, where's the Captain?" I shout up to the Ferris wheel. Candy #2 shrugs.

Beanpole points toward a passage carved into the rock. From what I can tell, there seems to be several tunnels branching off the main cavern, like spokes from the hub of a wheel. "He went in there," he says, pointing to a passage in the middle.

Holly runs toward it. I go after her and follow her inside. The corridor's dimly lit by a soft golden glow coming from the opposite end. It bends right, then branches off into a corridor on our right, and another one on our left. Holly passes the first, then stops and jumps backward.

"Did you see what's in there?" she asks. I peer into the dim light. It's too dark to tell.

"I can't," I say. She darts into the passageway. Apparently she can. I go after her.

She feels along the wall until she finds a control panel with a switch. She flips it, and a couple of bare light bulbs hanging from the ceiling turn on. It takes them awhile to warm up, and light gradually fills the cave.

We're in a long, rectangular cavern. I can't tell how far back it goes, since it's filled with piles and racks and rows of impossible things—helmets, underwater diving suits, laser fusion guns, plastic trees, stuffed lions, a giant metal robot arm. It's all familiar, and it's actually right in front of my eyes: a warehouse full of Pirates of Panzerfaust paraphernalia.

"We've found the prop house," says Holly quietly.

I think she's in as much awe as I am, as well anyone should be, since this is totally rad. I can think of about two million rabid fans whose brains would explode with joy if they even set foot in this room. I'm one of them.

She points to a set of domed metal bars. "There's the electric cage Viceicknick imprisoned Captain Bombardigo in when the Torqueod got frozen in Antarctic ice."

I recognize it. That was one of my favorite episodes, since the Captain tricked the guards into setting him free by pretending he had a highly contagious disease. I grab one of the bars. It's warm to the touch. It feels plastic.

"And there are the singing gorillas of Manachoowee," says Holly. She runs up to a pair of hairy gorilla suits standing up in the corner. Their eyes are just holes, so the actors could see what they were doing. Now they look like they're dead. She reaches out and feels the fur. I never saw that episode. It was one of the only ones I missed.

"But why is it here?" I say.

Holly browses the aisles. "I don't know. Sometimes studios sell off their props. Sometimes they store them for use on future episodes. But Pirates of Panzerfaust got cancelled, so they shouldn't need to keep them around anymore."

There are two iron double doors slightly ajar three rows down. They're bolted into the rock. They look like they've been rusting here for the last fifty years. I hear some grumbling—it might even be singing—coming from the other side. "In there," I say, and run up to the doors. I shove them open with both hands.

On the other side is a short passageway bathed in glowing yellow light. It opens into a hollowed out cave filled with mounds of golden coins. There are wooden chests overflowing with glittering rubies and golden goblets, all shining like a goose's golden eggs. There must be a trillion dollars' worth of treasure in here. I've never seen so much gold in my life. I didn't even know there was this much on the planet.

In the center of the room, surrounded by the gold, is Captain Bombardigo. He's draped over a magnificent gold and red velvet throne. He's holding a gigantic mug of foamy brown drink in one hand, staring up at the ceiling, singing softly to himself.

I charge down the red carpet that leads into the throne room. Holly's right behind me. "Why are we here?" she asks.

Captain Bombardigo looks up at us with drowsy, reddened eyes. "What? Oh, hello. It's you."

"Why are we here?" Holly repeats. She's not letting him get away with anything.

The Captain spreads his arms wide. "To collect the reward for your suffering," he says. "Betteravia is for healing sorrows, and restoring humor to the burdened soul. Have a root beer." He pats a small wooden barrel on a stand next to his throne.

"What humor? There's a massacre coming," says Holly.

"You promised you'd help us," I say.

Captain Bombardigo jolts up in his chair, exploding in a flurry of limbs and splashing his root beer across the throne. "What? I've already blown a ship to smithereens for you! What more do you want?" he yells, looking straight at me, like he's some all-powerful king, and I am merely a peasant.

I'm caught off guard. I didn't expect him to explode like that. What did I say? I'm just reminding him of our plan.

I look to Holly. Her face is set in determination, her red hair ablaze. If she's sure of herself, then I can be too. He has no reason to be angry with me. Whatever's wrong with him, I'm not backing down. "We've got to go back. We have to find a way to stop Frenzy Day," I say.

He throws his mug on the ground. It clatters across the floor. "What do you expect me to do, give a pickle to every person on the sand? Put every last shark in a cage?"

Again, I'm confused. I'm certain that was the exact plan he proposed in the first place. I try to flex my courage. "That's what you said we would do!" I shout. I'm getting mad. "It was your idea!"

"No! It's impossible!" he says.

"But you said . . . you said you would do something!"

"What do you want me to do?" he asks, holding out his arms. I don't think he wants the answer, even if I knew it.

"I don't know!" I say. "But I can't stay on some island, while everyone out there gets eaten."

The Captain flips around. He grabs another mug and fills it from the barrel. "No one's holding you here. You're free to leave whenever you want."

He knows that won't work. I've got no boat. It's an empty offer—just like his promises.

"Do you really want to go upset the natural order of things?" he asks. "This is the way it has been for eons! They're predators. They've always been that way. It's what Mother Nature wants." He motions out toward the lagoon. "Those people—did you see them? They were almost dead—they're happy now."

I don't understand him. He was more than ready to fire torpedoes on the Philanthropist. Maybe that was easy. All he had to do was press the button. There was little chance he'd fail. "I think you're scared," I say.

"You wouldn't get it," he says, and drains the contents of his mug down his throat. He smashes it to the ground. It shatters into pieces.

I look at the Captain, lounging on his throne, surrounded by his treasure; he's happy and safe here. There aren't many people who get to live like that.

I think of Dad. He and I could buy a house with this much gold. I reach down to pick up one of the coins. It's smooth and lighter than I expected—plastic. Disgusting. I drop it. It's a fake. I kick a pile of the gold, and the coins go flying. They're fake too, just like everything else here.

Holly frowns. "Let's go," she says. She turns on her heels and struts back the way we came.

I turn my back on the Captain. He was supposed to save us. That's not going to happen now. Lots of people are going to die very soon, and there's nothing we can do about it. I follow Holly through the double doors and out of the throne room.

▶ CHAPTER 21
DESTINY

Holly and I slam the iron double doors to the Captain's throne room behind us. I keep on going, to the end of the hallway and through the aisles and aisles of props. I want to put as much distance between myself and Captain Bombardigo as I can. He's the Captain, and he's failed us.

Holly follows after me. She's silent, but tense. "He's right, you know," she says.

That's not what I want to hear. I give her my sternest look. "How can you say that?"

"Because as much as he doesn't know what to do, we don't either," she says.

I stop. I wish we did. I wish this was like an episode of Pirates of Panzerfaust, where we come in with guns blazing and no one gets hurt, and everybody lives. They were always able to make things turn out all right, like some invisible force was guiding them down the right path, and they'd always succeed.

The Captain, as much as I pretended—even insisted—that I had out-grown him and the Pirates—maybe he was still my hero. I guess I kind of even had a secret hope—back when I was moving all the way to Hollywood from Idaho—that I would see him walking down the street or filling up at the gas station, because this town is supposed to be sizzling with stars, all the way from Santa Monica Boulevard to Rodeo Drive. All I wanted to be was him. I never told anyone that, especially not after the incident in the locker room.

But life has completely failed to turn out like an episode of the show. And the characters I love are just actors. I've already lost someone I knew, and who knows where we'll end up before we finally get our feet back on dry land again.

Albrecht is standing in the aisle, leaning against a shelf full of fake jetpacks. He's looking at an old map—the same one Captain Bombardigo took out of his jacket in the submarine. "You can't really expect the Captain to do much more than he's already done," he says, shaking his head. He looks a bit sad.

I wonder how long he's been standing there. "Why not?" I ask. As far as I'm concerned, he's as much at fault as the Captain is.

He shrugs. "Me and the Captain go way back," says Albrecht. "I've known him since we were young and new in Hollywood. Back then nobody knew our names, and we didn't have a dime. I got him the part on the show, actually."

It's hard for me to imagine a time before the Pirates of Panzerfaust.

"We used to surf together. Spend all day on the waves. We were just like every other surfer then. We told stories about sharks. We laughed at the kids on the sand who were afraid of them. Until we actually saw one. It came right up and bit a chunk out of my board. Sure, it didn't get us, but the Captain never went out in the water again. He got really into Hot Rods after that." Albrecht shrugs. "So I dunno, maybe he's spooked."

"Maybe," I say. But that's no excuse. I was in the water with three of those devils—they all tried to eat me too—and I went back in to get Holly.

"But he said he was going to help us!" says Holly.

Albrecht raises an eyebrow. "Did he now?" he asks. He seems to ponder that for a moment. "Was he all worked up in a fever, yellin' all sorts of heroic slogans, his hair standing on end and swinging around like a giant rabid bumblebee?"

I nod. That's a pretty good description, actually. My heart sinks. It sounds like he's seen Captain Bombardigo do this before.

"He's impetuous, the Captain. He follows his gut, that's for sure, even though it wrenches him about at times," says Albrecht.

"But he told us just today," says Holly.

Albrecht sighs. "I believe it," he says. "We were on the verge of finding Spanish gold last year. We'd been on its trail for months, when suddenly—without explanation—he turned the Torqueod around so we could join the Alaskan salmon migration. He dropped the whole quest, just like that. You never can tell what he'll do next. I reckon even he doesn't know."

He turns the map around toward us. "Look here," he says.

I can see the island better now that it's up close. The word "Betteravia" isn't printed on the map like everything else; it's been hand-written in calligraphy across the island in black marker.

Of course. Captain Bombardigo must have written that himself. That was some stunt. We're not standing on the island Cecil promised us, that supposedly didn't exist then suddenly did. Not even Captain Bombardigo could conjure that out of mid-air. We're not in Betteravia at all. "Then where are we?" I ask.

"Island CC800-670," says Albrecht. "It's not on the charts. Mr. Pengerwist, our generous trillionaire sponsor owns it." He points to a portrait on the wall. It's a painting of an old, stately gentleman with his hand on an enormous globe. His eyes are slightly crossed and an explosion of white hair is coming out from behind his ears.

"Mr. Pengerwist is a collector of sorts. This is where he puts the collections he doesn't know what else to do with. The rides are from some tiny Midwest amusement parks he acquired. The mermaids too. Then we've got some leftover torpedoes and explosives to arm the Torqueod—we don't normally make things go so kablooie—but we've got them on hand just in case anyway. The island's kind of our secret base."

"I don't get it," I say. "Then why would Captain Bombardigo bring us here?"

Albrecht shrugs again. "I dunno. Betteravia sounds more like a state of being than any particular island. Maybe the Captain wants everyone's dreams to come true."

Sure, I get that. But still . . .

"I bet the people on the shore have dreams of living into next week," says Holly grumpily. She's got her arms crossed.

Albrecht raises his eyebrow. "Admittedly, what you're asking him is hard. You want him to save an entire species from being eaten by another. It's like asking the human race to stop eating hot dogs."

So that's us: helpless. Up against a wall with no way over. Captain Bombardigo has failed us. I don't even know where in the sea we are, except for what we saw on that map. "We're leaving then," I say.

"Wish you could. You know we're even further out from shore than we were before," says Albrecht, "This island is mostly underwater—you can't see it from the surface. That's how it's remained hidden for so long. Only way in and out is by submarine. You have to go through the lagoon."

"I'll swim out," I say.

Albrecht tenses his jaw. "Eww. Not a good idea. It's too deep. Besides, there are more than glowing blue starfish out there—a gang of hammerheads lives in that lagoon."

I cringe at the thought. Hammerhead sharks are so sly, the way their eyes stare at you from those fins coming out the side of their heads. They'd chew me up for certain. No, I've had enough of sharks already. Going through the lagoon isn't an option.

"You can take us," says Holly.

"Not without the Captain's orders I can't. It takes a whole crew to man a submarine," says Albrecht, shaking his head.

It seems we've hit nothing but dead ends. Holly wrinkles up her nose, like she's thinking hard about things. "You said 'mostly' underwater," says Holly. She's got her arms crossed. She may be on to something there.

Albrecht smiles. Then there's a clatter, and a smash from the throne room. "Albrecht!" hollers the Captain from behind the distant doors. "Come at once! We have hefty matters of Betteravian defense to tend to!"

He turns and shrugs. "Duty calls," he says, and hurries off toward the throne room.

I watch him go. I'm glad that we can be alone. I need to re-sort the contents of my brain. I like Albrecht, with his easy manner, but I wish he would help us. He seems trustworthy at least.

I turn back toward the aisles; I want to search the props, just in case there's something there that can help us, some sort of relic that might actually be functional. There's a gold fish bowl, a pair of giant electrodes, and a tree with branches that are really machine guns.

Holly and I wander deeper into the tunnels, taking turns and twists as they come.

I go slowly at first—checking the props that look promising, but none of them actually work. All plastic. All just for show. We go through a half dozen more tunnels, some narrow, others big enough to park a school bus inside. They seem to go on forever; we're deeper into the maze of a warehouse than we've ever been, when we pass another wall of shelves and I see a familiar tentacle.

My heart gives a start. Around the corner, its many arms draped down and across the floor—all twisted around a set of dying mannequins—is a monstrous jellyfish with a head bigger than a one of those giant bean bags built for four, balanced atop the highest shelf. It's got a purple mass of brains and guts, all wrapped up in translucent slimy protoplasm—the very same giant jelly that was going to suck out Captain Bombardigo's blood. The very same one that was attacking me in the locker room that day with its toilet paper tentacles, even if it was only in my mind.

"The giant jelly from your video," whispers Holly. She recognizes it too.

It's odd, now that I'm seeing it here for real. I remember how Marcus's video seemed so important to me back then—how vital it was that no one saw it. I thought it mattered more than anything. I couldn't have people knowing what things were going on inside my head. I don't know, I guess I was just afraid that if people really knew who I was then we wouldn't have anything in common, and that, well, that I wouldn't have any friends.

And to tell the truth, before I came out to sea, I didn't.

If only people could see all this, I think, looking at aisle after aisle of props. All these props are real, and somebody—probably several somebodies—had to make them, and whoever did, well, we might have something in common. They might even get made fun of for liking what they do. I wouldn't make fun of them though. I'd think they were awesome. It's kind of nice, knowing that someone like that is out there.

I reach out and grab a white tentacle and wrap it around my arm.

In some ways, I'm surprised I ever cared so much about what others had to say. I look at Holly. I want to tell her something. I want to say things that I've never told anyone before, because I think that maybe she could handle it.

"Do you believe in destiny?" I ask her. It just spills out of me. I've never asked anyone that before.

She smiles mischievously. "Is that a pick up line?" she asks.

I put my hands up, like I'm trying to stop this conversation before it gets derailed. "No, that's not what I mean!" I say. I feel myself flush hot. "I mean for a person," I say.

She looks at me. "Oh, you mean, like something inside you that whispers to only you, and tells you that you were meant to do great things?" she says.

That catches me off guard. She's hit the nail on the head. I start to feel the heat drain out of me. I'm positive I've never told her that before. I certainly didn't write it down anywhere, so she couldn't have read it. She just knows, like she saw it on my sleeve. I wonder if she understands. I wonder if she has one too.

"I used to think I had one."

"What happened?" she says. I'm glad she'd care to ask.

Then I start to tell her. Maybe it's because we're so far away from home, or because we might not get out of this, but with Holly, something's different. I feel like I can say it. "I betrayed it. So now it's gone. That makes things different, without a Destiny. If there's nothing waiting for you at the end of the day then there aren't any promises. No guarantees. Things could go any which way. It's a lonely place, because things might turn out for the worse. It's scary."

Holly looks at me with her big eyes all squinted up and her mouth twisted to the side in a little 'O'. I don't think she gets what I'm trying to say.

"That's dumb," she says.

"Huh?" I should've quit while I was ahead.

"Yeah. Your Destiny," she says. She makes some air quotes with her fingers.

That makes me kind of mad. It's like she's making fun of me.

"Seems like life should be more about the choices you make rather than some stupid fate you've been given," she says.

I want to stomp my feet. Not her now too! I want to tell her she doesn't understand, that she's got it all wrong—that's not how it works. But I can't seem to figure out how to say it because . . . well, because what she's saying makes too much sense.

"But, what then, you want to be just an ordinary person all your life?" I ask.

"Who does extraordinary things," she says.

Just then, we hear a clatter, and a bucket of swords falls over at the end of the aisle. They scatter across the floor. Gumbo's standing there, looking like a bull. Marcus is with him—of course. That's the last person I want to see. Not here. Not now.

Marcus is looking in our direction. I can still feel the bump on my skull from hitting my head all too well. I look for something to fight with. The closest thing to me is a mannequin's arm. I grab it and hold it like a club. He's right next to the swords, but he hasn't picked one up.

"There is no victor in the Game of Chum," says Marcus. "The time for fighting has past."

I laugh, disgusted. Sure, he says that now.

He holds out his hands. His palms are empty. Gumbo's unarmed as well. They must be up to something.

"What are you doing here?" I ask. Holly picks up on my caution and moves back behind me.

"I came to tell you I believe you," he says. "About Frenzy Day. I heard you talking to the Captain about it."

He must've been outside the Captain's quarters. That's another surprise. I'm not sure if I can trust him. I wonder what his angle is. I stare him down with x-ray eyes; if there's a lying bone in his body, I want to spot it.

"And so . . .?" I ask. I remember what he did last time I turned my back. But I can't say that. I don't want to acknowledge that defeat. He'll just use it against me.

"Look, the Director was clear about it. This game was just a trick," says Marcus. "So there can only be one reason to bring us aboard. And that's Frenzy Day. Cecil has lost everything. Lying won't do him any good at this point."

I smile. Marcus is acting like he's the one who figured all this out, almost like he came to tell me about the secret.

Still, I have to give him credit. None of the other contestants have tried to piece it all together. But he has, and that can work to our advantage. I'm just glad there's someone else besides Holly and I who believes the danger is real.

"Do you even know what this is?" I ask him. I kick the jelly's tentacle.

"I dunno? A man o' war?" he says.

And then I realize how stupid I have been. Of course he doesn't know. He might not even remember if I told him. It's not like he watches the show. It's not his style. The only one who ever really cared about—or even remembered—that video is me. If Marcus doesn't even know what this jellyfish is, then how much less memorable was that little clip for anybody else?

I look at the swords, the laser guns, the jet packs. We're from two different worlds, Marcus Earl and I. Always have been. The funny thing is, right now, for the first time, the world we're standing in is mine. It may be hard to see, when you're on land, in school, or in front of your peers, but it's just as real as his.

And what does any of that matter, when at least we're alive? The internet can't kill you like a pack of hungry sharks can.

"There's something I have to show you," Marcus says.

I hold my ground.

"Levi, please. We have to help them." For the first time, he seems sincere. He stares at me, and I notice that his fake glasses are gone; they probably fell in the water. There's nothing but salty, smelly Marcus, his perfect shirt and jeans all tattered and stained by the sea.

He might really have something worth seeing. "Lead the way," I say. I drop the mannequin's arm.

He and Gumbo turn and head deeper into the storage tunnels, even further away from the lagoon than we've already gone.

▶ CHAPTER 22
A WAY OUT

The tunnel turns clockwise for a long time, like it's tracing a circle around some point—possibly the lagoon. The cave floor rises up higher and steeper the further we go. The racks and racks of props have given way to more practical mechanical equipment that hums and gives off heat as we pass.

Marcus is quiet as we go. I don't have much to say to him, and I want to keep my guard up—just in case. Whatever he's done to gain our trust, I have to be sure that it's for real.

Marcus stops at a narrow tunnel on the left. It's only as wide as a door. He and Gumbo duck inside. The passage is short. It dead ends in just a few feet.

"In here," says Marcus.

I don't see anything. There's nowhere to go. Then he grabs hold of a metal rung embedded in the wall and pulls himself up and out of sight. I look up to see where he went. There is rung after rung running all the way up a tight shaft hollowed into the rock. Marcus is ten feet up when Gumbo—he never seems to think much on his own—climbs up after his cousin.

Holly grabs hold of the ladder next. She's smiling. I think she's happy to do this. It might be one of those things she's doing just because it's new and challenging. She bolts up the rungs like a natural anyway.

I curl my fingers around the first rung and pull myself up. They're round, with a diameter that's just a bit too small to grip with any sort of security. They're slippery-smooth too. I climb up after them.

My bare feet curl around the rungs, but there's not much for them to grip. I keep going anyway, even though we must be about twenty or more feet high by now. I just hope Gumbo doesn't misstep and come crashing down like a wrecking ball on top of us.

It's dark. I listen for Holly's footsteps on the ladder, so I don't go too fast and run into her. We're up at least to forty feet by now. It's a long way to fall, so I concentrate on keeping at least three points of contact on the rungs at a time.

The air starts to feel fresher. I wonder where Marcus is taking us, and if we're just going to open up the wrong door into the sea somewhere and drown, when I see a faint light up above. Marcus crawls over an edge and disappears from view.

Gumbo and Holly do the same. When I get to the top, there's a metal railing. I grab hold and pull myself up onto flat level rock. I'm glad to be on solid ground again.

We're in a small cavern, about the size of a two-car garage. There's another small pool of sea water below us, with two heavy iron doors on the far side that look like they slide back into the rock, and equipment everywhere: gas cans, nets, cables, ropes, and tools. Not props, but actual working objects. It looks like a maintenance man's shed. The best part about it is floating on the edge of the pool—three jet skis.

Marcus did have something important to show us.

The jet skis are tethered by cables to the wall. They're about eight feet long and white with neon colored seats. Two purple ones and one bright green one, with splotches of color sprayed across their fronts. One of them has a rack mounted on the back, similar to the jet skis on the Philanthropist. It's more than I had hoped for. This could be our way off the island.

"See?" says Marcus. He's smiling from ear to ear. And for one second, I think he might just want some recognition. I'm surprised at that, because I didn't think he cared what anybody thought, least of all me. I have to be careful just in case.

I jump down the eight steps to the level of the pool. "But do they work?" I ask.

Marcus looks annoyed. "It's better than nothing," he says. "It might get us off the island."

I weigh what he's said. Could he actually be trying to help? I'm waiting to see if there's a catch.

"Let's fire them up and find out," says Holly. And then she catches my eye, as if she's noticed my concern. "We have to test them before we get any ideas though," she says.

"Of course," says Marcus. "There must be keys around here somewhere." He starts to rummage through the piles of junk.

I put a hand onto the throttle and jump aboard, straddling the seat like you would a horse. It rocks side to side, water sloshing up against the hull. The pool is surging softly up and down, lapping up against the rock. There's a coiled cord leading from the jet ski's dashboard to a small red knob stuck into the handle.

"You mean keys like this?" I say. I turn it and push a button labeled 'start'. The motor coughs, and sputters, turns over, then dies.

Marcus looks at me. "Good find, Big B," he says.

I try it again. It doesn't sputter as much this time.

"Gumbo, see what you can do," says Marcus. Gumbo lifts the front hood of the jet ski and sticks his head down inside. He tinkers around a bit, then grabs a wrench from the work table and attacks the fixtures inside. I can't tell what he's doing, but one thing is clear now: he and Marcus really want to help.

The thought occurs to me that we might actually be getting out of here. It's a long way to land, but if we are going, I want to be ready. There's something I need from Doctor Wissenschaft.

"Marcus, I've got to get a couple of things from the Torqueod," I say.

He nods. "Sure. Gumbo is a decent enough mechanic. If anyone can get them running, he can. Let's get ready to get out of here."

I jump off the tiny boat and head for the ladder. Holly winks at me before I go, her dimples shining with a victorious glow. I turn back. "And Marcus," I say.

He looks at me. "Yeah?" he says.

"Thanks," I say. And I really mean it. He nods. There's no smile. Just a nod, but he looks like he might be glad that I said it.

I drop down the ladder, going from rung to rung carefully, but quickly, because now I've got a direction. It takes half the time to get down as it did to go up, and in a minute or two I'm back on the cavern floor, running down the hallway, past the machines, and circling toward the lagoon.

I'm afraid to even think about what it is I'm going after, but I would rather not leave without it. It could save my life.

I pass the giant jellyfish, then the aisle with the giant robot arm and the domed cage. I'm careful to memorize the path—there are so many twists and turns—so I can find my way back to the shaft again.

When I get to the lagoon, Captain Bombardigo is there, blasting out a humdinger of a guitar solo from the top of the Ferris wheel. It echoes through the cave, and Candy #2 is bouncing up and down like a groupie, while Touchdown and a dozen other contestants are holding lighters in the air or throwing hot dogs into each other's mouths. I don't even stop to watch or consider how disappointed I am. It doesn't surprise me like it used to.

I find Doctor Wissenschaft aboard the Torqueod in his lab. I burst into the room. Cecil is still handcuffed to the wall. Specs and Mushroom Cloud are gone. "I need the ampullae of Lorenzini!" I shout, panting; I'm almost out of breath.

Doctor Wissenschaft looks up from his work. He looks confused. "Why?" he asks.

"Because," I say—and I can hardly believe what's about to come out of my mouth, "I'm going after the Shark King."

Doctor Wissenschaft's jaw drops open. I didn't expect he would think it was a good idea. "You can't! For what? Are you insane?" he sputters. His hands start shaking. "He'll kill you."

"I'll stay out of the water," I say. I'm so full of adrenaline, it doesn't matter what they think. I'm going to do this.

"Then how are you going to stop him?" he asks.

"I don't quite know," I say. I know killing him won't do any good. We've already decided that much.

Doctor Wissenschaft stares at me from behind his wire rimmed glasses. His collared plaid shirt is wrinkled, and he looks distressed. I can tell he's been up all night.

"Unless you have any ideas," I say.

He throws up his hands. "None!" he says.

"We have to do something."

He turns, pulls the white lunchbox-like object out from a disheveled pile of papers, and hands it to me with both hands. There are wires and chords hanging from it—not unlike the giant jelly's tentacles. "Take it. It should last a day without charging." He plugs a set of headphones into a jack on the side of the box. "Put these on when you want to listen to the sea." He points out a black 'on' switch, a red 'record' one and a blue 'play' button. "This switch flips it on, this one records whatever signals you receive, and this one broadcasts through the water. But it only has a limited range of course, when it's not hooked up to the Torqueod."

I nod. It's straightforward enough. Just like recording a voice memo on my phone. As much as I hate the sound of those sharks' voices, I want to know what's coming after me when I'm out there. I'll need as much warning as I can get.

Cecil reaches over and touches my arm with his stump. It feels like a giant toe, and it makes me feel all squeamy.

"Find the trail of blood from the Philanthropist," he says, his cool gray eyes ablaze. "Follow it to shore. The tides will sweep it there. Then look for the place with the most people in the water. If the Shark King is anywhere to be found, he'll be there."

He smiles his approval. But I'm not doing this for him. I never would have known about the coming doom of Frenzy Day if it weren't for Cecil and Doctor Wissenschaft, but that still doesn't mean I condone Cecil's methods. I'm doing what I know that I have to do, because those people out there need me, and not because anyone told me to, or may ever know.

I gather up the wires and tuck the lunchbox under my arm and turn to go. "Wait," says Doctor Wissenschaft. He takes me into the kitchen and opens the fridge. He pulls out three small jars of pickles and hands them to me. He looks scared.

"Thanks." I take them, knowing full well what it might mean.

I grab a plastic trash bag from underneath the sink and stuff the lunchbox and headphones inside. With three jars of pickles, a pair of headphones, and an oversized lunchbox, I climb out of the Torqueod's hatch and run up the gangplank, not even pausing to watch as Captain Bombardigo swings from the top of the Ferris wheel on a rope, spraying root beer from a fire hose onto the contestants below.

I head back into the tunnels. When I pass the double doors to the Captain's throne room, I stop myself short, turn back, and go inside. I set one of the pickle jars on the seat of his throne.

I know it won't matter, that he's already made his choice, but I need to leave him a tangible reminder of the kind of consequences that lie ahead. I need him to know exactly what it is he should have done.

And maybe, just maybe, because I hope that when he sees it, he will remember who I was.

I leave the throne room and zigzag through the aisles. I'm just arriving at the giant jelly. It's a clear shot from here, just past the rest of the props, then the machines, and up the tunnel to the shaft, when something hard swings out from behind a pile of props and smashes me in the face. I go down hard to the ground.

▶ CHAPTER 23
DELUSIONS OF GRANDEUR

I'm on my back. I've dropped the lunchbox and the pickle jars. My nose feels like it's been shattered, and my face is throbbing, sending me signals of pain in bright white flashes. I desperately try to figure out what just happened.

My head's on the ground. I blink as fast as I can, trying to regain my vision, but my eyes are all fuzzy. I barely make out two pickle jars rolling off the giant jelly's soft tentacles then across the floor. Then there's a shadow above me, standing over me.

"You stole my chance!" shrills a voice. My head is throbbing. It sounds like Glamour Sequins.

"You ruined the game! I was supposed to win!" she screams. "Do you know how long I waited for this?" She's crying. "They were going to give me my own spinoff series!"

My head is foggy, muddled. I'm trying to understand why she's saying what she's said. She feels entitled. She feels robbed. I'm almost certain Cecil told her the same thing he told me—the same thing he told everybody else. Only she believed it, maybe even more than I did. And for some reason, despite the fact that Mr. Director himself told her it was a trick, she still thinks the game was real.

"You heard the Director!" I say. "The game was just a hoax! There was no show!" I put my hands to my face. Blood runs all over my palms. It's gushing out my nose.

She raises something over her head. I can see it now. It's a robot arm. "That's what you want me to believe, isn't it!"

She swings it down at my face like a hammer.

I roll to the side as fast as I can. The arm crashes onto the cave floor. This woman might actually be trying to knock my head off. She pulls the robot arm back behind her, like she's setting up to swing at a baseball, only my face is the target. I can't take another blow to the face. I'd be knocked out for sure.

I kick out wildly. My heel catches Glamour Sequins in the back of the leg and she stumbles, giving me just enough time to scramble backward on my hands and knees.

"I was the lead in my high school play! They told me I'd be somebody!" she cries. She's sobbing. "It's been twenty years!" she screams. I catch a glimpse of her curly dark locks and her gleaming pearly white fangs in the chandelier overhead, her face twisted up like a broken seashell.

She leaps forward for another attack. This time I'm ready. I push myself onto my feet and spring into the aisle, grabbing the nearest prop I can find. My hand closes around an old stuffed squirrel, which is not what I had hoped for. I throw it at her, and it bounces harmlessly off her sequined shirt.

I'm trapped. The aisle is a dead end. I frantically search the shelves for something I can defend myself with. A cowboy hat, a rubber ducky, a pile of plastic grass. My hand closes around a white tentacle. It leads up to the giant jellyfish.

Of course. I pull as hard as I can; the humongous body scrapes along the shelf an inch. It's not enough.

Glamour Sequins cocks the arm back, ready to take another swing at me. I grab a second tentacle, and pull on both of them. The giant jelly teeters, then tips over the end of the shelf, its flubbering body of protoplasm flopping down, smashing her on the head. She screams. It knocks her to the ground.

Her feet are sticking out from under the jelly, toes curled. I won't have long before this wicked witch wakes, so I scramble up and over the mass of mucus, grab the two pickle jars and the lunchbox and bolt down the passageway as fast as I can. I can't help but smile to myself—the giant jellyfish, for as much trouble as it caused me in the past, just came through in a big way.

When I get to the ladder I stop to make sure nothing's damaged. The pickle jars seem intact, and so does the ampullae of Lorenzini.

My nose is another matter. It's sore, and still gushing blood. I hold it between my thumb and forefinger and wait for the bleeding to stop. It takes a whole three minutes before the well dries up.

I put the pickle jars in the trash bag and tie it to my shorts to free up my hands for the climb. I feel weak and dizzy, so it takes me longer to climb the ladder than before. I keep going, holding as tight as I can, until I've finally scrambled to the top. I pull myself over the edge and skip down the steps to the level of the garage.

Marcus, Gumbo and Holly are there waiting. They've packed three red gas cans onto the jet ski with the rack and cinched them down. Its motor is running. I've never heard such a pleasant sound, not on all the playlists in the world.

"What happened?" Holly says. She's looking at my shirt. It's covered in blood.

"I met a fan," I say. I try to catch my breath. "You couldn't get the others working?" I ask.

"Doesn't matter either way," says Marcus. "Gumbo says these things eat up fuel really fast. We don't exactly know how far out from shore we are. We can't risk running out of gas in the middle of the ocean."

That makes sense. It could be forty miles back to shore. That's a long way to drift. We might never get picked up.

But that also means that only one of us can go. "I'll do it," I say.

Holly opens her mouth to object. "What if you have to swim?" I ask her. I'm starting to wonder if it will come to that.

"Fine," she says. I can tell she doesn't want to stay behind.

I don't think Marcus wants to go himself. Otherwise he would've fixed the jet skis and left already, without ever telling us that he'd found them. And then for the first time, I realize he really truly does believe me. Maybe he even wants me to succeed.

"Marcus, how did you know I'd be on the show?" I ask.

He almost laughs. "I work in the mail room at the network. My dad's an exec there. I saw some papers I shouldn't have. That's how I knew you were coming, and how I got the Chum cards."

Wow. I didn't expect such a straight answer from Marcus; he's just told me everything.

Then a thought frightens me. "Does the network know about all this?" I ask.

Marcus shakes his head. "I doubt it. From what I could tell, Cecil set up Chum Studios on the sly."

That comforts me a little I guess. But it also means that no one else out there knows about Frenzy Day but us. In the whole wide world, there's no one to help. It makes me feel so alone.

"But you came anyway?" asks Holly.

Marcus shrugs. His hair is a tangled mess. "I didn't know I was getting tricked into being bait. I was going to vlog the whole thing. I wanted to make a viral video sensation. My dad doesn't believe me when I tell him TV is a thing of the past."

I think of Marcus's phone, how it's down at the bottom of the Marina. It sounds kind of like he wanted to be famous too, just in a different way.

I jump aboard the jet ski. Gumbo unhooks it from its tether and I secure my plastic bag inside the rack then press a button that says 'reverse'. I press the throttle softly while I turn the handlebars, and the jet ski rumbles backward in the water. I rode one of these once, on a lake back home in Idaho. This one's not that different.

Marcus and Gumbo turn a crank next to the wall and the heavy metal doors slide apart a foot at a time. There are sun beams streaming past the garage, reflecting off the water slantways, but we're still in the shade. It must be early morning. I had no idea what time it was, we'd been underwater for so long.

"Good luck, you hero," says Holly. She's trying to smile, but her dimples don't show. She must be as scared as I am.

I salute her, then press the throttle as hard as I can. The engine buzzes and whines, and I blast out of the garage onto the open waves.

⏵ CHAPTER 24
THE YOUNG MAN AND THE SEA

There's nothing but a plane of infinite water stretching out from me to the end of the world. I understand now why people used to think they might fall off the edge of the map.

I don't see the sun, so I turn the jet ski around and try to get my bearings. There's a chunk of gnarled rock sticking up out of the water where I just came from—the only small speck of the island that's not submerged. It's just big enough to contain the garage, with two open metal doors and nothing more. The Pirates' underwater base is well-hidden.

Beyond that, there's a very faint strip of land in the distance where the sun has barely risen. It seems so far away, and my little jet ski seems so small, a mere mosquito trying to fly though space to the moon.

I point my boat at the sun—I'll have to navigate by sight alone—and give it full throttle. It lurches, speeding off across the water, as I hang onto the handlebars with everything I've got, the waves beating on the jet ski's hull.

Thud. Thud. Thud. It's like driving across speed bumps. I hope the boat can take it. I slow down for a bit, and try to get a better grip on the seat with my thighs. It's going to be a voyage and a half before I get to shore.

I get settled and give it full throttle, bouncing across the waves. The needle on the speedometer points to 52. The gas tank is full. The wind is in my face, the engine is spewing out water behind me. Everything tastes salty. It feels good just to move.

I speed along, wondering where Dad is. I'm certain he'll be going in the water today. He's loved it ever since we moved here.

I guess that's one of the reasons I'm doing this. Sure, it's for everybody on the beach today, but most of all for him. I wonder if I've been too hard on him. He's had a rough job making ends meet sometimes, but he's always worked hard, and shown more discipline than anyone I know.

Maybe that's why he never had much imagination. He was too worried about reality. Maybe that's why he never understood my dreams. He doesn't think much of action figures—I nearly laugh to myself—especially the Pirates of Panzerfaust ones I used to own.

I wanted the kids at school to like me. I didn't think it was so much to ask. I thought they owed it to me, considering how astonishing I am. I mean look at me. Right now I'm Blackbeard, a super-spy, and Jacques Cousteau all wrapped into one. Again, I chuckle at myself.

That's what's strange. If I'm going to do what I think I am, then none of them—the people at school or anyone else for that matter—will ever know about it. Nor will they ever care, even though it may save their everlovin' lives.

Their feet will be dipping in the water soon, like rows of meaty corndogs, just waiting for the harvest.

It's probably too late to go for help. And now I think I'm going to—I can't think about it. Not yet. First things first. I have to find the Shark King.

I stop the boat to eat a pickle. Then I have half dozen more. They taste awful, so it's not because I'm hungry, even though I am.

It's not too long before I'm off at full speed again, headed straight for the tallest mountain I can see. There's no way to tell exactly where I'll land, I just need it to be close. I wouldn't want to have to hitch a ride or catch a bus once I get to shore. No time for that. It's not like I can plan to ride up the coast for very long, either. There's no telling how long my fuel will hold out. The tank is more than half empty already.

The sun is rising higher in the sky. It's just the sun and I, in the middle of a million blue-green waves. I've never been so utterly alone.

I spot something small and yellow floating on the water. It can't be a fish, otherwise it would've darted away already. I slow down and approach it cautiously. It's round and yellow, with a blue and white body—a Chum!

It must be from when we wrecked the Philanthropist. Good. At least this means I'm on the right track.

I pick him up—out of mercy I guess—and look at his smiling face. What a little trooper. It's good to see him. Chums are omens of survival.

I turn him over and check the button on his back out of habit. There's a tiny picture of a sword there. A thrill grows inside me. I don't know what that does, but a Sword Chum could be useful. I decide not to press the button just yet. I want to use this when it will count. I stash my Sword Chum on the rack behind me.

Another hour and I can definitely notice the shore getting closer. My tank's near empty now, so I stop again and climb out to the front carefully—I do not want to go in the water—and pop the hood. The gas cap is inside. I unscrew it and retrieve the portable red plastic gas tank from the rack. I straddle the jet ski, facing the back, and pour the fuel into the tank until it's all gone.

It isn't enough. The jet ski wants more. I've still got two more red tanks, but I decide to keep going anyway. I'm nervous about getting to shore in time. I swing myself back to the seat, stash the empty red fuel tank, and close the hood. The needle says we're three-quarters' full.

I hit the throttle again—smoother this time, so I don't waste gas—and speed toward the pointy mountain. I pass another Chum, then another. Then three more.

Then I see a red streak on the water. Blood. Oozing toward the shore. It's got to be from the Philanthropist too.

I jet around it, then alongside it. I'd rather not get too close, but it gives me a perfect indication of the tides. Cecil said to follow it. This is good.

I do. I put another mile or so behind me, curving along the stream of blood. The trail of red widens as it spreads toward the shore. I'm at full speed now, with my head low, my chin stuck out, my knees absorbing the bounce of the boat, when my heart jumps. I see them, just below the waves: sharks.

At first it's a pair of them, all stealthy and gray, flitting along beneath me, their tails rippling back and forth—smooth, deadly and effortless. Then it's a dozen gliding along in a pack. After another mile it's even more.

They're swarming.

I stop the boat. A jet ski is rocky—I saw Dad flip one last summer—so I make sure to stay low and make my movements count. I can't afford to fall in now. Carefully—oh so very carefully—I turn around and pull the lunchbox from the sack. I put on the headphones as the shadows flit around below me, mere inches from my feet. The sharks don't seem to care that I am there, as long as I stay on my boat.

I lower the box into the water by a cable attached to its top and flip the switch to on.

"Hungry. Hungry. Hungry. Hungry," the voices blast into my ears. There are more than a dozen different tones, all shouting over one another, trying to be heard. They're vicious. They're angry.

"Kill them. Kill them. Kill."

I rip the headphones off my head. I'm shaking. My blood is pounding past the backside of my eyes. I touch my forehead to the seat, panting, trying to regain my breath. I'm sweating, despite how cool the breeze has been. I should have known what to expect.

Get a hold of yourself, I think. I pull the lunchbox out of the water and stash it on the rack. I'll try again a little later, when I'm closer to shore. I'm not sure what it'll sound like, but I'm hoping that somehow, when I find him, I'll be able to tell.

I unscrew the first pickle jar and wolf down everything that's left. It makes me want to puke. I eat everything in the second one anyway.

I sit there gazing into the water below for a long time. I think it makes sense now, what I have to do. My history teacher told me about Kami-kaze fighter pilots in class last year. If they got shot down, they'd crash their planes into the enemy battleships so they could sink them. They wanted to make dying count. It's strange, because I never understood them before. Now I do.

I fire up the jet ski again and point it toward land. Half a tank left. I've taken the long way to get here, that's for sure—I probably zigzagged more than I wanted—but at least shore is getting close; I can even see some buildings now. I'm actually going to make it.

And there I will find him.

Instead of making me happy, it makes my stomach turn. It means I'm going to have to do what I set out to do.

I'm going to sacrifice myself to the Shark King.

► CHAPTER 25
BATTLE AND BITE

The blood trail turns gradually toward the north, paralleling the shore. I'm so close now I can see cars, and even people, as tiny dots in the distance. I wish I could yell to them, tell them to run.

I follow the blood due north. The water's clear, which lets me see the gathering mass of sharks below me. There must be hundreds: pale gray-blue ones, others with gray-green stripes. Some are much bigger than the rest, maybe as long as a dozen feet or more.

There's a pier with a gigantic Ferris wheel and a roller coaster just a little ways off. I've been to it before. The rest of Los Angeles stretches out behind it.

I slow just for a second, and the faint whine of jet skis fills the air. I stop and look up the shore, where there are a few of them whizzing back and forth, weaving between each other near the pier. My first instinct is to warn them.

But wait, I've seen those jet skis before. I can make out the stocky form and grizzled gray beard on Captain Poursport's face. He's laughing, pouring something out the back of his boat from a big red container—it looks like a fuel tank—as he rides. There's Killjoy and the other crewmen, each on their own jets doing the same.

I can't deal with them now. They'll ruin everything. They're darting toward shore, then back again, working their way toward me. I don't think they've seen me yet. I have to keep going. Maybe I can slip past them.

A sailor—I think it's the same jerk who sawed my plank—zips closer than the others. Mr. Jerk-saw stands up, emptying the rest of the contents of his red jug into the sea. Now I can see what's inside all too well. It's not gas. It's blood. Just like from the ship.

They're baiting the waters. Which can only mean one horrible thing—they're here to make Frenzy Day worse.

"Ay! Look over there!" shouts Mr. Jerk-saw to the others. He points in my direction. They've spotted me.

There's nowhere to hide. Mr. Jerk-saw guns it, jetting toward me. I get low and pour on the gas—I only have a quarter tank or less—and my jet ski rises out of the water. I jet hard left.

Mr. Jerk-saw's coming so fast he zips across my wake mere yards behind my boat, jumping into the air.

Two more jet skis come from my right. The others have joined the chase.

I slow down, sinking the boat a few inches lower in the water, then hit the throttle again, putting all my weight over one knee and cranking the handlebars hard to the right. The two sailors' boats pass by at full speed on either side, inches away from mine. They're so close that I recognize their angry faces.

There are three more jet skis ahead. Captain Poursport is riding one of them. He pulls his sword from the scabbard on his belt, and points it forward, toward me, like he's heading up a cavalry. But his boat doesn't move—not yet.

"You came back to collect your just and fitting end, did you boy?" he yells. "You should have died when we first threw you to the sea!"

My insides growl. Had Cecil put me up to this? Did he know they would be here?

"Your boss is through, Poursport!" I shout. I'm trying to sound big and grown up, even though he's twice my size and decades older. I can't let him know how scared I am.

The Captain laughs, his beard bristling like fire, spit flying from his crooked teeth, his eyes burning like magma under the Earth. "Ha! You think I'm doing this for him?" he shouts. "He'll never enjoy it like I do! Good riddance to his Weakness!"

So Cecil doesn't know Captain Poursport's doing this? The Captain sounds like he's here to jumpstart the frenzy, and nothing else. That's what Cecil said—Poursport's cruelty knows no bounds.

Captain Poursport turns his sword until the blade is flat. I need something to defend myself. I reach back into the rack and pull out the Sword Chum.

Don't fail me know, my little Chum, I think as I press the sword button. The Sword Chum's head splits open at the jaw and swings backward like a gaping frog's mouth. Inside there is a familiar looking handle with a guard on it. I grab hold and slide it free from the head. A silver metal tube about as thick as a half dollar springs out of the handle guard, nested segments sliding out like a telescope until they lock into place, measuring over four feet long.

I take a practice swipe with it. Thank you, Sword Chum! A spark club—longer than any I've seen before. Exactly what I need. I toss the empty Chum into the water.

Captain Poursport guns it, his sword pointed at my heart. I would turn, but I can't—the two boats flanking either side of him are coming at me too. There's nowhere to go without crashing into them at breakneck speed.

I lean to one side and duck.

Light glints across steel as the blade flashes toward me. I swing the spark club up to block my head. I press the trigger, but nothing happens. It must have been damaged in the water.

There's a thwack, and I'm knocked backward into the rack as Captain Poursport zips by.

There's a pain in my chest, and I struggle to breathe. Captain Poursport's knocked all the wind right out of me. I push myself up. My spark club is bent and chipped, but still useable. That Sword Chum saved my life.

Captain Poursport and his cronies are turning around, so I pour on the gas and speed away. I can't run out of gas now—that would be disastrous.

There's no way my jet ski is faster than theirs—it's probably a decade old. I get low and bounce across the waves.

I chance a look downward. There's something strange going on below me—the sharks are swimming back and forth, parallel to the water's edge, but no closer to it than I am, like there's an invisible barrier between them and shore. I need to hear what they're saying. I've got to get far enough away that I can lower the lunchbox and listen again.

I point my jet ski straight for the pier. It's risky. The wooden beams holding it up are as thick as tree trunks, with only four or five feet between them. It's like a forest in there, there are so many support beams, and the waves are rising and falling so drastically in the shadows, going in there would be worse than riding your bike across the freeway in traffic.

I ease off the throttle just as I pass between the first pair of pillars. I blink at the sudden lack of sunlight, when a wave comes crashing in, roaring and echoing underneath the wooden pier. It raises me up and smashes the back end of my jet ski into a second set of pillars. I scramble to hold on and drop my spark club. It sinks. No!

I won't make the same mistake again. I duck and turn my boat so it's perpendicular to the shore. When the next wave comes, I'm ready, and I give the jet ski just enough gas to keep the wave from knocking me backward. There's a lull before the next wave, so I press the throttle halfway and wind through the pylons and out the other side.

There are people on the pier yelling at me, but I don't care. The sailors would be stupid to follow me. I'd be stupid to follow me. I've got just enough time before they take the long route around the tip of the pier to see what's going on below.

I stuff the headphones over my ears, grab hold of the cable, and drop the lunchbox down into the water, all the while keeping one eye on the far side of the pier.

"Hungry. Hungry," say the sharks. I grit my teeth and bear it. Then a new word, one I haven't heard them speak yet.

"Yours."

I press the headphones to my ear. I think I heard that right.

"Yours. Yours."

I did. Doctor Wissenschaft's machine is learning. When I think about it, what they're saying kind of makes sense. As much as it could anyway—they're waiting their turn. They're giving priority to someone or something else that gets to be first in line.

I catch a glimpse of the poor people on the sand. There are hundreds of them. All bare and pink, with nothing but swimsuits on—playing Frisbee, building castles, wading, laughing—all tender for the slicing. And I'm one of them. Suddenly, I feel very small and weak.

The crew's jet skis are rounding the end of the pier and closing in. They're only sixty feet off and coming fast. I yank up the lunchbox and set it on the rack. There's no time to secure it – they'll be on me any second—too bad I dropped my spark club.

I gun it for the count of twenty to put some space between us. I cut toward the shore to give myself a wide berth, then go back out to sea. I'm going to slice diagonally across their path.

Captain Poursport adjusts his course, pointing his boat at me. I turn south. He turns too. It's a game of chicken and the stakes are death.

I hold my line. We're twenty feet apart, now ten. Whatever I do, I have to stay on my boat. I cut the gas and turn sharp left, punching it again. I zoom out of the water and miss him by a hair.

Then something suddenly slams into my boat from the side and I'm hurled through the air. I splash down on my back, punching through the water. I'm a few feet underwater; I pull myself to the surface, sputtering for air, wiping my eyes, trying to figure out what happened. A second boat jets away. It must have struck me from behind. A third boat cuts in front of me.

I look for my jet ski—it's only five feet away, and I take two long, quick strokes to get myself to the runner as soon as I can. I don't want to be in the water. Not like this. My legs are too exposed—inviting—like I've stuck them into a viper's hole.

Then I see it: the empty rack. The lunchbox isn't there. It must have been knocked loose in the crash. There it is, behind me, sinking below the surface. I splash over and reach for the cable, but it's already too late. "No!" I shout. It sinks down, down, down. I've lost it.

And the sharks must be closing in. It's a wonder they haven't got me yet.

I see Captain Poursport and his crew—they look bigger from down here in the water. They turn their jet skis around like a swarm of bees, darting in and out between each other, headed straight at me; they're going to try to run me down.

I have to get the lunchbox.

I catch a breath, tear my shirt off and throw it on the runners, then dive head-first into the water like a missile, just as Captain Poursport's jet ski is on a crash course for my own.

I feel him pass above me, inches from my feet. It was close.

It's silent now that I'm diving underwater, except for what sounds like the distant whine of engines on the surface. Under here, they seem oh-so-far away. They can't touch me; I am finally alone.

The water is clear, which is good so I can see, and the sun has risen high now, striking the turquoise green water so that it's bright and golden. I'm in a different world. For a moment, I wish I could swim away.

But I know I have to get the lunchbox. I kick my legs as hard as I can, then stretch out my arms and pull, willing myself downward, a sleek and speedy dolphin, a rocket in outer space.

For just a moment, I'm in my element—then I see the first one. It's out of the corner of my eye. He's six feet long, a greenish-gray, with a short snout, his teeth all bristling out like a chainsaw.

He circles me, curious, looking, waiting. If only I had the headphones on, I could hear what it is he's saying.

Down. Down. I have to ignore him. The pressure squeezes painfully on my head. I hold my nose and blow gently to clear the air from my ears. It works, and my head clears. That feels better. I have to focus. I have to pretend he's not waiting to kill me. I can see the sand below; little flecks of it glint in the sun like gold. It ripples off in endless snaking s's.

There's another one, just to my left. He's just a little smaller. This one's gray. Still big enough to kill. He flits away behind me, out of sight. I hate it when they hide.

Kick, pull. Down. I must be thirty feet under. That's a lot of water over my head. It's the deepest I've ever dived. I still don't see the lunchbox. My lungs begin to shrink, and it feels like an elephant is standing on my chest. I don't know how long they'll hold.

Then I see a third shark. Light blue. And a fourth. Darker gray. I can't tell how big they are now. It's too hard to take it all in. Shadows. I just know they're big enough to kill. They're closing in their circles. Probably fighting for the right to bite me first.

I turn onto my feet and hit the bottom, knocking up a cloud of sand, eroding the delicate formations. I look left, then twist around behind me. There it is—the lunchbox—settled on the sand nearly ten feet away.

My lungs are burning now, and my body screams for air, but I refuse to give in. I take a giant step toward the box; the water slows me down, like I'm in a dream, or walking on the moon.

A shark bumps me from behind. I panic. No! That's bad. Any moment now. They always do that before they strike.

I push off again, this time leveling out to kick. One strong pull and I'm there. I grab the lunchbox and clip the cable to my shorts, so I can keep both hands free. I plant both feet in the sand, bend my knees, then push off powerfully with both legs and rocket toward the surface.

Good. Have to breathe soon. Lungs hurt. Drown for certain.

Then something smashes me in the legs and dozens of spiny knives clamp down on my flesh.

▶ CHAPTER 26
PURPOSE AND PAIN

Bursts of pain stab up my bone and through my heart. I . . . I . . . Giant bubbles escape my lungs. It hurts so bad.

I look down before I drown. There's a shark—the green-gray one—thrashing my lower right calf back and forth. What. Pain. Can't. My leg . . . Clouds of blood. All I see are things in flashes, split seconds as they happen.

There are his fins, his tail, his pulsing gills. He whips his head back and forth—he's got a vice grip on my leg—I can't tell which hurts more, the teeth, or the pressure from his jaw.

I try to get away, to swim upward, but that just makes the tearing worse, like an iron anchor latched onto my leg. It's killing me . . . the pain . . . help . . . .

Then I see his beady hollow eye. It doesn't stare, nor focus; it's rolled back, callously, indifferently, into its sadistic head. He doesn't seem to care what it is he's doing. It just wants to hurt me! And suddenly how much I want to kill him explodes across my mind.

I pull back my fist and slice my hand down through the water as hard as I can straight toward his eye, but it's like in a dream, where everything is slow, and I feel weak.

My fist glances off his eye. So I do it again. And again. This time, it's soft and squishy, and it feels like I've damaged something. I strike again. Then again. In the gills. Then again, in the eye. The gills! The eye! I unleash a fury of blows, striking at him madly. It'll never be enough. My eyes are closed.

He lets go. I don't know how. I see the sky above. I can't let the others take their turn. Somehow, I pull myself up the last few yards, and my head breaks the surface, and I struggle, gasping desperately for air, coughing up the sea.

I splash toward my jet ski, and heave myself on board. I have to get out before the others come. I pull myself up by the handlebars and throw my left leg on the runner. I step up with my right, and shots of unbearable pain shoot up my leg and scream through all my flesh.

I scream again. I force myself to look. My calf's a mangled bloody heap. Somewhere under it is bone. I grit my teeth to stop the pain.

I grab my shirt—it's still on the runner—and tie it around my leg to form a tourniquet, then cinch it down as tight as it will go. It's soaked red in seconds. It's the best I can do. It seems to take an hour.

The lunchbox. The cable's still clipped to my shorts. I haul it up, trying hard to ignore the bursts of pain. I have to keep myself from fainting.

I rip it out of the water, then clip it to the rack. As I do, something tall and dark gray-blue rises out of the water beside my boat and slices through the waves like a giant triangular blade. The fin must be as tall as I am, with notches all down its curved back and shiny black skin as hard as armor.

The Shark King. He's here, I think. He's real. And then another fin—it must be his tail—follows all too far behind. He's massive, maybe the size of a bus, a gray-blue shadow below my boat. The waves from his wake lap up against the runners, rocking my jet ski back.

I look down. The smaller sharks—which is all of them—swim away like guppies, abandoning the water all around him, giving his Majesty his space.

I'm frozen with fear, respect, and awe. Even though I see him, I still can't believe he's real.

Then I remember the box. I drop it in the water, keeping it clipped to the rack this time, and jam the headphones on my ears.

"Soon," sounds a deafening voice. "Soon."

It is as deep as a canyon, with the finality of kings. It shakes my very bones, and for a moment, I forget my pain. All I want is to obey.

"Soon."

The dark mass swims slowly along the beach, between my jet ski and the sand, inching ever closer towards the people there.

And then Captain Poursport comes back around again—he must've thought I was dead. He's near, between me and the shore. And suddenly I remember where I am. They'll have me surrounded for sure. I'm in no state to fight them off again. I'm as good as dead.

I look to the shore. There's a little boy and girl splashing each other, knee deep in the water. There's a kid in a yellow hat building sandcastles. There's a middle-aged man with a boogie board and mustache—it looks like Dad, but it's not—wading up to his chest.

I stand and wave to them, frantically. There are hundreds and hundreds more, strewn for a mile or more down the beach, as far as I can see. Somewhere in there is Dad, defenseless and unaware. They have to get back on the sand. One of them waves back—a little boy—he's smiling. He doesn't understand. They're too far away.

They need to be protected. They need me.

And then I hear another motor—this one's further out, with a deeper pitch—coming from behind. I turn and see a red speedboat about fifty yards out. Standing there, all straight and tall like Washington on the boat's pointed bow, his arm raised at his chest, his sword drawn, his curly locks draped over his shoulders and his brass buttons gleaming, is none other than the great Pirate of Panzerfaust, Captain Bombardigo.

Holly's with him. And Albrecht's at the wheel. I feel a surge of hope. I've never been so glad to see them. They can help. This doesn't change what I have to do—it just buys me precious time.

"Ho, you! You would poison the sea with unjust rewards!" Captain Bombardigo hollers at Captain Poursport. His voice booms across the waves. "Your deeds are known. I bring retribution with me!"

Captain Poursport hears him and scowls. These waters aren't big enough for two captains. Poursport shakes his beard and revs his engine. As mad as he is, he looks happy to see someone who he can fight. He smiles with all his jagged teeth, then waves his sword toward the red speedboat.

His crew responds. Killjoy, Mr. Jerk-saw Sailor, and all the rest turn their jet skis hard and charge the speedboat.

Mr. Jerk-saw Sailor reaches the speedboat first. He butts the side of his jet ski up against the speedboat, scraping it, then leaps aboard. He lunges at Captain Bombardigo, both hands stretched out like claws, clutching at the Captain's neck. Captain Bombardigo sidesteps him, then stomps down on Mr. Jerk-saw's back with his boot, knocking him to the deck. Serves him right.

Two more sailors board the speedboat from behind; one leaps over Albrecht at Captain Bombardigo and draws a knife. He lands on the bow of the boat and takes a stab at the Captain's chest. The Captain dodges backward—it's close—the knife slashes his coat, but it looks like it missed his vitals. Albrecht springs up from behind, with a metal fire extinguisher raised high, and clubs the sailor in the head, knocking him down. Albrecht turns and smashes the second sailor in the gut, then shoves him in the water with his shoulder before he can draw a weapon.

"Thanks," says Captain Bombardigo, then turns. Killjoy roars in on his jet ski, drawing his sword and baring his silver, pointy teeth.

Captain Bombardigo draws his sword too, the blade flashing and singing as it slides from his scabbard. He gets low into a fighting stance, and holds the blade up in front of him, ready to attack.

Moving like a missile, Killjoy reaches Captain Bombardigo and swings his sword. The Captain swings his own blade to meet it, and smashes into Killjoy, like two cymbals clashing with colossal force.

The impact shoves Killjoy backward, knocking him from his jet ski. He splashes down hard into the water, then disappears below the sea. I'm elated. It feels so good to see Killjoy go down. The jet skis sputters, slows, and settles in the water.

Captain Bombardigo leaps from the bow of the boat onto the empty jet ski, landing on it like it's a horse, splashing white foam out from under it like a cannonball, nearly sinking it as he lands. He turns his steed around. He jets right for Captain Poursport, his sword drawn and aimed straight ahead like a jousting knight's lance, his curly black locks waving behind him like a cape.

Captain Poursport guns his engine, and points his sword straight at Bombardigo's heart, building ferocious speed, like a terrible black knight, jousting at war.

I can only hope the best for Captain Bombardigo. Two seamen on collision course at breakneck speed. They're both insane. A perfect, unwinnable clash—unstoppable cannonball versus immovable wall—one that I won't stay to see.

I know what I must do. I grip the lunchbox tightly, seal my lips with my last breath, and throw myself over the side headfirst, splashing into the sea.

I sink down, down. Again, I'm underwater, and it's quiet, almost tranquil as I leave the battle up above behind. With each sinking fathom, somehow, I feel peace inside me grow. I'm protected from the fight above, and in a moment, all the things that worried me are gone. And I see a vision inside my mind of Destiny. You're beautiful, but wispy as a breeze, fading away like the ocean foam. And I realize you never knew what you would do for me; you never had a plan. It was always up to me. The choices I made—whether mediocre, or heroic—are what will forge my mark on history.

A shadow blocks out the sun. I know what it is.

"Now."

The voice is loud and deep, and echoes all through the sea. I know that what he says is true. I turn.

"Now."

There he is—I see all of him now, for the first time. The Shark King— as wide as the world itself, not so much in the sea as carrying it on his back, a mass of the darkest blue holding up the water.

He's extraordinary. He's twice as tall as I am and as long as an airliner; his fins are like a rocket's wings, his gills like pulsing vents. His skin is scarred and mottled from battles gone by, his mouth ever open, with teeth lined up in rows like rank after rank of soldiers' spears. He seems to settle deeper in the water. I've never seen a thing so big.

I see his eyes. They're black and so very, very deep. They're different than other sharks', like they've seen the centuries. And now what they see is me. And for this moment, we seem to understand each other.

"Pinky. Kill you."

I nod. I know. My blood must smell so good to him. I feel a twinge of guilt for how bad I'm going to taste.

I press record on the box. I die now for the people on the shore, for Dad. Someone will have to find this box. Perhaps then there can be a way to stop the future frenzies.

I spread my arms and calm myself.

The Shark King opens wide.

I'm ready. He flicks his tail.

"Kill you," he says.

Then there's a crash as two jet skis rip up the surface overhead and smash into each other in a clank of a hundred twisting, ripping metal-plastic parts that explode right through the water.

Two unlucky seamen—the Captain and the Captain—punch through the surface, sinking down between the shark and I, their limbs locked in battle with one another.

Captain Bombardigo smashes his elbow into Poursport's face, then doubles over, a curved sword stuck in his side. He's stabbed! Poursport falls away, limp.

Captain Bombardigo puts both hands up to his ribs, examining—almost admiring—Poursport's sword, a cloud of blood spurting from his wound. Then he looks at me, and with shiny ivory teeth, he smiles. He looks so innocent in this moment—like a kid brother—with his baby-smooth face.

He opens his jacket toward me and points inside. There's an empty pickle jar. One I can only assume he emptied himself. The one I left on his throne.

He winks, turns, and with one arm stretched out like a flying superhuman, kicks himself through the water, straight into the Shark King's open jaws.

In a moment he's there, and I'm wracked with disbelief. The Shark King hovers closer, then snaps forward, biting down in a burst, swallowing the

Captain whole. His teeth clamp shut, and he chomps again, then settles into stillness.

And just like that, Captain Bombardigo is gone.

Then, the Shark King turns. He makes one tight circle, swimming slowly with his massive body inches from my own. I can see tiny sucker fish and barnacles attached to his side he's so close. He's going to eat me. It's my turn now.

Then he darts, and I brace for impact. But it doesn't come. In a thrashing fury, The Shark King snaps at Poursport's unconscious body, bites down with a vice-like grip and tears him into pieces.

"Kill you. Kill you!" He thrashes. The noise is deafening. He's mad for human blood.

I look back. There's a school of sharks behind me, hovering back and forth, waiting for their turn. I'll be next for sure.

"Kill you Pinky!"

The Shark King slows his maddened thrashing. He stops, arches his back, and for a moment, is still.

Then he shivers.

"Pinky! Dirty!"

He opens his mouth and heaves, almost like a cough. "Pinky! Dirty! Dirty! Dirty!" crackle the headphones in my ears.

The sharks are circling around, unsure. They pause—all of them, like they're waiting for more advice.

"Dirty!" booms the Shark King's voice. It makes me tremble—I'm almost certain I feel the electricity shoot out from his pores.

The pack behind me shakes and shivers, mimicking the King. "Dirty! Dirty! Pinky dirty," say the voices to each other in agreement.

They dart back and forth. "Dirty! Pinky, dirty!" they say. It echoes in my ears like a thousand voices crying all at once, like an angry mob, shouting over each other, fighting to be heard. It's so loud, it hurts.

Then a gray shark turns around, shakes himself, and swims away toward the open sea, leaving the rest behind. "Dirty!" says a green striped one a second later, and follows. Then a brown one, and then another, and another. Gradually, one by one, they all turn away from shore, and head out to sea. In seconds, all of them are gone.

I'm shocked. They're leaving me alone. They're letting me live. That's when I frantically realize I have to breathe.

The burning! I push off the bottom, and scramble upward, my arms flailing almost helplessly. I'm flopping like a tired dog, struggling, fighting, one arm on the lunchbox, when I finally break the surface again—something I thought I'd never do—and gasp for air, but all I get is water, and I'm swallowing it, and coughing up my lungs, and trying to swim, but I lack the strength, and I fall back into the sea. All is black.

▶ CHAPTER 27

THE CAPTAIN

My head hurts. It feels like a stack of bricks fell on it. Everything is dark. I try to remember where I am. I can't.

I see flashes of my past. Betteravia. The Shark King. Holly. Captain Bombardigo. Cecil. The Captain. A swarm of sharks. Captain Bombardigo. Gone. A fog of sadness creeps through me and settles in my chest. Captain Bombardigo. I feel numb.

There's something else I'm trying to remember, something very important. A tiny light, no bigger than the head of a pin, flicks on inside the darkness. It starts to grow. The Captain. The Shark King. The box. The ampullae of Lorenzini. A recording. The lunchbox. The lunchbox!

"Doctor Wissenschaft!" I cry, sitting up straight in bed. I'm in a small room, my lower half covered in a white sheet, tubes stuck in my arm. It looks like I'm in a hospital, only the room is too small for that. There's a small round window letting daylight in from the outside.

There's a fresh bandage on my arm, from where Poursport stabbed me days ago, and my nose is sore. I can't feel my right leg. No! I need that leg! I pull back the sheet – I'm afraid of what I'll see. Luckily, it's there, covered in a tight, white gauze. It's just numb.

Holly is sitting next to me. She looks clean. She's wearing a set of denim overalls, and her hair is brushed neatly. "Levi, it's okay," she says calmly.

"But the recording," I say. There's no time. "It's on the box. We have to get it to Doctor Wissenschaft. He'll be able to use it."

Holly smiles. "Already done. We gave it to him first thing, after we pulled you out of the ocean."

I sit back, calmed a little. Holly. She always knows.

"It wasn't hard to figure out what you were trying to do, once we saw you clinging to the box. The Torqueod arrived shortly after we did, so we got Doctor Wissenschaft to broadcast the recording underwater, just in case there were any sharks still left. Most of them were already gone."

A narrow door opens inward. Doctor Wissenschaft sticks his head inside. "Ah, you are awake! I see the medicine has done you well, plus the eighty-eight stitches." All of his grumpiness has somehow washed away. Come to think of it, I don't think I've ever seen him smile before. He's even wearing a clean yellow shirt.

"What about the rest of the coast?" I ask.

"The Torqueod's heading out on patrol tomorrow. We're going to sweep the whole shore, from Canada to Mexico, broadcasting the Shark King's words. The Pirates have never had a mission of such grave importance! They've never been so needed! In a matter of days, every single shark out there will know how much he hates the taste of people meat, and he'll never have to bite a human for himself. All because the Shark King told them so!" He laughs. "Your recording of the Shark King—it's like nothing I've ever heard before! Do you know what this means for science! It's on par with fetching the first rock from the moon!"

He clenches his fists. He's shaking, his eyes bright beneath his wire-rimmed glasses, his lips pursed together in a tight smile that stretches across his cheeks. "We've solved it, Levi! All the sharks will know to stay away! It's a brilliant ruse! And we already know that it works!"

"And Frenzy Day?" I ask.

Doctor Wissenschaft shrugs. "You saw them turn back. It's gone and done, and no one died, thanks to you."

That's good—for the people on the sand—but it's not entirely true. Not everyone survived. Not Captain Bombardigo. I feel a stab of pain, but not from my wounds. He's gone. He was eaten right in front of me.

"The Captain!" I say. I flush hot. I know we were at odds, but he didn't deserve that.

"I know," says Holly. "He was daring in the very end."

"What happened?" I ask. "Why did he come?"

"Not really sure. It was kind of a spontaneous thing," says Holly. "After you left on the jet ski, Marcus and I went back down to the lagoon to see if we could find another way out. That awful woman with the sequin shirt came screaming into the party, tearing down lights and knocking over everything in her path. She was shouting something about it all being fake. How there never was a game. How the props were plastic and the Pirates were all nobodies. The Captain came out of his throne room and just kind of snapped. He told everyone they had twenty seconds to get aboard the submarine, or they were getting left behind to rot."

So she wounded his identity. I wonder too, if the jar of pickles had anything to do with it. I don't mention that I left it there.

"Once we were all up on the surface, the Captain stopped the Torqueod and commandeered a passing speedboat." Holly laughs. "You should've seen their faces—the Pirates of Panzerfaust coming straight up out of the ocean, then the Captain hollering for them to stop in the name of humankind. We were lucky they came by."

I stare at nothing. Captain Bombardigo, for all his unexplainable ways, in the end, he came back for me. For that I owe him my life.

Holly puts her hand on my arm. It's cool to the touch. "Levi, I think he knew what he was doing," she says. I look at her. She's probably right. Somehow, he must have known. The way he looked so proud of himself, with his empty pickle jar in hand—maybe he even knew how it would all end. I think he wanted to sacrifice himself.

"You're right," I say. "Saving people no matter what—that's what the Pirates of Panzerfaust do." It feels good to say it, because I know that finally, it's true. No episode can match the feats Captain Bombardigo dared to do today. He might just be the bravest man I've ever known.

"There's something else," says Holly. She flips the switch on a small TV sitting atop a table in the corner.

The evening news flickers on. It shows the bird's eye view of a jet ski in the ocean near the shore. Someone's swimming toward it, and there's the clear outline of a shark below him, swimming away.

"In an astonishing story of man versus wild, a local boy survives a shark attack by punching a shark in the gills," says the anchorwoman. The boy pulls himself aboard the jet ski. They're looping the clip so that it plays over and over. I look closer. To my surprise, it's actually me. I was on camera.

"Reports from an eyewitness said that the shark grabbed the boy by the leg, and he was actually able to free himself with his bare knuckles. The boy is currently being treated for a severe leg wound and loss of blood, but is in stable condition."

"I'd hate to go a few rounds in the ring with him, Susan," jokes the anchorman. The anchorwoman laughs.

"They've been playing it over and over," says Holly. She turns it off. "It's all over the news."

I'm all tingly from my innards to my skin. The story makes me look like some kind of super-guy—even though I know I'm not. Something I thought no one would ever see somehow ended up on TV. At least a couple thousand people probably watched that clip, maybe even more. It could even be on the internet.

I shake my head in disbelief. "But how?"

"The news chopper got you on camera, and Marcus leaked the details to his father. With his studio connections, it was on the air within an hour."

Marcus Earl did that for me? First the jet ski, now this. He's really come through more than once, both times in a very big way. "But how did he know what happened?" I ask.

"You talk a lot in your sleep," says Doctor Wissenschaft.

That's embarrassing. I wonder what else I said.

Which reminds me, I have no idea how long I've been unconscious. Outside the window, the sun is getting close to the horizon. "What time is it?" I ask.

"Almost sunset. You've been out for a couple of hours," says Holly.

"Where are we?" I ask. The room doesn't look like familiar. We're definitely not on the Torqueod.

"It's Mr. Pengerwist's yacht," says Doctor Wissenschaft. "It has all the luxuries we need, plus we got you the necessary medical supplies. Mr. Pengerwist himself will be here tomorrow. He wants to meet you in person."

Me? What would I say to a rich and powerful trillionaire? How do you do? I guess. Or maybe I'll ask if he's ever been to Africa.

Doctor Wissenschaft looks at his watch. It's a humongous calculator one, twice the size of Holly's. "But it is indeed time for us to go. Nurse!" he calls back over his shoulder.

A young blond woman in blue scrubs comes into the room with a wheelchair. She gives me a robe to wear over my hospital gown—thankfully Holly looks at the floor while I change—then helps me into the chair. She's especially careful with my leg, but I bump it on accident anyway, which hurts. At least I know I'll get the feeling back.

The nurse wheels me out of the room behind Doctor Wissenschaft. Holly's right behind us. I'm not sure where they're taking me, but it doesn't matter; I want to look around a bit. Two Pirates are waiting at the end of the hall. They lift me up a short staircase out onto the deck of the yacht.

The ship is absolutely magnificent. It's at least a hundred or more feet long, gleaming white with sapphire blue windows and antennae and radar pointing to the sky. It looks like it came from the future.

We're just offshore, near a lonely stretch of beach I don't recognize.

Holly wheels me around to the west side of the ship. The Pirates of Panzerfaust are all there—except for one of them of course—Albrecht, Friedhelm, Hugo, Dieter, and rest of the crew. They're standing at attention, with smooth army-green bazookas in hand, leaning vertical against their shoulders. They're staring out to sea at the sun as it sets, fiery and crimson on the water.

Doctor Wissenschaft stands with them. I push myself up out of my chair and stand on my one good leg beside them. Holly and Marcus are there too. So are Handlebar, Candy #2, Touchdown, and all the rest. Glamour Sequins is there as well. But she's handcuffed to the railing on the ship.

I nod to Marcus. He nods back. That says it all: we're kind of almost friends.

Albrecht draws his sword and points it at the sun. "Donald J. Warnickshire," he says, "Known by most as Captain Bombardigo, captain of the Torqueod. A longtime, loyal friend. He was just a little too big for this world, and so we send him on to the next."

The other Pirates shoulder their bazookas and aim them out to sea. On Albrecht's mark, they fire. Flames blast out the back of each metal tube with a bang. Two seconds later, somewhere out in the distance, at the end of several twisting trails of smoke, the rockets explode. It's like fireworks on turbo-charge.

They reload, then fire again. Then one more time, and the rockets explode with finality. A twenty-one bazooka salute for Captain Bombardigo.

I'm sad, but I think I might understand the Captain, perhaps in a way that no one else can. I saw him in his final moment. He was determined, and doing what he does best—looking for a destiny.

They take me back to my quarters and hook me back up to my tubes. A doctor comes in to take my blood pressure and look over my vital signs. He tells me I'll have quite the scar, but other than that, I should be just fine.

They serve me a dinner of tender beef and mashed potatoes. There's a pickle on the plate—I don't think the cook meant anything by it. I toss it out the window.

That night Holly comes in to tell me that we're coming in to port. I look out my window and see the Marina where we boarded the Philanthropist.

Then Hugo and Albrecht and the rest of the pirates are hauling Cecil and his two scientists away in handcuffs to a waiting police car. Doctor Wissenschaft says he's pretty sure Cecil will be put in jail for life. The FBI can close the cases on a whole slew of missing persons over the last several decades now that they can trace them back to the Philanthropist.

The contestants are being sent home. I can see Touchdown, Candy #2, Marcus and Gumbo, and all the rest walk down the gangplank and get on the bus or jump in taxis. Even Glamour Sequins goes. Handlebar leaves last. I wave to him. He gives me the thumbs up. I'm glad I knew him.

I'd go too, but the doctor wants me to stay on board one more night to keep an eye on me, just to be safe. Besides, in the morning I have a meeting.

"You're one wild riot," says Holly, punching me softly in the arm. Her dimples are smiling at me. She leans down to whisper in my ear. "I'm Holly Hendershot," she says, "Look me up and friend me." And just like that, the girl who wants to ride her scooter all the way up to Oregon walks out the door. I think I will friend her, and not just in the cyberspace kind of way, but in realspace, since I have a feeling I'm going to see her again soon enough.

I sleep deeply that night. I was tired, after everything that happened over the last few days. When I wake up the next day, it's well past nine am. Doctor Wissenschaft has called my Dad, to tell him I'm okay. I can only imagine the earful I'll get when I reach home. Maybe the clip on the news will increase the chances of Dad letting me leave the house ever again; maybe it'll make them worse.

The medical doctor says I can use crutches now, so I put them under my armpits and hobble my way onto the deck after a good strong breakfast of pancakes.

There's the sound of helicopter blades beating the air, and a great big black whirlybird with a 'P' painted on the side hovers down and lands on the deck. An old gray-haired gentleman opens the door and hops out. He's got crazy chameleon eyes that point every which way at different times. He's the guy in the painting—Mr. Pengerwist.

He walks straight to me, brisk as can be for such an ancient guy, and extends a slender, wrinkled hand. I shake it. His cufflinks shine like diamonds. His suit must be worth more than my Dad's car.

"Levi Middleworth?" he asks.

"Yes?" I say.

"I've heard of your exploits in detail. This is a distinctive pleasure," he says. His lips smack together as he talks. Only one of his eyes seems to look at me at a time.

I try to remember all the lines I made up to tell him. "Thanks," is all I say. This is the guy who owns the Torqueod, and the Island, and this giant yacht. "I borrowed your jet ski," I say.

"HA!" he laughs. He smiles, kind of like a grandpa would. "And it's a good thing too!"

He takes me to a bench and we stare out to sea, and he tells me he has plans for me. "Levi, when the Torqueod returns from their patrol, they'll need direction. They'll need a vision." He wrinkles up his face. He really does look like a grandpa. It makes me want to trust him. "I'll admit, it was kind of a hobby, setting up this whole pirate masquerade—with the sub, the uniforms, the tiny details. I didn't tell them that, of course." He chuckles, "But it's gone beyond personal amusement. Now I see how much they can really do. And you've shown a measure of grit I never did see."

I'm not sure what he's getting at.

"Levi, I'd like to offer you a job," he says and tells me what it is.

I'm flabbergasted. "But I can't," I say. "I'm just thirteen."

"Consider it an internship," he says.

Ten minutes later, I'm standing on deck in a silver, knee-length coat and matching pants with big important brass buttons sewn to my chest and a pair of binoculars slung over my head. Mr. Pengerwist pins a small brass insignia with two crossed bazookas on my collar, and then presents me with a sword. He really must be crazy, but I don't argue, because it's a sword, and I've secretly wanted one for my own anyway. So I accept it. All the Pirates are lined up behind me, polished as can be, standing at attention.

Mr. Pengerwist looks at me with only one of his crazy eyes and says, as if I were the King of England, "Do you Levi Middleworth, swear to set sail for a noble course, to seek adventure beneath the waves, to right the wrongs that befall mankind, wherever they be found?"

"I swear," I say, taking the sword in both hands. I'm having a hard time believing that any of this is real, but I mean what I say. It's the destiny I choose.

"Then I hereby grant you the rank of Captain, and charge you with all the heroic duties associated therewith, and place the Torqueod and its crew under your command."

He salutes me. I salute him. The Pirates of Panzerfaust salute me back. It's a salutefest, and I kind of wish it could go on forever.

Lucky for me, Albrecht has agreed to take me under his wing and show me the ropes on the submarine. Mr. Pengerwist even said he'd explain things to Dad before we set sail again.

But that won't be for a while yet. For now, I've got to go home and let Dad know that I'm alive before he kills me. I don't mind. I'll just be glad to see him. Besides, he's got nothing on the Shark King.

Come to think of it, neither does anyone I've ever met at school either. It's a slippery slope to slide down, once you've been sub boat Captain for ten minutes in your life. Things like eighth grade don't seem half so ferocious as they used to. I'm in my groove—I've seen the open seas and everything beneath. What's more, I know people like Marcus and Holly. Nothing's as scary as it used to be, when you know you've got some chums.

I hobble down the gangplank, and set both feet on solid ground again, soaking up the total magnificence which is my life.

ABOUT THE AUTHOR

In between books, Adam Glendon Sidwell uses the power of computers to make monsters. Robots and zombies come to life for blockbuster movies such as *Pirates of the Caribbean, King Kong, Pacific Rim, Transformers* and *Tron.* After spending countless hours in front of a keyboard meticulously adjusting tentacles, calibrating hydraulics, and brushing monkey fur, he is delighted at the prospect of modifying his creations with the flick of a few deftly placed adjectives.

Adam has swum dozens of miles in the open sea, so feels very qualified to write this book. He recently moved his family away from Los Angeles to the safety of the mountains, because bears are less scary than sharks.

Connect With Adam:

Facebook.com/AdamGlendonSidwell

Instagram: @adamglendonsidwell

Youtube.com/Evertaster

www.evertaster.com

Want Adam to come to your school?
Contact: publicity@evertaster.com